RED MOON RISING

RED MOON SERIES, BOOK TWO

ELIZABETH KELLY

EK PUBLISHING INC.

RED MOON RISING

(BOOK TWO, RED MOON SERIES)

A wounded spirit. A healing touch.

Bree has spent her entire life struggling to survive in the world built from the ashes of the Great War. Captured and forced into slavery by the Lycans, her worst fear comes true when she is chosen as the prey for their monthly hunt. She is released into the woods and the hunt begins.

Wounded and dying, Bree is rescued by a half-Lycan named James. Unique not only for his red hair but also his ability to heal, James is horrified to realize her wounds have been caused by his own kind.

Healed by James and taken in by his family, Bree slowly begins to realize that not all Lycans are cruel. Confused by her attraction to the Lycan who saved her life, she must learn to trust James and his family in order to save her enslaved brother.

CHAPTER 1

S he stumbled through the forest, her body trembling violently, and her vision blurred. The sun was setting, and she could see her breath in the cold air. She had used her shirt as a bandage but the blood from the wounds on her side had already soaked through it and dark rivers of blood were streaming down her leg.

She was dying. She'd managed to kill one of the beasts, more from luck than any kind of skill, but not before it had wounded her mortally. She staggered on anyway. The other two would soon discover their dead brother and it would not take them long to find her. They would smell her blood and track her down. If the gods were merciful, she would already be dead before they found her and ripped her body to pieces.

She stopped and leaned against one of the thick trees, the bark scraping against her bare back as she took shallow, gasping breaths. The small dog at her feet whined nervously and pawed at her leg.

"Tia." Her voice was thick, and she coughed weakly, moaning when it made her sides burn. Blood coated her lips and slipped down her chin. Her ribs were broken, she was sure of it. She had both heard and felt the crack when the beast threw her against the tree.

She raised her hand and touched her face gingerly. Her battle with the beast had left her face battered and bruised. One eye was swollen shut completely and her lips were bruised and swollen from having her mouth punched. She touched her front teeth experimentally with her tongue, wincing when they wiggled loosely in their sockets. She was surprised they hadn't been knocked out completely.

"Tia." She tried again. "When I die, you have to leave me."

The dog stood and rested its small paws on her shin. It whined again and she tried to smile at the dog. "Don't stick around. They'll kill you if they see you. You have to -"

She coughed again, moaning and crying out with the pain as fresh blood poured from the wounds on her side.

"You have to run away. Find a new family, all right?" she whispered.

The dog barked once, shrilly, and she winced. "Hush, Tia."

She made herself push away from the tree. Oddly enough the pain was a little better. It had been replaced by a curious feeling of numbness. She pulled the sodden material of her shirt away from her wound and stared at the blood spurting from the four deep slashes.

"That can't be good," she whispered and then laughed weakly. She replaced the drenched material against the wounds, why she bothered she didn't know, and stared down at the dog.

"Do you hear me, Tia? Find a new family. Don't stay with me." She stared into Tia's soft brown eyes. The dog cocked its head, stared into the trees, and bolted away.

"I'm not dead yet, damn you," she muttered.

Her heart squeezed painfully. The little dog's abandonment hurt more than her broken body did, but it was for the better. She swiped a shaking hand across her mouth, stared dully at the blood on her fingers, and lurched on.

They would bring her head back and stick it on a pole beside the others. She cringed at the thought that her brother would see it. He'd screamed and raged and begged the beasts to allow him to take her place in the hunt. They laughed and sneered at him. He was too valuable to be used in hunting.

They'd stopped laughing when he attacked and killed one of them with his bare hands. Valuable or not, they would have torn him apart if she had not gotten on her knees and begged Draken to spare his life.

They hadn't let her say goodbye to him, hadn't let her hug him and tell him she loved him. The last time she had seen him he was pinned to the ground, his face red and his muscles straining against his captors as he fought to get to her.

She swallowed, tasting the metallic tang of blood as tears slipped down her cheeks. She was suddenly so weary she couldn't take another single step. She collapsed to the ground, her breath wheezing in and out as her lungs laboured to draw air into them.

She was cold and exhausted. Her eyes slipped shut and she pictured her brother's face - his strong jaw and clear blue eyes. His eyes had once danced with laughter, but it had been many months since there was anything but anger and sorrow in them.

There was snuffling beside her and a warm, wet tongue licked her forehead. She forced her one good eye open and stared at the small dog.

"Tia," she whispered.

Tia whined and looked behind her. The dying woman

3

followed the dog's gaze, squinting at the two figures behind the dog. Dread filled her body. They had found her.

One of them crouched beside her and she realized with a faint thread of relief that it was not one of the beasts. The man was as big as her brother, his shoulders broad and heavily muscled. His eyes were a dark brown and his hair was a rich, dark red.

The second figure knelt beside him. He was blond and blue eyed and almost as big as the redhead. Even with only one eye working properly, she could see the horror and disgust on his face.

"Gods be damned, James. What happened to her?"

The redhead grunted. "I don't know, Nicky." He leaned over her. "What is your name, girl?"

She ignored his question and with the last of her strength reached up and brushed his face with her bloody fingers. "Tia. Please help her -"

A sudden, stabbing pain shot through her chest and she screamed hoarsely. Darkness crept across her vision and the last thing she saw before it overtook her, was the redhead reaching for her.

THE THUMPING IN HER HEAD WAS LOUD AND IRRITATING. With her eyes closed, she reached up and massaged at her temple. It didn't help. The thumping continued - a solid constant beat that demanded her attention.

She wanted to ignore it. Her side and head ached, and she was exhausted. She wanted to drift back into sleep, but the thumping wouldn't allow it. She frowned. Her bed was moving. Only a little, but it was definitely moving.

She forced her eyelids up and her mouth dropped open

with surprise. Her bed wasn't a bed at all but a human being. She was sprawled across the body of a man twice her size. Moving carefully, she lifted her head from his chest. The thumping stopped, and she realized that it was the solid beat of his heart she had been hearing.

Not daring to move anything but her head, she looked around. She was in a tent. Cold sunlight was filtering through its walls and although she could see her breath, she wasn't the least bit chilled. The man beneath her radiated heat. It surrounded her entire body and –

She realized with sudden horror that she was completely naked, and the gods help her, so was the man underneath her. She froze, her pulse thudding and her eyes widening, as she stared at the man's broad chest. It was covered in a layer of reddish-brown hair and despite the cold weather, he was deeply tanned. His chest was rising and falling evenly, and she risked a glance at his face. He was sleeping soundly, and she studied his face. He had a broad nose and wide cheek-bones, and freckles covered his tanned cheeks.

He looked to be around her age, and he was a handsome man, she decided. He was also huge. Her small frame fit neatly on top of him with room to spare. He would be at least a foot and a half taller than her, her feet barely reached his knees. If she –

For the gods sake – what are you doing? In case you've forgotten, the man is very naked and very much a stranger. Get your naked self off of him and get out of his tent before he wakes.

Excellent advice. Moving slowly, she slithered off his body onto the blanket beside him. He snorted, his hands twitching by his sides, but didn't wake. She almost screamed out loud when a cold nose poked into her back. She twisted her head, flinching at the pain in her face, and stared into the face of the small dog.

"Tia," she breathed. The dog licked her face, her entire body wiggling.

"Hush, Tia," she said before turning back to the man beside her. She started to slide out from under the blankets that covered them and then paused, reaching for the edge of it.

What are you doing? Have you gone mad? What do you think he'll do if he catches you staring at his naked body?

She ignored the voice and lifted the blanket a little. In all of her nineteen years she had never once seen what was between a man's legs, and curiosity was winning out over her fear. She lifted the blanket higher, squinting to see in the dim light below it. Before she could fully see what was between his legs, he muttered in his sleep and turned away from her.

She stared at his naked back and ass for a moment before gingerly scooting out from under the blankets. Away from the heat of his body, she started to shiver as the cool air brought goose bumps to her skin. Her clothes were nowhere to be seen, but his were piled neatly on the ground and she picked out his shirt and slipped into it. The material was cold but soft, and it fell past her knees. Tia scratched at her legs and she reached down and petted the small dog, wincing at the pain in her side.

Lying in the Red's bed she had felt tired but there was only a dull ache in her side and her face. Now, sharp pain was radiating from her side into her back and her face was throbbing dully. She touched her face gingerly, realizing for the first time that she could see out of both eyes. The one that had been puffed shut was tender and sore, but not swollen the way it was before. She pressed her tongue against her front teeth. They didn't move and she frowned a little. They were loose last night. She was sure of it.

The evening came flooding back to her. Her fight with the beast, the agonizing pain in her side and back when he had thrown her against the tree. She paled and reached for the hem of the shirt, lifting it up and studying her side carefully.

It was swollen and bruised, and she could see four barely-scabbed over gashes where the beast had swiped her with his long claws. She blinked in astonishment. Last night they were wide, gaping slashes with blood pouring from them.

"What's happening to me, Tia?" she whispered fearfully as she dropped the shirt.

She decided that for the moment she didn't care. What mattered was getting out of here before he woke up. Her side was burning and throbbing, but she would have to move quickly. She needed to put as much space between her and the stranger as possible.

"Come, Tia," she whispered. Her eye fell on the sword lying next to his pants. She hesitated and then picked it up. It was heavy and it hurt her side to hold it, but she would take it anyway.

"Good morning."

She screamed and whirled around. The cuts on her side split open and fresh blood dripped down her side as she lifted the man's sword and held it in front of her.

The Red was sitting up in his nest of blankets. He yawned and stood, and her eyes dropped automatically. She flushed scarlet at the sight of his penis. It was partially erect and as big as the rest of him.

He walked toward her, and she stumbled back, holding the handle of the sword tightly in her hand and giving him a warning look. He ignored it and reached for his pants, slip-

7

ping into them and smiling a little at the redness of her cheeks.

"Do you know how to use that?" He pointed to the sword in her hand.

"Aye," she lied.

He reached out with terrifying quickness and knocked the sword from her hand. It clattered to the ground, barely missing her bare toes, and he scooped it up. He held it out to her, handle-first and grinned at her. "Try again."

She glared at him and snatched it from him. Her sudden movement ripped open the barely-healed cuts on her side even more, and she fought back the wave of nausea that went through her as blood soaked into his shirt. She swayed a little and he frowned.

"You're not fully healed yet." He held out his hand. "Come to me."

She backed away toward the opening of the tent.

"Do not be frightened of me, little one. I only wish to help you."

"Stay away from me," she said.

"Tia - that is your name is it not?"

She frowned in confusion at him as the dog at her feet perked its ears up and then ran to the man. Her tail wagged happily, and she rolled onto her back when the man reached down. He rubbed the dog's belly. She whistled softly and the dog, after licking the Red's hand, bounced to her feet and ran back to her.

"We're leaving. If you try and stop me, I'll kill you," she whispered.

She backed out of the tent. The man made no attempt to follow her as she stepped into the cold morning air. She trembled violently and pressed her hand against her side. It was getting hard to breathe again, and she felt weak and faint. She took a deep breath and turned to flee into the forest. The blond man, an amused expression on his face, was standing behind her.

"Good morning." He stared at the sword in her hand. "Are you planning on hunting for our breakfast?"

She lunged forward, lifting the sword and jabbing it at him weakly. He sidestepped her easily and she tumbled to the ground, crying out at the bolt of pain that went through her side. Dimly she could hear Tia barking and the blond man cursing, and then the Red's face was above hers and he was staring at her gravely.

"Stay away from me," she whispered as he plucked the sword from her limp hand.

"We won't harm you, little one," the man said.

Black edged her vision and then swallowed her whole.

CHAPTER 2

J ames sat down on the fallen log and pressed the girl's
tiny body against his naked chest. Nicholas dropped a
blanket around his shoulders, and he nodded his thanks
before wrapping it around them both.

He stroked the girl's long blonde hair. It was tangled, and
leaves and twigs were knotted throughout it. He stared at her
pale face. The bruising around her eye was almost gone, and
her formerly swollen lips had returned to their normal size.

She was so thin and frail. Last night when he had stripped
her of her pants and underclothes, he had been shocked by
how emaciated she was. Her breasts were nearly non-existent,
and her body was nothing more than skin stretched over bone.

As Nicholas cooked breakfast, he gave James a solemn
look. "Those wounds on her side, James – they were from our
kind."

"I know," he replied. He pulled the woman closer, and she
sighed and nestled into him.

"How do you feel?" Nicholas asked.

"Fine," James grunted.

It was true. Although the woman had lain on top of him

the entire night and her injuries were grave, he felt as robust and healthy as he always did. There was some pain when he first pressed her naked body against his, but that faded quickly.

He sighed and stared into the small fire. There was something about the tiny, fragile woman in his arms that made him feel unsettled. It was just the shock of seeing her on the forest floor, bloodied and bruised and nearly dead, he decided. Of course, it didn't explain the odd pressure in his chest whenever he held her, or his sudden desire to protect her from harm. His blood boiled as he thought about Lycans tearing into her fragile body. What kind of Lycan would attack an innocent woman?

He didn't realize he had spoken out loud until Nicholas replied.

"I don't know. I've never seen Lycans behave in such a manner. We'll have to speak to Dad about it. Perhaps he will know."

"Perhaps," James said and pulled the woman closer.

When she woke for the second time she was back in his arms. The Red was sitting on a fallen log and she was sitting on his lap. A blanket was wrapped around them both, and her entire body was warm and tingling pleasantly. She raised her head from where it was nestled against his shoulder and stared at him in terror.

She tried to struggle away from him, and his arms tightened around her. "No, Tia. Stay with me."

She realized quickly that she was no match for his strength, and she sank back against him, staring around the campsite with wide eyes. The blond man was crouched next

12

to a small fire. The body of a rabbit was roasting on a spit over it and as the smell of cooking meat drifted to her, her belly growled loudly.

The blond man grinned. "Someone's hungry."

"When was the last time you ate, Tia?" The Red's voice rumbled above her.

"Bree," she whispered.

"What?"

"Tia is the dog. My name is Bree."

"Oh. Sorry, I thought you said your name was Tia." The man smiled at her in a friendly way, but she tensed when his big hand rubbed her back. He was still shirtless despite the cold air, but at least she wasn't naked. She squirmed a little on his lap.

"Please let me go," she said softly.

He shook his head. "No, little one. Believe me when I say that sitting with me is the best thing for you right now."

The blond man pulled the rabbit from the spit and tore it into sections. Tia sat at his feet, her tail wagging hopefully, and he tore a back leg off and blew on it before tossing it to her. She snatched it out of the air and gnawed at it contently.

"My name is James. That man is my brother and his name is Nicholas," the man said.

Bree stared curiously at them. "You do not look like brothers."

Nicholas laughed. "Aye, Bree. We do not. I'm much better looking than him, and I have a far better sense of humour."

He winked at her and she flushed, making him grin.

James was still rubbing her back and she wished he would stop. The pain in her side had subsided again, and the feel of his hand on her back was causing not entirely unpleasant tingling in her lower body. She squirmed again and gave him a pleading look.

"Please, let me go."

He actually pulled her closer, pressing her head back into the curve of his neck. "Try and relax, Bree. It will help."

Help with what, she wondered as Nicholas piled three plates with rabbit meat. He carried them to the log and sat down beside them. James carefully folded down the blanket and took one of the plates Nicholas offered him. He held it out in front of Bree.

"Here, little one."

She refused to take it at first and kept her hands clenched tightly in her lap. He held it patiently until, unable to ignore the delicious smell any longer, she reached out and took it from him.

Her fingers trembling, she took a small piece of meat and chewed delicately at it. It tasted amazing, smoky and sweet, and after a few seconds she was wolfing the meat down. It had been nearly three days since she had eaten last and over a month since she had eaten meat. She forgot about both James and Nicholas and stuffed her face as fast as she could.

After only a few minutes her plate was clean, her belly full, and her fingers and mouth shiny with grease. She sighed contently and then burped. Her face turned red as she covered her mouth and gave James a guilty look.

He was grinning and Nicholas actually laughed out loud. "The gods be damned, James. The girl can eat."

James set his plate on one wide leg and, keeping one arm firmly around Bree, began to eat. She leaned against him and watched Tia gnawing at the leg Nicholas had given her. The food in her belly had made her feel better, more alert, and she reached down and touched the cuts on her side through the shirt.

She hissed quietly, touching them made them burn a little, and James moved her hand away. "No, Bree. Do not touch them. They've stopped bleeding but they haven't healed over entirely yet."

She felt her face, pressing on her mouth and then around her eye. Neither caused any pain and she wiggled her tongue against her front teeth again. They were as solid as ever. She had been dying last night, she knew that as well as she knew her own name, and she had no idea why she was alive and healing.

"Do you remember what happened to you, Bree?" James asked.

He had finished eating and was staring curiously at her. She shook her head quickly as Nicholas gathered the plates.

"Are you sure?"

"I don't remember!" There was a hint of hysteria in her voice, and James immediately rubbed her back soothingly.

"All right, little one, all right."

She twitched against him. "I have to go to the bathroom."

He stood up, lifting her as though she weighed no more than a feather. He left the blanket lying against the log and carried her toward the trees before setting her down next to a large clump of bushes.

"I'll be waiting right here for you, Bree. Do not try and run. Do you understand?"

She nodded, her skin breaking out in goose bumps as she moved carefully around the bushes and squatted. She was tired and cold and by the time she had finished and stood up, her side was throbbing. She staggered a little as she rejoined James, and he picked her up and carried her back to the log. He wrapped the blanket around them both and sat down. She rested against him, watching quietly as Nicholas cleaned up from breakfast.

15

Tia stood at James' feet and whined. He reached down and scooped her up, placing her on Bree's lap. The dog curled up on her lap and stared adoringly at her.

"What kind of dog is she?" James asked. Tia was small with short brown hair and large ears.

Bree shrugged. "Just a mutt."

"Where did you get her?"

"She was a gift."

"How old is she?" he asked.

"Two."

"She's a friendly little thing."

"How did you find me?" she asked suddenly.

"Your little mutt dog actually," James replied. "We were traveling through the forest and she came running up to us, whining and crying and trying to get us to follow her. She led us straight to you."

He rubbed the dog's head. Tia licked his hand before staring at Bree again.

"Why are you in the forest?" Bree asked.

"We were visiting friends and are on our way home."

"Do you live close to here?"

He shrugged. "It's about a day and a half by foot."

She frowned. "You don't have horses?"

Nicholas laughed. "We like to walk."

James studied Bree. "Is your home close to here?"

She immediately tensed. "I – no, it isn't."

"Where are you going?"

She hesitated. "Um, I…"

He was staring at her curiously, and she blurted out the first thing she thought of. "I am going to visit my aunt."

"Where does she live?"

"In Vanden."

He frowned. "The city? It is a long way to walk, little

one."

"I like to walk." She mimicked Nicholas and James snorted softly.

"We should get going, James." Nicholas had washed and packed the dishes, and was extinguishing the fire.

"Aye," James agreed.

He stood and set Bree gently on her feet. "How do you feel, Bree?"

"Fine," she replied. "May I have my pants back please?"

"Your clothes were soaked with blood. We burned them last night."

She frowned. James' shirt would not keep her warm enough. "May I trouble you for the blanket?"

He nodded and handed it to her. She wrapped it around her body and whistled softly for Tia. The dog stood at her feet and she gave James and Nicholas a small smile. "Thank you for your kindness and for breakfast."

She turned and walked away. James followed her and snagged her arm through the blanket.

"Where are you going, Bree?"

"I told you, to my aunt's house." She attempted to tug her arm free.

"You're not travelling alone. It isn't safe."

She straightened her shoulders. "I'll be fine."

He arched his eyebrow at her. "Fine? If you think we're letting you leave so you can be raped and beaten again, you're mistaken."

"I wasn't raped!" she said hotly.

"I thought you said you didn't remember what happened," he replied.

She flushed at being caught in her lie. "I – I know I wasn't raped."

He continued to stare at her, and she cleared her throat.

"Thank you again. Please, I need to get going."

James sighed impatiently. "I was not joking when I said we weren't leaving you to roam the forest alone, Bree. There are both faeries and leeches in these woods. You are not fully healed and wouldn't stand a chance against either of their kind."

She could feel the blood draining from her face at the mention of faeries and leeches.

"You can travel with us until we reach our home." Nicholas smiled encouragingly at her. "You are more than welcome to spend a few days at our home while you recuperate, and once you're feeling better, we'll give you supplies and a horse. It'll take you moons to get to Vanden on foot."

"Why are you being so kind to me?" she asked.

Nicholas frowned. "Well, because it's the right thing to do, Bree. Also," he glanced at James and grinned, "our mother would kill us if she knew we let a little slip of a thing like you wander the forest alone."

Bree sighed and bit at her bottom lip. They were right – she wouldn't stand a chance alone in the woods. She took a deep breath, ignoring the twinge of pain in her side, and smiled shyly at the two brothers. "Thank you."

Nicholas smiled with delight and James gave a grunt of satisfaction.

THEY WOULDN'T LET HER HELP PACK UP THE CAMP. THEY made her sit on the log, the blanket wrapped firmly around her as James pulled on a shirt, and they packed up the two small tents and their supplies into two large leather bags. The bags had long straps and Nicholas picked up one and crossed it over his body. He glanced at Bree and then at James.

"It is too far for her."

"Aye," James agreed.

Nicholas took the second bag and slung it over his left side. The handles of the bags criss-crossed his broad chest, and he shifted them slightly as James walked towards Bree.

He held his hand out to her. "Come here, Bree."

"Why?" She gave him a suspicious look.

"It's too far for you to walk."

"You're not carrying me," she protested.

He turned until his back was facing her. "You can ride piggy-back."

"What?"

Nicholas tugged her to her feet and led her to where James was standing patiently. Before she could protest, his hands were on her hips and he boosted her up and pressed her against James' back. James wrapped his large hands around her thighs as Nicholas moved her arms around his thick neck.

"I'm too heavy," she protested again.

James laughed. "I've carried my younger siblings around for hours on my back, and they both weigh more than you, Bree."

Nicholas wrapped the blanket around her, tucking it around her slender frame as Tia danced excitedly around James' feet.

"Ready?" James turned to look at her, his warm breath washing over her face, and she flushed and nodded. The warmth and the tingling were back, and she shifted a little as his hands tightened on her bare thighs.

Her calves and feet weren't covered by the blanket and Nicholas patted her on the back. "Tell us if your feet get too cold all right, Brcc? You'll have a hard time getting to Vanden if you lose your toes to frostbite."

CHAPTER 3

"D o you smell them, James?" Nicholas asked.

"Aye," James replied.

Bree shifted closer to James, straining to hear their quiet conversation. They'd been walking for nearly half the day and she had dozed off a few times. James showed no signs of tiring, and she was amazed by his strength and stamina.

"How many do you think there are?" Nicholas muttered.

"Two, maybe three."

"Shall we wait for them to attack?" Nicholas' eyes were dancing with something Bree couldn't recognize.

"No," James said, and Nicholas actually clapped his hands with glee.

The two men stopped, and Nicholas removed the bags, setting them on the ground, as James slid Bree off his back and set her gently on her feet.

"What's going on?" She asked as James bent and picked up Tia. He handed the small dog to her and she clutched her to her chest, petting her when the dog whined.

"Hush, Tia."

"We have company." James stepped in front of her and Nicholas stepped behind her.

Bree glanced around. She couldn't see any movement in the trees, but James was standing completely still. She watched as he lifted his head and inhaled deeply. The familiar stance made her stomach drop, and she backed away until she bumped into Nicholas.

"Easy, Bree," Nicholas murmured.

"Show yourself!" James suddenly shouted.

She jumped and squeezed Tia until the dog whimpered.

Two large and naked men stepped out from the trees and adrenaline pumped through Bree's veins.

"No," she whispered.

James gave her a brief look, a frown crossing his face.

"Good afternoon, gentlemen!" Nicholas called merrily. "How are you on this fine day?"

"You have something that belongs to us," the largest of the men snarled. "Return her to us and we will not harm you."

Nicholas stepped forward until he was standing next to James. He looked around innocently. "I see nothing here that would belong to the likes of you."

The smaller man bared his teeth and growled low in his throat. "Give her to us now!"

The larger man put his hand on his companion's arm, quieting him. "She is a slave. She killed our brother and she will be punished for it. Give us what is rightfully ours and walk away, or we will kill you."

Nicholas sighed. "Uh oh – now you've done it. My brother here has never cared much for the "s" word. I mean, I don't like it either, but it makes him seriously angry. You know the Reds – they have such tempers."

"Stop your foolish talking and hand the slave over before we kill you and the half-breed!" The man shouted.

A low growling was rising from James' chest, and Bree watched as he unbuckled the scabbard around his waist. He dropped it and the sword within it and stretched lazily. She could hear the bones in his spine cracking, and she stepped back. His entire body seemed to be growing, the sleeves of his shirt straining against his arms. As she watched, the back of his shirt ripped with a low purring sound. His previously smooth back was now covered with hair, and she moaned low in her throat and backed away.

"If you want her, come and take her." His voice had deepened, becoming a growl, and the two strangers snarled loudly and shifted into their wolf form. James and Nicholas shifted immediately, their clothes tearing apart and falling to the ground in tatters, and they howled in unison.

As the Lycans raced towards each other, Bree turned and fled into the forest.

BREE HELD HER SIDE GRIMLY AND FORCED HERSELF TO RUN faster. Tia, tucked under her arm, whimpered and squirmed against her. She held the dog tighter. The wounds on her side split open for a second time, and fresh blood trickled down her side.

Behind her, the sound of the Lycans fighting was growing steadily dimmer. She cried out when she ducked around a large tree and a stray branch swiped across her forehead. It drew blood and some of it ran into her eye, making it sting painfully.

Squinting to see, she wiped at her eye and then screamed

when a hand grabbed her arm. She was yanked to a stop, Tia tumbling from her arms as she was whipped around.

She screamed again at the sight of the thin, pale leech standing before her.

"Ooh, a wood nymph running through the forest!" He grinned at her and wrapped one strong, cold hand around her neck.

"I heard the Lycans fighting and thought it would be best if I skirted around their silly little fight." He rolled his eyes and sighed dramatically. "They're so dreary. Always fighting like dogs. The world would be much better without their wretched kind stinking up the place."

Bree screamed a third time, and the leech gave her a look of distaste before squeezing her throat. "Oh, do stop your awful caterwauling would you, dearie? It's giving me a headache."

He jerked when Tia bit at his leg through his pants. "Ugh. Dogs are just as bad as Lycans."

He bent quickly and picked the small dog up by the scruff of the neck. Tia snarled and bared her teeth at him, and the vampire hissed and bared his own fangs at the dog.

"Please, let her go," Brie choked out.

The vampire laughed and hurled the small dog into the tree beside them. Tia's body hit the tree with a loud thud and fell to the ground. She whimpered once and was silent. Bree screamed with rage and punched and kicked at the vampire. He laughed and hauled her closer, licking the blood from her forehead.

"Delicious," he whispered.

He wound his hand through her long blonde hair, yanked her head back and sunk his fangs deep into her neck.

THE LARGE RED WOLF LOPED THROUGH THE FOREST. HE inhaled deeply as he ran, searching for her scent. He had just caught her scent when she screamed hoarsely. The fur on the back of his neck stood up, and he raced through the trees.

He ran past a large tree and howled when he saw the leech drinking from her. The leech dropped the woman and turned toward him, his eyes widening with fear. "No! I beg you! Do not -"

Growling viciously, James leaped on him and knocked him to the ground. As he buried his mouth in the leech's throat, the vampire grabbed his shoulders and tried to sink his long nails into his skin. Before they could penetrate the thick pelt, James ripped his throat open. The vampire clutched at his throat, making a weak gurgling noise as blood flowed thickly from the hole. Already the wound was trying to heal itself and, snarling loudly, James tore the leech's head from its body.

The vampire exploded into ash and the wolf turned to the woman lying on the ground. He approached her slowly and, crying and gasping, she shuffled backward and held her hands out pleadingly.

"No, please, stay away…"

He whined and shifted into its human form. He knelt beside her and reached for her. She twisted away from his grasp and, still crying, crawled to Tia's body lying motionless on the ground.

"Tia, oh please, oh, Tia," she moaned as she reached the dog.

Incredibly, the dog was still alive, but it was panting harshly, its body twisted in an unnatural shape and blood trickling from its mouth.

Bree screamed with grief and reached for the dog with a trembling hand. Before she could pick her up, James pushed her aside. He picked the dog up and it shrieked in agony. Bree pounded weakly on his broad back.

"Stop," he said. "I'm trying to save her."

He held the small dog to his chest and turned away, shielding Tia from her view. Bree sobbed loudly as Nicholas ran up beside them. He was wearing just pants and he crouched next to Bree and held her against him, rubbing her shoulder.

"She'll be okay, Bree," he muttered.

———

BREE SWALLOWED DOWN HER GRIEF. IT HAD BEEN ALMOST twenty minutes and she knew in her heart that Tia was dead. She had to be by now, but James still stood quietly with his back to them. Bree shook and shivered against Nicholas. He was as warm as James and she leaned into him, trying to absorb his warmth as she stared at James' broad back. Tears leaked continually down her face, and she couldn't stop the small keening noise from escaping her throat.

Her breath caught in her throat when Tia whined softly. James grunted with satisfaction and turned around.

"Tia?" Bree whispered.

The dog was lying in James' arms and at the sound of Bree's voice, her tail wagged. Bree stared in shock and disbelief as James knelt and placed the dog on her lap. Blood still stained the fur around the dog's mouth, but her body and limbs were straight and smooth.

"The gods be damned," Bree said faintly as she lifted Tia. The dog licked her face enthusiastically, and Bree stared at James with a touch of fear.

"What – what did you do?" she whispered.

"I'll explain later. Come, we must keep moving," James said.

He looked to Nicholas who nodded. "They're both dead."

"Good."

He leaned down and scooped Bree up, ignoring the way she cringed, and scowled at the holes in her throat. He strode quickly through the trees until they returned to the spot where the other Lycans had appeared.

He placed Bree on her feet and dug through one of the leather bags, pulling out a pair of pants. He put them on, picking up the sword and scabbard from the ground and buckling it around his waist. Bree put Tia on the ground. She watched in amazement as the dog ran to James and barked excitedly.

Nicholas was pulling on a shirt and he frowned. "Quiet, fuzzbutt. There may be others."

Bree blanched at the sight of the two dead Lycans lying a few feet away. She felt weak and confused, and the sight of their bodies was making her feel nauseous. She couldn't believe they were dead. She took a few shaky steps closer until she was standing over them. The larger one had been particularly cruel to her and she heard James and Nicholas grunt with surprise when she spit on his face.

She staggered away from the bodies and stared at the two brothers.

"Bree, are you all right?" Nicholas asked.

She didn't reply. They were Lycans and although they'd been kind to her, she knew what they were capable of. She backed away as James approached her.

"I won't harm you, Bree. I promise." He held his hand out to her.

"Stay away from me," she whimpered.

"I won't harm you," he repeated.

27

"Don't touch me."

"Please, little one. We need to go. I will explain later." He smiled reassuringly at her, but she continued to stare at him, her face pale with fright and blood loss.

Nicholas had circled around until he was behind her and she was trapped between them. Her body trembled and swayed like a frightened deer, and she realized that she was dangerously close to fainting once again.

"No," she moaned as Nicholas and James closed in on her.

"It's okay, little one," James said.

The world spun wildly, her stomach rolled, and everything went black.

JAMES WATCHED AS BREE'S EYES ROLLED UP IN HER HEAD and she pitched forward. He caught her before she could hit the ground and lifted her into his arms.

"Gods – the girl can't catch a break," Nicholas said.

"We have to keep moving." James started forward and Nicholas held up his hand.

"Wait, brother. You cannot carry her like that the entire way. You're strong but your arms will tire eventually."

"What do you propose we do then?"

Nicholas stared thoughtfully at him for a moment before rummaging through one of the bags. He pulled out a length of rope. "We'll lash her to you. It will save your arms and help her heal faster."

He paused. "How do you feel? She's been sucking a lot of your power for nearly a day."

James shrugged. "I'm fine."

"Are you sure?"

"Aye. I'm a little tired but sleeping tonight will help."

"Not if you're still trying to heal her, it won't," Nicholas said.

James scowled at him. "I said I was fine, Nicky. She's little. It won't take long to heal her."

Nicholas rolled his eyes. "Not if we can't keep her from being injured for longer than a few hours at a time."

"Enough. The sooner we get moving, the better. Lash her to me."

Nicholas picked up the blanket from the ground. It was dirty and bits of leaves were stuck to it, and he shook it briskly. "Do we undress her?"

James hesitated. "Aye. It'll work better that way."

Nicholas reached for her shirt and James knocked his hand away. "Turn around, Nicky. She doesn't need both of us seeing her naked."

Nicholas turned away and James slipped his arm under her shirt and held her around the waist. He used his other hand to tug the shirt from her pale body. Her side was oozing blood again, and the blood the vampire had taken from her had left her even paler than usual and cold to the touch.

He turned her until she was facing him and held her against his broad naked chest like he would hold a small child. Her legs dangled limply as he kept his arm around her waist.

"The blanket," he said. Nicholas held it out without turning and James draped it over her body, tucking it in around her sides and under her ass.

"Okay."

Without speaking, Nicholas worked quickly to wrap the rope around Bree's blanket-covered body. With James' help, he raised her legs around his waist and wound the rope around them until they were held firmly against James'

29

narrow waist, and then wrapped the rope around both hers and his brother's upper body until they were lashed together. He tied the two ends together in a knot at the small of her back and stepped back to admire his handiwork.

"How's that?"

Cautiously, James dropped his hands. Bree's body stayed firmly against his and James nodded. "That's good."

Nicholas eyed his brother's naked upper body. "You want me to try and wrap the blanket around you as well?"

James shook his head. "No, I'll be fine. Let's go."

Tia whined as Nicholas hooked both bags around his body, and he scooped the small dog up and deposited her into one of the bags. Her head poked out of the top of the bag, and she peered around curiously as Nicholas petted her head. "Let's go, fuzzbutt."

CHAPTER 4

S he was naked again and pressed up against him as intimately as a lover. She kept her eyes closed, feeling the sway of his body against hers as he walked briskly. Her small breasts rubbed against his chest, and she was embarrassed to realize that her nipples were hard.

"How are you feeling, Bree?"

She thought about pretending to be asleep but abandoned the idea quickly. He knew she was awake. She tried to move her legs, but they wouldn't budge from around his waist. She opened her eyes. Rope crisscrossed her legs and she wiggled her entire body experimentally. More rope was across her blanket-covered back, and they were so tight she couldn't push her body away from his.

"Why am I naked?" she asked.

"Skin-on-skin contact helps heal you faster."

"How – how are you doing this?" She couldn't look at him. She wondered if he could feel how hard her nipples were. New heat rushed through her body. She didn't even want to think about the fact that he had seen her naked twice now, and that her crotch was rubbing against his hard abdomen. The feel of his stomach against her naked center was making her pulse flutter in an alarming way.

Her eyes suddenly widened. "Tia! Where's Tia?"

"Right here." Nicholas pointed to the bag thumping against his hip, and she sighed with relief when she saw the top of Tia's head sticking out.

She stared over James' shoulder into the growing darkness.

"How are you doing this?" she asked again.

"I'm a healer. When I touch people who are hurt or sick, I can heal them."

"How?" she asked.

He shrugged. "I do not know."

"We should make camp for the night," Nicholas said. "This looks like a good spot."

James nodded and stopped as Nicholas dropped the bags to the ground. Tia jumped out and peed before sniffing at a cluster of bushes.

Bree stiffened against James. The funny warmth in her stomach disappeared and fresh fear flooded through her. The two Lycans had saved her life, but that didn't mean she could trust them. James had not raped her the first night only because she was close to death. Now that he had used his powers to heal her, she would not be so lucky tonight. Perhaps the brothers would take turns using her.

She shuddered and choked back a quiet sob. All her life her brother had protected her, kept her safe from men and beasts alike. Now she was alone, and she was too weak and afraid to defend herself.

Don't be ridiculous. Do you really think either of these men will hurt you? They have been nothing but kind to you. They fed you, protected you against the Lycans, and James saved you from the leech. They may be Lycans, but they seem different from the others.

Her brain knew it to be true but after months of being abused by the Lycans, she couldn't seem to control her fear of them. Her heart was pounding so hard in her chest she thought it might explode.

She gave a short cry of fear when she felt Nicholas' hands at her back.

"Easy, little one," James murmured. "He's just untying the rope."

Nicholas unwound the rope and James set her on the ground. She wrapped the blanket around her body and stared at the two men with wide and frightened eyes.

"Bree, do you feel better?" James made no attempt to touch her.

"Aye," she said, "I feel much better."

Could they tell she was lying? Gods, she hoped not. She needed to appear strong and brave. Moving slowly, she backed away from them until she was leaning against a large tree. She sunk to the ground, wincing and pressing her hand against her side, before she tucked the blanket around her bare legs and feet.

As James built a fire, Nicholas set up the two small tents. Bree watched them silently, her body trembling. When the fire was crackling loudly, she crept closer to it and sat cross-legged in front of it. Tia climbed into her lap, wagging her tail enthusiastically when James approached them.

"You should sit with me for a while longer, little one."

"I don't want to." She cleared her throat. "I don't need any more healing."

James frowned at Nicholas who made a small shrugging motion.

"Please, may I borrow one of your shirts?" Bree asked.

He dug through his bag. He pulled out two shirts and handed one to her before slipping into the other one. He turned away to give her some privacy. A groan of pain slipped out when she eased into his shirt and James glanced at her over his shoulder.

"Bree, is your side bleeding?" He moved a little closer and she shrank back.

"No."

"Show me."

"I told you, it's -"

"Show me," he said loudly.

She flinched and raised her arm to shield her face.

"I'm sorry." He lowered his voice and crouched beside her. "I need to see your side, Bree. Just for a moment."

She kept the blanket wrapped firmly around her hips but raised his shirt. He stared at her pale side. There was no bleeding, and three of the four wounds had disappeared completely. The fourth was a healing scab.

"It looks much better." He gave her a warm smile that she didn't return. She pushed his shirt down and wrapped herself up in the blanket again, wincing as she did so.

James frowned. "Where does it still hurt, Bree?"

"It doesn't," she said.

JAMES KNEW BREE WAS LYING BUT HE DIDN'T PRESS HER. He stood and walked over to Nicholas, saying in a low voice, "She won't let me touch her."

He stared at his own hands in frustration. "I don't understand why it's taking so long to heal her."

"Hmm, let's see – maybe it's because when we found her, she was minutes from death. The gods only know how many internal injuries she was suffering from. Then she had a good deal of her blood sucked out of her by a leech," Nicholas said.

"I should still -"

Nicholas held his hand up. "You've been sleeping on the ground for nearly four nights. We've been traveling for days and it's been what – six moons since you had a healthy woman warm your bed?"

James flushed. "Why exactly are you keeping track of my night time activities?"

Nicholas laughed. "All I'm saying is that you may have both Lycan healing powers and our mother's healing gift, but even you get tired every once in a while."

He glanced over at Bree. "The woman nearly died, James. You've never tried to heal someone that close to death before. She's so malnourished I can't believe she even survived with your help. It's not surprising that she's still not fully healed."

"She won't heal if she won't let me touch her," James muttered.

"The way she is reacting to us now, touching her is likely to do more harm than good, brother. Leave her be for the night. She isn't dying, and I'm afraid that knowing we are Lycans means she will never trust us," Nicholas said. "Frankly, I don't blame her. What they did to her..."

His face darkened as he remembered the way Bree had looked when Tia had led them to her.

"I know." James glanced behind him at Bree. "She needs food. I'll go hunt something for dinner. Keep an eye on her, all right?"

Nicholas nodded as James disappeared into the darkness.

"IT'S TIME FOR BED, LITTLE ONE." JAMES VOICE DRIFTED across the campfire.

She blinked rapidly. "I'm not tired."

Nicholas smiled at her. "You are, Bree. You're practically falling asleep sitting up."

"No, I'm fine," she said.

James tried not to show his frustration. They had finished eating the rabbit he caught, and he'd been watching her nod off for the last ten minutes. Weariness was etched into her thin face. He had considered just letting her fall asleep and then carrying her to his tent, but he worried about her reaction if she woke up to find him touching her. Still, he was anxious to try and finish healing her.

Everything Nicholas told him was true, but it frustrated him that he couldn't quickly and easily heal the small woman in front of him. After dinner he leaned against Nicholas for a while. It made him feel stronger, and he was positive that one more night of sleeping against him would help heal Bree completely.

Kissing her would help.

He snorted to himself. That might be true, but she would never allow it. She was terrified of both him and Nicholas, despite their gentleness with her.

He stood and held his hand out to her. "Come to my tent, Bree."

She shook her head, her nostrils flaring and her eyes wide. Tia, sensing her mistress' distress, left the bone she was gnawing on and climbed into her lap. "I'll sleep out here by the fire tonight."

"No, Bree. It's not safe and you'll be too cold," James said patiently.

"I'm not going in your tent with you." Her body was trembling, but her voice was steady enough.

James gave Nicholas a helpless look.

"You can have the tent to yourself, Bree." Nicholas smiled at her. "James and I will be taking turns keeping watch anyway, so we can share my tent."

"Nicholas that won't -"

"Be quiet, brother." Nicholas' voice was unusually harsh.

James glared at him, but Nicky shook his head before turning to Bree.

"Neither of us will come into the tent. You have my word on that. You may take my dagger if it makes you feel better." He moved toward her and held out the short but sharp knife.

She took the knife from his brother. As she stood, she swayed and stumbled forward but Nicholas made no effort to touch her.

She weaved carefully to the tent. "Good night."

She disappeared into the tent, Tia at her heels, and James turned on Nicholas.

"Nicky! What are you doing? She needs me."

"Aye, brother, she does. But she does not realize it yet. It is better to leave her be for the night."

James growled with frustration and Nicholas clapped him on the back. "I will take the first watch. Get some rest."

"IT IS NOT MUCH FURTHER NOW, BREE," NICHOLAS said encouragingly.

Breathless and her side hurting so much she thought she might faint, Bree nodded. They had been walking for most of the morning, and she wasn't entirely sure how much longer she could continue to walk.

James had wanted to carry her on his back again, but she refused. She felt well enough when they started out, but now each step she took sent a jolt of pure agony through her ribs and into her lungs. She was lagging further and further behind. She stared grimly at the ground below her feet and forced her tired legs to move one step at a time.

There was soft muttering ahead of her. She heard Nicholas telling James not to, and then James was standing beside her and lifting her into his arms. She knew she should tell him to put her down, but she was so weary that she let her head drop to his shoulder and closed her eyes. She would just rest for a moment and then tell him to release her.

She woke when she heard the woman's voice. She blinked and squinted at her surroundings. James and Nicholas were standing in a large room with an enormous fireplace. A couch was placed in front of it, and a fire crackled in the fireplace. The woman standing next to the couch was tall with long dark hair and dark eyes like James'.

"You were supposed to be home yesterday. Mom was ready to send out a search party."

"We ran into a bit of trouble." Nicholas grinned at her. "Nothing we couldn't handle though."

She ducked back when Nicholas tried to ruffle her hair. "Stop it, Nicky." She eyed Bree curiously. "Who's the girl?"

"Her name is Bree. This is my sister Sophia." James gave no other explanation, and Sophia didn't press for details.

"Hello, Bree." Sophia smiled a bit guardedly at her before looking down at the dog sniffing at her boots. "And who is this little fuzz?" She reached down and petted the dog.

"That's Bree's dog. Her name is Tia." Nicholas looked around. "Where are Mom and Dad?"

"They're upstairs having a nap." Sophia emphasized the word nap and Bree, her mind tired and her body throbbing, frowned in confusion.

"Gross," Nicholas replied cheerfully.

"We'll have another sibling soon if they keep that up." There was a hint of laughter in James' voice.

Sophia studied Bree. "When did she eat last?"

"She ate last night," James replied. "She's been badly injured and needs rest."

Still carrying Bree, he left the room and carried her down a long hallway. The house was bustling with activity. James passed at least three people who all bowed and murmured, "welcome home, my lord". He greeted them politely by name as he moved further into the house.

He stopped in front of a door and opened it. The curtains were drawn, and Bree strained to see in the dim light. A fire had been started in the fireplace and the room was deliciously warm. She tensed when she realized that James was carrying her toward the bed.

"No! Put me down!" She pushed weakly at his shoulders.

"I'm not going to join you in the bed, little one."

He set her down and unwrapped the blanket from her body. He pulled back the covers on the bed and steadied her with a hand on her elbow as she climbed into it. The bed was large and soft, and she sank into it with a happy sigh. It had been two years since she had slept in a bed and even then, she had never had a bed as comfortable as this one.

James patted her awkwardly on the shoulder as he tucked the blankets around her. "Go to sleep, Bree. You're safe now."

CHAPTER 5

"Hello."

Bree blinked at the young girl sitting on the end of the bed. For a moment she wondered if she was dreaming.

"What's your name?" The girl spoke again.

"Bree." Her voice was hoarse, and she cleared her throat as she sat up. She flinched a little as the girl watched her carefully.

"Where am I?" She looked around the large room.

"You're in my brother's bed. You've been sleeping almost all afternoon," the girl said.

She scooted a little closer and raised her head, inhaling deeply. "You're a human!" She announced with delight.

"Are you..."

"I'm a Lycan. Well, a half-breed, but I can shift just as well as Sophia and Nicholas and Papa can. At first, I had a hard time controlling it but I'm really good at it now. Look!"

Bree watched wide-eyed as the little girl stared down at the bed for a moment. When she looked up, her formerly dark eyes were glowing green and a dark layer of hair covered her cheeks and forehead.

Bree moaned and shifted backward until her back hit the headboard. The little girl frowned and shook herself all over.

"What's wrong?" Her eyes had returned to their normal colour, and the hair on her face had disappeared.

"I – nothing," Bree whispered.

The door to the room opened and a woman with hair the same shade of red as James', walked into the room. "Leta, my love, I asked you to leave her alone."

"I just wanted to see what she looked like," Leta said cheerfully. "She's really skinny. And she's dirty and kind of smells bad."

"Leta," the woman said, "you're being rude."

"Sorry, Mama." Leta looked sufficiently chastised as the Red stood next to the bed and smiled down at Bree.

"Hello, Bree. My name is Avery."

"Hi," Bree whispered as Avery sat down on the bed beside her.

"How do you feel?"

"Fine." She felt better than this morning but the constant pain in her side was still there. She wondered if it would ever go away.

Leta squirmed her way onto her mother's lap. Avery smiled down at her. "Soon you will be too old to sit on my lap."

"Nu-uh," Leta disagreed. "I'm only ten, Mama."

She stared at Bree. "She's a human."

"I know, my love." Avery kissed the top of Leta's head. "Will you run to the kitchen and ask Marian to make up a plate of food for Bree? Have her put lots on it."

"All right." Leta slid off her mother's lap and skipped to the door. She paused and smiled shyly at Bree. "Your dog likes me. She sat on my lap earlier."

Before Bree could reply she had slipped out of the room. Avery smiled at her and reached for her hand.

Bree snatched it away and Avery said, "I won't hurt you, my sweet."

Bree didn't reply, and Avery stared thoughtfully at her for a moment. "Would you feel better if I told you that I was as human as you are?"

Bree visibly relaxed and studied Avery. She was wearing a plain white blouse with a long, dark green skirt, and she was beautiful. Her skin was as pale as Bree's and smooth and unblemished. A small smattering of freckles covered the bridge of her nose and her eyes were a clear green.

"Are you – are you James' mother?" Bree asked.

"I am," Avery said.

"But he's a Lycan. Was he bitten?"

"No. His father is a Lycan."

Bree's mouth dropped open. "You are married to a Lycan?"

Avery laughed at her surprise. "Aye. His name is Tristan and you'll meet him soon. But first, you need a bath and some food."

She held out her hand and after hesitating for a moment, Bree took it. Warmth and tingling started in her hand, and Avery smiled at her as she tugged her to her feet. "Come, my sweet Bree. The tub awaits you."

Bree took a step and stumbled, falling against Avery. Immediately, the Red put her arms around her and held her tight. She stroked Bree's back through the shirt. "Are you all right, my love?"

Bree's entire body was tingling now, and she couldn't stop herself from putting her arms around the woman's waist. She leaned against her and rested her head on her shoulder.

Avery rocked her back and forth. She stroked Bree's hair,

picking out bits of leaves and twigs as Bree fought to keep from crying. The last two days she had been touched and held more often than she had in her entire life. Before James and now Avery, the only person she had really ever hugged or been close to was her brother.

It felt strange and uncomfortable, but it also felt unbelievably wonderful. Avery's body was soft and warm, and Bree thought she could hug the woman forever and still not tire of it. Tears leaked from her tightly-closed eyes, and a soft sob escaped her throat.

"There, there, sweet Bree," Avery murmured. "You're safe with us. I promise you."

The door opened and Nicholas stuck his head into the room. "Mom, have you -"

Bree pushed away from Avery and stared at him.

"Hello, Bree." He waved at her.

"Have I what, Nicky?" Avery asked.

"Have you seen Dad and James?"

"I believe they're at the barn." She smiled at Nicholas and he blew her a kiss before closing the door.

She held her hand out to Bree. "Follow me, my love."

Bree followed her down the hallway. Avery opened a door and ushered her into the room. Bree stared in amazement. The room was small, but it had an indoor toilet and a large tub. It was already filled with water, and steam rose lazily from its depths.

"We have both electricity and running water." Avery smiled at her as she lit some candles. "Although my husband does like to conserve so we use candles for everyday use. Do you need to use the bathroom?"

Bree nodded and Avery left the room. "I'll be in the hallway if you need me."

"Thank you." Bree closed the door y and rubbed absently at her aching side.

"BREE?" AVERY KNOCKED ON THE BATHROOM DOOR. "MAY I come in?"

At Bree's soft yes, she opened the door and smiled at her. "Shall I wash your hair for you?"

Bree nodded gratefully. She had tried to wash her hair but lifting her arms over her head made her side hurt too much.

Avery knelt next to the tub and using a metal jug, poured water over Bree's hair until it was soaking wet. She lathered her hands with soap and massaged Bree's scalp, working the lather through the long, wet strands.

Leta popped into the room. "I put the food in James' room, Mama."

"Thank you, Leta."

Leta leaned against the sink and stared at Bree. "How old are you?"

"Nineteen," Bree murmured.

"Oh. I'm ten. I'm big for my age, aren't I, Mama?"

"Yes, you are, my love."

"I'm almost as big as Evan and he's fifteen," Leta said proudly.

As Avery rinsed Bree's hair, Leta leaned forward. "You're not very big at all."

"Leta," Avery said warningly.

"What? I'm only telling the truth. She isn't very big."

Bree blushed, and Avery turned to Leta. "Go and find your sister and ask her to help you look through the spare closet for some of her clothes. They'll be too big, but Bree needs something to wear other than your brother's shirt."

"Aye, Mama." Leta kissed her mother's cheek and left the room.

"How many children do you have?" Bree asked tentatively as Avery finished rinsing her hair.

"Tristan and I have five children."

"Are they all Lycan?"

Avery nodded. "We weren't sure about Leta at first. Lycans usually start shifting around two years of age, but she was nearly seven before she shifted for the first time. I'm still not convinced she didn't do it from sheer willpower alone. She was terribly jealous of her sibling's abilities."

"You look much too young to have five children," Bree said.

"Why thank you, sweet Bree." Avery stroked her wet hair. "I do seem to be aging well but in fairness our two oldest, Sophia and Nicky, are not my birth children."

Bree blinked in surprise as Avery squeezed the water from the ends of her hair. "Sophia was seven and Nicholas nearly a year when I married their father. Sophia and Nicky are full blooded Lycans like Tristan, but Nicky is not Tristan's child."

"He isn't?"

Avery shook her head. "No. We do not know who his father is. But in our hearts, he belongs to us, and that's really what's important isn't it?"

She finished squeezing the water from Bree's hair and stood up, reaching for a towel that was on a shelf on the wall. "Stand up, Bree. The water is cooling."

Bree stood and Avery wrapped the towel around her slender body. She used a smaller towel to bundle up Bree's hair and then led her back to the same bedroom. A short and chubby woman was just changing the sheets on the bed.

"Thank you, Laura." Avery replied.

"You're welcome, Avery." The woman plumped the pillow and set it on the bed with a flourish. "It's going to be a cold night tonight."

"Aye, I believe you're right. How is Leo feeling?"

"Oh fine, fine. The cut healed up overnight without any trouble," Laura replied. "He was grumbling that in his youth the cut would have healed in hours, but he's not a young Lycan anymore is he?"

Avery laughed as she led Bree to a chair in front of the fireplace. "No, I suppose none of us are young anymore."

Laura left the room as Avery took a comb and carefully detangled Bree's hair.

"Who was that woman?"

"That's Laura. She's a human who works for us."

Bree stiffened. "You mean she is a slave?"

Avery shook her head and rested a gentle hand on Bree's shoulder. "No, my love. We have no slaves here. Everyone who works for us earns a wage, and they are free to leave at any time."

Bree mulled this over as Avery combed the tangles from her hair. After a few moments she glanced up at the Red. "Are you – do you need more workers? I am looking for a job. I am very good at cleaning, and I'm stronger than I look. I could do outside work if necessary."

"I thought you were going to Vanden to visit your aunt?" Avery said. "James and Nicky said you were."

Bree flushed. "I am. I just – I could use some extra money."

Avery smiled at her. "We do not need any more help around the house and besides, you are a guest of my son's. You will not work while you're visiting us."

She brought the tray of food over and placed it carefully

on Bree's lap. "Eat some food, Bree. Leta is right – you are too thin."

Bree tried to eat politely, but after only a few minutes she was eating ravenously. Avery pulled a chair up beside her and watched silently as Bree chewed and swallowed the meat, cheese, and fruit was piled on the plate.

When the plate was empty, she set the tray on the ground in front of her and leaned back in the chair. She rubbed her belly and sighed contently. Avery handed her a glass of water.

"Drink this up, my love."

She drank obediently and Avery took the empty glass back as Bree sat up straight. She flinched and grabbed at her side. At Avery's sympathetic look, she dropped her hand and looked around the room. "Whose room is this?"

"It's James' bedroom."

Bree tensed and gave Avery a cautious look. Her initial fear that she would be raped and forced into slavery had subsided, but she was uncomfortable at the thought of sleeping in his bed. What if he decided to join her in the night?

Avery patted her knee. "James will be sleeping in the guest room down the hall."

Bree flushed. "I can take the guest room. He shouldn't give up his room."

"Nonsense. The guest room does not have a fireplace and is much cooler than this room." She smiled. "Lycans run hot. My son has no need for a fireplace."

Bree thought back to the heat that had radiated from James when she was lying against him in his tent. He had been as warm as an oven.

"Bree, may I ask a favour of you?" Avery said.

Bree nodded. The woman had fed her, washed her hair, and been extremely kind to her. She owed her.

"Will you tell me what happened in the forest?"

"Do I have to?" Bree whispered.

"No, my love, you do not," Avery said kindly. She reached out and took Bree's hand, squeezing it gently before releasing it. "But I believe you would feel better if you did."

Bree stared down at her lap, opened her mouth to say she would be fine, and found herself sharing the truth instead.

CHAPTER 6

They quieted when she walked into the kitchen. Tristan stood and hurried forward. "Avery? What's wrong?"

Avery gave him a trembling smile and leaned against him. "I am fine, my lord."

She sat down at the table, folding her hand into Tristan's as he sat beside her and cupped the back of her neck. She stared gravely at Sophia, Nicholas and James.

"Did she let you heal her?" James asked.

Avery shook her head. "No. She let me hug her for a bit, but I did not tell her I share your healing powers. We were interrupted before I could heal her fully."

"Sorry, Mama," Nicholas said.

Avery smiled at him. "It's fine, my sweet Nicky. But we will have to convince her to let one of us heal her, James. Although I don't believe her injuries will kill her in the next day or so, they will kill her eventually. The marks on her skin have faded which means the injuries are to her organs."

James swore under his breath as Sophia leaned forward. "Did she tell you what happened to her?"

Avery nodded. "Aye, she did."

She was starting to tremble and, without speaking, Tristan pulled her from the chair and drew her onto his lap. His large hand rubbed her back soothingly, and she kissed him on the mouth before turning back to their children.

"She was a slave in the home of a Lycan named Draken. She'd been there for nearly two years. Apparently this Draken has many human slaves. He collects them and keeps them like cattle."

Avery's face was pale, and she took Tristan's hand. "Draken and his pack, they – they hunt humans. It's why they have so many of them. Once a month, they release one or two of them into the woods and hunt them."

"The gods be damned," Nicholas said as Sophia gave her mother a horrified look.

"You haven't heard the worst of it." Avery shuddered. "Bree said she knew she had been chosen for the next hunt because they deny their chosen prey meat for the month before. Two days before the actual hunt, they stop giving them food all together. It makes them weaker, she said. Makes it easier for the Lycans to hunt them."

James slammed his fist down on the table. "Have they gone mad? What would make them do such a thing?"

Tristan sighed. "It used to happen all the time, James. Twenty years ago, it was not uncommon for packs of Lycans to release ten to twenty humans deep into the woods, and then spend the next few weeks hunting them down systematically one by one. It has gotten better, but I am not surprised that there are still a few of our kind who participate in such hunts."

"I can't believe she survived," Nicholas said, staring down at his tightly-clenched fists.

"She got lucky," Avery replied. "Three Lycans hunt one human. They give the human a three-hour head start, and then the first Lycan goes after them. If, after another three hours the Lycan has not returned with the human's head, they send the next one. Three hours later, the third one goes on the hunt. They bring the head back and hang it on a pole for the other slaves to see."

She sighed and leaned against Tristan. "The first Lycan caught up to her quickly. It taunted her for a bit and then when she fought back, beat her badly. She doesn't remember everything that happened, but she knows that it ripped her side open and threw her against a tree and broke her ribs. She was lying on her stomach on the ground and there was a fallen branch beside her. She picked it up and rolled to her back just as the Lycan was leaping onto her."

She shivered a little. "She was extremely lucky. The branch pierced the Lycan's heart and killed it instantly. She staggered to her feet and kept going. She told me that she knew she was dying. She believed walking would kill her faster than lying on the ground would. She wanted to be dead before the other two Lycans found her."

The others were staring at her, their faces pale and sick looking, and she rubbed at her forehead. "She's only nineteen years old."

James cursed again and stood up, moving jerkily back and forth in the kitchen. "Gods, no wonder she is terrified of us."

"When she found out that we had no slaves and that we paid humans for working, she asked me if she could have a job with us. She told me that she was good at cleaning or could work outside." Avery shook her head. "She said she was stronger than she looks."

"A strong wind would blow her over," Sophia said. She glanced at her brothers. "I thought you said she was going to Vanden to see her aunt."

Nicholas shrugged. "That's what she said."

"I don't believe she has an aunt in the city," Avery said. "She is young and afraid, and she believes that we will treat her like the other Lycans have."

James gave her a frustrated look. "I don't know how to change her mind."

"I think our biggest concern right now is healing her," Tristan said. "Is she frightened of you, Avery?"

Avery shook her head. "No. When she found out I was a human she was obviously relieved. Although she thinks it is strange that I am married to a Lycan and bore his children." She smiled at Tristan who squeezed her thigh.

"Aye, but there are many humans who think that way. We will stay away from her and let her spend time with you this evening."

"Actually, my lord, I think it might be better for her to see us interacting as a family. If she sees that you and the children are nothing like the Lycans she has always known, perhaps it will help her to not be afraid," Avery said.

Tristan thought carefully and then nodded. "Aye, you are probably right." He gave his children an affectionate look. "Be on your best behaviour. I want none of your usual squabbling at the dinner table."

BREE CLOSED THE DOOR TO JAMES' BEDROOM AND LEANED against it. Her side was throbbing and burning, but her stomach was full, and she was more relaxed then she'd been in months. The door had no lock on it, but even that didn't bother her. After watching James with his family, she was sure he would not come to his room without her permission.

"Come, Tia," she murmured to the little dog. The dog followed her eagerly to the bed and she bent, her face tightening with pain, and picked up the dog. She plopped her on the bed, and Tia circled three times before curling up into a ball.

"It's nice here isn't it, Tia?" She took off the dress that Sophia and Leta had found for her. She slipped into James' shirt. She didn't need to wear it any longer. The Lycans had found several pairs of pants and shirts, as well as under-clothes and a few dresses, that were big but weren't falling off her. Leta had even found a long white nightdress for her to wear to bed. But wearing James' shirt comforted her in a way that she didn't understand, and she rubbed her hands along the soft fabric as she curled up in the bed.

Avery had encouraged her to nap for an hour or so before bringing her downstairs to the large common room. There she had met Avery's husband Tristan and their youngest son Evan. He was fifteen, and tall and lanky with his mother's eyes and his father's dark hair. He seemed to be the shyest of the siblings, and he gave her a small nod before immersing himself in a book by the fireplace.

She joined them at the dinner table, sitting between Avery and Leta. She wasn't sure she would be able to eat at first, but the smell of the roasted duck and the heaping piles of pota-toes and vegetables on the table changed her mind quickly.

She had kept her head down and eaten hugely. She felt guilty for eating their food but couldn't stop from eating a second plateful. The Lycans hadn't seemed to notice. They had an easy dynamic between them, and a few times she found herself smiling as Nicholas teased all of his siblings mercilessly.

Sophia and James were the quietest of the siblings. She thought Sophia to be beautiful with her dark hair and eyes, and her straight white teeth. Although Avery was not her birth mother, it was obvious there was great affection between the two of them and it made Bree's chest ache. She barely remembered her mother, and she was deeply envious of the love Avery had for Sophia and the rest of her children.

Other than the red hair, James was the spitting image of his father. He was a little taller and a little broader than his father, and he kept his hair short instead of long like Tristan did. She found her gaze returning repeatedly to his hands, remembering the way they had stroked her back and examined her injuries.

Evan and Leta favoured Avery in looks although neither had her red hair. Leta chattered nonstop through the dinner, and more than once Avery or Tristan had to remind her gently to stop talking and eat her dinner.

Bree had listened closely when James and Nicholas spoke at length to Evan about his sword training. Apparently, they were teaching him to fight, and although she wondered inwardly what need a Lycan had for a sword, she did not ask.

By the time dinner was over and they had retired back to the common room, her nervousness had disappeared. She curled up in the chair next to the fireplace and watched as Nicholas got down on all fours, and stalked a shrieking, giggling Leta around the room. Barking excitedly, Tia had bounced around them, nipping a little at Nicholas' arms until he pinned the small dog down and rubbed her belly roughly.

Bree sighed and curled up into a smaller ball in the middle of the bed. Avery had offered to stay with her in James' room tonight. She was shocked by the offer and almost said yes before her brain caught up to her mouth. She had only hugged Avery for a few moments, but she could still remember how nice it felt.

She wasn't surprised at how often Leta stopped her play to crawl into Avery's lap for a while. She'd had to stifle the urge to crawl into Avery's lap herself. All of the siblings were affectionate and friendly with each other and their parents.

After a moment's hesitation, she had turned down Avery's offer with a weak smile. It would be hard for her to sneak out of the house with Avery in the same bed. She stared at the flickering candle beside the bed.

As nice as the Lycans were, she couldn't stay with them. Forgetting that they were Lycans, she needed to go back and rescue her brother. It would be faster and easier if she took a horse, but she had never ridden a horse by herself, and the thought of trying to control it made her nervous.

Her side throbbed and she rubbed at it. She would sleep for a few hours and then sneak out just before dawn. She would be gone for hours before the Lycans realized she'd left. She glanced at Tia and choked back a sob. She would leave the dog here. It was too dangerous for her and she would have a good home here. Leta was already in love with her.

BREE, DRESSED IN PANTS AND A LONG-SLEEVED SHIRT, CREPT quietly through the common room. The Lycans did not have shoes that would fit her, but she had torn up one of the shirts and bound her feet with them. She slipped a little on the floor and grabbed at her side. It was hurting even worse this morning. It was a constant deep and aching throb that made her feel sick to her stomach. She'd almost abandoned her plan to leave, but she thought of her brother and forced herself out of the warm bed.

The large house was quiet and still, and she squinted as she crossed the room. The fire was low in the hearth and, afraid of tripping over furniture in the semi-darkness, she moved slowly.

"Going somewhere, little one?"

She gasped and whirled around, slipping on the floor again and nearly landing on her ass. A bolt of agony ran up her side and tears came to her eyes. She held her side and tried not to moan as James rose from the large armchair beside the fireplace.

"I – I told you that I am going to see my aunt in the city," she said.

"Aye, you did. I thought you might stay with us for a few days," he said.

"I cannot. She is expecting me."

"Fair enough. Goodbye, little Bree. Best of luck."

She blinked in surprise. She thought he would try and prevent her from leaving, or at the very least argue with her, and a strange ripple of disappointment went through the pit of her stomach when he didn't.

"Um, goodbye. Thank you again and please, will you thank your mother for being so kind?"

"Aye."

She smiled weakly at him and turned away. Before she could leave, he called her name.

"Will you give me something before you leave?" He smiled at her.

"What?" She asked.

"A kiss."

She turned red and backed up a step. "I – I don't…"

"Just one kiss, Bree. As payment for everything I have done for you."

Shame rushed through her. He had been very kind to her. He had saved her life and the life of her dog, and welcomed her into his home. A kiss was a small price to pay. He was right - she did owe him.

Liar. You want to kiss him because you've never kissed a man before.

True. Mind you he was not really a man - he was a Lycan. Of course, considering she was headed toward what was most likely a slow and agonizing death, what difference did it make? It would be her last chance to kiss anyone – human or Lycan.

She swallowed and took a few steps toward him. He stayed where he was, his hands folded behind his back, and smiled encouragingly at her. She dropped her bag to the floor and approached him gingerly.

"Where is Tia?" He asked.

"I – I thought I would leave her here, if that's okay? I'll come back after visiting my aunt and pick her up," she replied.

"That's fine."

She was standing in front of him now, and she stared silently up at him. She studied his mouth and blushed at the excitement that was growing in her belly. It dulled the pain in her side, and she stepped closer until she was nearly brushing against him.

He bent until his face was only inches from hers but kept his hands behind his back. He didn't say anything, and she licked her lips nervously and then pressed her mouth against his. His lips were warm and firm. She started a little when his mouth opened, and his lips pulled gently at her bottom lip.

She moaned softly and he pulled his head back. He smiled at her and she took a deep breath and pressed her mouth against his again. The kiss had been too brief, barely even recognizable as a kiss, and she wanted to try it again.

He didn't object and returned her kiss. She swayed toward him and he put one arm around her waist and drew her up against his hard body. His tongue traced her lips and she parted them, a small whimper escaping her mouth.

He slid his tongue into her mouth, sweeping along her teeth before pushing past them and stroking at her tongue. Bree shuddered and gripped his broad shoulders with her hands. The pain in her side had faded, and she barely noticed when James pulled her gently toward the armchair. Without breaking the kiss, he sat down and drew her onto his lap. She straddled him, pushing her tongue into his mouth enthusiastically.

She explored his warm mouth with her tongue as his hands stroked her back through her shirt. When his hand slid to her front and cupped one small breast, she arched her back and gripped the back of his neck. He pulled his mouth from hers and trailed warm, wet kisses down the slender column of her throat.

She didn't even notice when he unbuttoned her shirt. One moment his hand was cupping her breast through the fabric of her shirt, and the next it was touching her bare skin. His large, tanned hand completely covered her tiny breast. She had lost so much weight while being held captive by the Lycans that she was embarrassed by how thin and sickly she looked.

The embarrassment cut through the desire, but before she could pull away his thumb rubbed along her nipple. It hardened immediately and his low groan, the first sound he had made since they started kissing, brought a new surge of desire to her insides. He pinched her nipple lightly and she jerked and stared at him with wide eyes.

"I'm sorry. Did that hurt?" he rasped.

She shook her head and he brushed her shirt back until both of her breasts were bared to his hot gaze. He cupped them both and moved his thumbs in lazy circles around her nipples. Embarrassed by the small moans and whimpers coming from her mouth, she buried her face into his neck. She wanted to taste his skin and he angled his head so that she could lick a slow path down his throat. She nipped experimentally at his warm flesh and was delighted by the sharp inhale of breath and the way his hands tightened on her breasts.

———

JAMES TOOK A SHUDDERING BREATH AND CONTROLLED HIS urge to thrust his pelvis against the woman on his lap. He had coaxed Bree into kissing him as a last-ditch effort to heal her before she ran. He sucked in his breath when she nibbled at his throat. He hadn't expected to feel such a strong pull of need for her, or to be so excited by the feel of her mouth on his. She was obviously inexperienced, but the way she so sweetly responded to his touch had made his cock rock hard.

He stripped the shirt from her upper body. She blushed and tried to cover herself, but he tugged her hands down and kissed her collarbone, sliding his tongue across her flesh. She moaned and arched her back, pushing her pelvis against him as he kissed between her tiny breasts. When his mouth closed over her nipple and pulled lightly, she cried out and her nails dug into his broad shoulders.

"James, please," she moaned.

He released her nipple and quickly pulled off his own shirt. He pressed her upper body against his and sucked her earlobe into his mouth. She made a soft cry of pleasure and turned her face towards him.

"Kiss me, please," she pleaded.

———

BREE'S EMBARRASSMENT AT BEING HALF NAKED IN FRONT OF James had disappeared completely. When he sucked on her earlobe, she cried out and turned her face toward his. "Kiss me, please."

He kissed her immediately, his tongue thrusting deep into her mouth as he cupped one breast and squeezed and kneaded it gently. Bree squirmed on his lap. There was a strange heaviness between her legs, a throbbing that wasn't exactly painful, but she couldn't stop rubbing against James, trying to find relief from it.

James was kissing her slowly and thoroughly, and each stroke of his tongue was sending delicious shivers up and down her spine. She could kiss him forever, she thought dimly. She had never felt so good in her life. Her entire body was tingling and buzzing, and for the first time in months she felt no pain.

He rolled her nipple between his thumb and finger before pulling on it. It sent a throb of pleasure straight to the area between her thighs, and she made another soft moan of need. She ran her hands over his broad chest, threading her fingers through the coarse hair that covered it, and he made his own quiet noise of need.

"Your skin is so soft, Bree," he whispered against her mouth. "So warm and so soft."

"James, I need …"

She stared at him anxiously and he stroked her hair back from her face. "What do you need?"

"I don't know. It aches so much. I can't stand it," she moaned.

He frowned. "Where does it ache?"

She blushed furiously. "It aches between – between…"

A look of understanding dawned on his face. "Between your legs?"

She nodded. Her face was so red she could feel herself starting to sweat.

He kissed her again. "I can help you with that ache, Bree. Come to my room and I'll make the aching stop."

"Do you – do you promise?" she whispered.

"Aye," he pressed another kiss against her mouth, "I promise."

She stared into his dark eyes and nodded her agreement. He started to rise and then froze before sitting back abruptly. He pulled her forward until her breasts were mashed against his chest as Nicholas strolled into the room.

"Gods be damned, it's cold in here. Why haven't you built up the fire, you lazy red bastard? I can see my breath."

He stumbled to a stop and stared in surprise at Bree and James. "Sorry to interrupt, baby brother. I'll uh, just go now."

Before he could leave, Leta came bounding into the room and Bree felt, more than heard, James' low groan. "Nicky! Mama says that I -"

She skidded to a stop and stared in astonishment at James and Bree. "What's going on? Why isn't Bree wearing a shirt?"

Bree stared wide-eyed at James. She wanted to die of humiliation. Just when she thought it couldn't get any worse, Avery, followed by Tristan, entered the common room.

"Mama! Bree's sitting on James' lap and she's not wearing a shirt! Why isn't she wearing a shirt?" Leta squealed.

Avery didn't hesitate. "Leta, you know that the healing works best with bare skin. Remember the time you fell and skinned your arm? James let you rest it right against his bare chest, didn't he?"

"Aye," Leta said.

"Well, Bree is hurt as well. Only her injuries are on the

inside and much more painful than a skinned arm. In order for your brother to help her heal better, she had to take off her shirt." As she spoke, Avery crossed the room. She took the blanket from the back of the couch and wrapped it around Bree before tucking it behind James' back.

James grunted his thanks and Avery smiled at the two of them. "I'm so glad you decided to let James help you heal, my sweet Bree. We were worried about you."

Bree looked down in embarrassment. She suspected Avery knew exactly what they had been doing, but Bree was grateful for her pretense.

Avery clapped her hands briskly. "Leta, go and wake your sister and brother please. Nicholas, could you build up the fire? It's chilly in here."

Nicholas nodded as Tristan cleared his throat. "I'm uh, I'm going to go find out what's for breakfast."

"I will join you shortly." Avery smiled warmly at him before squeezing Bree's blanket-covered shoulder.

"James and Bree, you stay right where you are. It's important that Bree starts to feel better. I'll send Nicky for you when breakfast is ready."

CHAPTER 7

Nicholas built up the fire without speaking to either of them and then, after a cheeky grin at his brother, left the common room.

Bree couldn't look at James, and she didn't object when he cupped the back of her head and urged it toward his chest. She rested her cheek against his skin and listened to the steady beat of his heart in her ear.

"Do you feel better, Bree?"

"Aye, other than wanting to die of embarrassment," Bree muttered.

"You have nothing to be embarrassed about."

She snorted. "Nearly your entire family saw me half-naked and kissing you but no, I don't need to be embarrassed. Thank the gods your mother is a fast thinker and told Leta you were helping me heal."

He chuckled. "I am helping you heal."

"What do you mean?"

He shifted under her. "Kissing me, touching me, helps you heal faster. I don't know why it does, but my mother was speaking the truth when she told Leta that."

Bree didn't reply. Her stomach was burning with shame. James had only kissed her in order to heal her. She thought he had kissed her and touched her because he wanted her. She swallowed her disappointment. Believing someone like James would ever want someone like her was ridiculous. Besides, it was for the best. He was a Lycan and she hated Lycans.

Still, she couldn't help but recall the way it had felt when James had touched her. She shivered lightly at the memory of his deep voice promising to help her with the ache between her thighs.

"Are you cold, little one?" He hugged her closer to his warm body.

"No," she said. "I think you can let go now. My side isn't hurting at all."

He tightened his arms around her. "Are you trying to get me in trouble with my mother? She told us to sit here until breakfast and that's what we're going to do."

She could hear the grin in his voice, but she refused to look at him. "Will this be enough to heal me completely?"

"I don't know. We'll find out when I let go of you. Of course, since you have a tendency to lie to me about how you're feeling, I'll probably have to join you in my bed tonight just to be on the safe side."

She stiffened against him. "No! You promised me you wouldn't."

"I'm only teasing you, little one. I'm sorry. I did not mean to frighten you," James said immediately.

"I'm not afraid. I'm just – I'm very tired. Can we please stop talking now?"

"Aye," he said.

She stared into the fire, trembling lightly against him.

"How do you feel now?" Avery sat down on the couch beside her and rested her hand on Bree's leg.

"Better, I think."

It was just after breakfast and Avery had invited her to sit in the common room with her for a bit. The others had disappeared, and Leta was thrilled when Bree gave her permission to take Tia to her room to play.

"Are you sure?"

"Aye. My side doesn't hurt anymore."

Avery smiled. "Why don't you let me hold you for a while?"

It was a strange thing to offer but Bree didn't really think about it. The idea of being held by Avery was very appealing to her, and so she scooted her butt across the couch as Avery opened her arms. She snuggled into the redhead, resting her head on Avery's shoulder and sighing happily when Avery wrapped her arms around her.

She closed her eyes as Avery stroked her long hair. "You have very pretty hair, Bree."

"Thank you. I like yours better," Bree said shyly. "I have never seen a Red before I met you and James."

Avery laughed. "We are uncommon."

"I do not believe the stories you know."

Avery continued to stroke her hair. "Sadly, there are still plenty who do. Five years ago, men from a nearby village attacked our home. There had been some strange animal deaths, and they blamed James and me. They wanted to burn both of us at the stake."

"What happened?" Bree whispered.

"The humans are no match for Lycans – even half-breeds," Avery replied.

"Did they – did they kill them?"

"No, of course not. Tristan would never kill a human unless given no other choice. Our children have been taught that all life has a value, and we need to respect those who are different from us."

They were quiet for a little while and Bree shifted closer to Avery. "Am I too heavy?"

"No. You probably weigh less than Leta." Avery laughed.

"It's so nice to sit with you," Bree murmured.

"Is it? I'm glad," Avery replied.

Bree leaned into her. She felt so calm and happy. Sitting with Avery felt almost as good as sitting with James. Her eyes popped open and she stared wide-eyed at Avery.

"You're a healer too."

"Aye, little one. I am." Avery smiled down at her. "Although I believe James is more powerful than I when it comes to healing."

"What do you mean?"

"When I help to heal someone, I often have to rest afterward or sit with someone who is healthy. Both James and I can absorb a person's good health as well as their illness. James doesn't seem to need to though. He can heal someone and still feel strong and healthy himself. I've never seen him look tired or unwell until he and Nicky arrived home with you."

A thread of guilt went through Bree. "That's my fault. If I had known it would hurt him, I would never have -"

"Do not be concerned, Bree. James was perfectly fine after a night of sleep," Avery said. "Of course, it probably also helped that Leta missed her brothers terribly and was clinging to him for hours. She's as healthy as a horse that one."

"Do you know why he's more powerful?" Bree asked.

Avery shook her head. "No. Although perhaps it is the combination of the healing power he inherited from me, and his natural Lycan healing abilities."

"Do all of your children have this ability?"

"No. But our healing gift does not reveal itself until puberty. We discovered that James had the ability to heal when he was thirteen. Evan is fifteen and shows no signs of it, but Leta is only ten. She may still develop the ability."

As if she heard her, Leta, followed closely by Tia, barrelled into the common room. "Mama, can I please go to the barn and see Papa?"

"Yes, you may." Avery smiled at Bree as Leta left the room. "Why don't I take you around and introduce you to everyone? I assume you're staying a few days with us before you travel to your aunt's home?"

Bree gathered Tia in her arms and petted the dog nervously. "Um, I haven't decided what my plans are."

Avery didn't push her for details. She linked her arm through Bree's and tugged her to her feet. "That's fine. You can let us know when you decide."

BREE SMILED UNCERTAINLY AT TRISTAN. IT WAS HER FOURTH day here and every morning when she tried to sneak out of the house, she had stumbled across a different family member. The second morning it was Avery. She'd caught Bree as she was sneaking past the kitchen and asked her to join her for a cup of tea. Afraid of hurting the redhead's feelings, she agreed. By the time Avery made the tea, both Tristan and Sophia had joined them in the kitchen.

Yesterday morning it was Nicholas. She had actually

made it out the front door that time. Before she could close it quietly behind her, Nicholas, yawning hugely and pulling a jacket over his thin shirt, had staggered out behind her.

"Lovely morning for a walk!" He'd said cheerfully, rubbing the sleep from his eyes. "Do you mind if I join you?"

She'd shaken her head no, and then spent an hour wandering Tristan's and Avery's rather large and impressive estate as Nicholas chatted to her.

This morning, Tristan was waiting in the common room when she slipped quietly down the hallway. She sighed. Her plan to sneak away was obviously not going to work. She would just have to gather her courage, thank them for their hospitality and tell them she had to leave.

"Have you been given a tour of the barn yet, Bree?" Tristan asked.

She shook her head no and he offered her his arm. "I'm heading there now. Why don't you come with me?"

She took his arm, not registering that even three days ago she would not have touched him unless forced to, and he led her outside to the barn. They entered the warm and steamy building, and she stared around in surprise. It was a large barn but there were more horses than she had expected.

"Good morning, Tristan."

A man was walking down the wide aisle in the center of the barn. Bree thought his name was Jeffrey, but she couldn't remember if he was human or Lycan. As he approached, she shrank back against Tristan and he patted her arm gently.

"You're fine, little one." He sounded so much like James that she smiled. They really were very similar.

"Good morning, Jeffrey." Tristan nodded to the man.

"Going for a ride?" Jeffrey gave Bree a friendly smile and she looked away shyly.

"No, just showing Bree the barn. She hasn't been in here yet."

"I'm heading to the smaller barn. Ian says that Bella should be ready to give birth any day now."

"Let me know when she goes into labour."

Jeffrey nodded and, whistling under his breath, left the barn.

"Who is Bella?" Bree asked timidly.

"One of our mares. We bred her with Samson, and she'll be giving birth soon."

"Oh."

Tristan led her down the aisle of the barn, telling her the names of the different horses they passed. When they were halfway to the end of the barn, she cleared her throat nervously. "May I ask you something, my lord?"

"Call me Tristan, and yes you may."

"Why do you have so many horses? It seems strange for Lycans. Where I – where I was before they didn't use horses at all. Do you not move faster than horses when in your Lycan form?"

Tristan laughed. "Aye, that is true, Bree. We do move faster than horses." He stopped in front of a stall and reached in to pet the small grey horse that was standing in it. The horse snorted quietly and nudged at his hand with its broad nose.

"I have loved horses since I was a boy. My father had no use for them, but he indulged my love and allowed me to have a few when I was growing up. About fifteen years ago, Avery convinced me to do what I had always wanted to do and breed them. I've been breeding and selling horses for nearly ten years now."

"Is that why you are so rich?" Bree blurted out without

thinking. She stared at him in horror, afraid she had insulted him, but he threw back his head and laughed.

"We are not rich, little one."

Bree gave him a doubtful look. Their home was large, they had not one barn but two, and they paid their slaves to work for them. She was two when her parents died and her brother, only twelve years old, had somehow managed to keep them both alive. Even before they were captured by the Lycans, they'd never had enough to eat. They'd slept in abandoned buildings and in fields, and she had never once had more than a few coins to her name. The most stable time of her life was the three years they worked as slaves for a human family that lived just outside of the city.

Her brother had gotten them into the household, she had no idea how and he wouldn't say, and she'd worked in the house while he worked the fields. They weren't paid, but they were given one meal a day and beds in the slave quarters.

Her face darkened. Draken's pack had attacked the home and taken the humans as their own slaves. She'd spent the next two years living in fear, never knowing when she would be chosen to be hunted.

Tristan was staring at her and she gave him a timid smile. "I am sorry, my lord. I did not mean to offend."

"You didn't," he replied. "My father did very well for himself. When he died his wealth passed to me. I have lived a very fortunate life."

"Is your mother still alive?"

"Aye. She lives with us, actually. She is visiting my adopted brother Marshall and his family at the moment."

He stopped in front of a stall that held the largest horse Bree had ever seen. It was completely black in colour except for a white blaze on its forehead. Its coat looked silky soft, and she took a nervous step back when it hung its large head over the stall door and snuffled at Tristan's coat.

Tristan rubbed the horse's forehead. "Are you afraid of horses, Bree?"

She licked her lips. "No."

"Do you know how to ride?"

"Of course," she said.

He gave her a stern look. "I would prefer if you tell me the truth, little one."

Her mouth dried up and she took another step backward. Even though Tristan had not raised his voice and his body language was relaxed, she could feel her pulse speeding up.

"Don't be frightened, Bree," Tristan said gently. "I know why you fear my kind, but I promise no one here will ever harm you."

When she didn't reply he took his own step backward, putting more space between them. "Have you ridden before?" he asked again.

She was opening her mouth to squeak out an answer when a familiar voice spoke behind her. "Good morning."

She whipped around, her body sagging with relief when she saw James. He frowned at the look on her face and put his arm around her, pulling her slender body against his. "What's wrong, little one?"

"I've frightened her," Tristan replied. "I'm sorry, Bree. I did not mean to."

"What did you do?" James snapped at him.

Tristan stared at him silently, and James flushed before looking away. "Sorry, Dad."

"He didn't do anything," Bree said. "It's me. I'm just um – a little nervous that's all."

She took a deep breath and gave Tristan a shaky smile. "No, my lord. I do not know how to ride a horse."

"Then I'll have James teach you," Tristan replied.

"Teach her what?"

Still keeping his arm around Bree, James turned to see Nicholas and Evan ambling down the aisle of the barn.

"I'm going to teach Bree how to ride a horse." James squeezed Bree's shoulder and smiled at her.

She knew she should be stepping away, but the gods be damned, it felt so good to be standing against him. She wanted to wrap her thin arms around his waist and bury her face in his chest. The only time she didn't feel afraid was when she was near him.

He shifted her against him, and she leaned into his warm body and stared up at his mouth. Kissing him had excited her in a way that she didn't understand. She wondered what it would be like to share his bed, to straddle him and feel his hardness rubbing against her. She would –

"Bree?" James was looking at her curiously, and she blushed and pulled free of his embrace.

James was kind to her, and he was the most human-like Lycan she had ever met, but she needed to remember that he was still a beast and not to be trusted. He had saved her life, and sooner or later he would demand some type of payment for it.

What if he demands you join him in his bed? What if his idea of payment is taking your innocence?

Instead of being horrified at the idea, a tremor of lust went through her belly. For his size and strength, he was surprisingly gentle. There was a secret part of her that wanted him to take her to his bed. She wanted to be under him. She wanted his hands on her body and his mouth –

"Bree?" James took a step toward her and she backed away. What she was thinking was madness. Her brother, at great risk to his own life, had protected her from the Lycans who had wanted to rape her. Now she was betraying him by hoping the Lycan in front of her would take her to his bed.

"You're fine, little one," James murmured soothingly. He reached for her, and she stumbled back until she ran into the solid wall that was Nicholas.

Nicholas patted her shoulder awkwardly as she staggered away from him.

"I'm sorry. I didn't sleep well last night," she muttered.

"Is your side hurting?" James frowned.

She shook her head. "No, it isn't. I swear it."

She hoped he could see the truth on her face. She really was feeling better. Nothing hurt at all, and just four days of eating three meals a day had already made a difference in how she looked and felt.

He studied her carefully for a moment and then nodded as Evan stared at her curiously. "How come you don't know how to ride a horse, Bree?"

"I just never learned." She stared at the sword he was casually swinging back and forth.

"Oh." He turned to Nicholas. "Are we going to work on sword training this morning or just hang out in the barn?"

Nicholas punched him lightly on the shoulder. "Be careful, Evan. Your cheekiness will get you extra push-ups."

She gathered her courage. "Would you train me to use the sword, Nicholas?"

Nicholas blinked in surprise and then looked to his father. Tristan gave Bree an appraising look before nodding at Nicholas.

"Aye," Nicholas said. "I'll teach you."

"No," James said. "She does not need to learn to use a sword."

Nicholas frowned at him. "And why not, baby brother?

Sophia and our mother both know how to use one. As will Leta when she is big enough."

"Bree is too little. She can barely lift a sword, let alone swing one." James scowled at Nicholas.

"She can build up her strength, James. There is no reason she can't at least try," Nicholas protested.

"I said no," James snarled.

"I heard you the first time," Nicholas said cheerfully. "But if father says I can train her on the sword then I will."

"Do not try my patience, Nicky," James growled. "Bree does not need to learn sword fighting. I will protect her and keep her safe."

"Travelling to Vanden with her then, are you?" Nicholas raised his eyebrow.

James flushed. "No sword training, Nicky."

Nicholas laughed. "It's not your decision to make."

"It's not yours either," James replied.

"Do the two of you realize how incredibly insulting you're being to Bree?" Sophia had joined them in the barn.

She gave her brothers a look of disgust. "Bree is a grown woman. She does not need either of you making decisions on her behalf."

Tristan grinned. "Your sister is right."

"Dad, I -"

Tristan held up his hand. "Enough, James. If Bree wants to learn sword fighting, then Nicky will teach her."

James swore violently, making Bree shrink back, and he stomped from the barn without looking at any of them.

"He's so dramatic." Sophia rolled her eyes and held her hand out to Bree. "Come, Bree. Mama and I are going to town with Jeffrey and she wants you to come with us."

"I'm going as well," Tristan replied.

"Papa," Sophia gave him a loving look that was tinged

with exasperation, "it was five years ago, and the attack came from the village to the south. The people in this town have always been welcoming."

Tristan shrugged and gave the giant black horse one final pat. "I'm still going with you, Sophia."

CHAPTER 8

"No, I don't need them." Bree crossed her arms across her chest and shook her head.

Sophia frowned. "Bree, you can't walk around barefoot. It's just going to get colder and none of our shoes will fit you."

They were standing in a small store on the edge of town. The shelves in the store were stacked high with clothing for both men and women, and there was a small section at the back that carried shoes and boots.

While Sophia and Avery looked through the clothing, Tristan and Jeffrey went next door to the food supply store. Although they grew most of their own food, Marian had requested a certain type of spice and Avery needed more tea.

Bree was fascinated by the glass display case that ran the length of the counter. It was filled to the brim with necklaces and bracelets and rings that sparkled and shone under the weak light. She was almost as fascinated by the lights as she was the pretty jewels. She had never been in a building that had electricity, and she had stared for some time at the bulbs that glowed in the ceiling before directing her attention back to the display case.

"Do you like them, girl?" The store owner leaned over the counter and grinned at her. She gave him a polite smile and held her breath. He was smeared with grime, and the smell of ripe cheese was wafting off of him.

He was missing both of his front teeth, and he'd touched the tip of his tongue to the gums as he grinned. "Perhaps you'd like to try one on, Miss?"

She shook her head. "No thank you. I'm only looking."

"Are you sure?" He'd wheedled. "These pretty pieces come from the old city they do."

She'd stared doubtfully at him. She knew of the old cities but had never actually seen one. There was a rumour that the buildings of the ancients towered so high into the sky, you couldn't see the top of them. She had often wondered what it would be like to walk among the ancient's structures, but she would never do so. Too many people who visited the old cities or lived too close to them, died horrible deaths. They vomited for no reason and lost all of their hair. At least that's what her brother had told her. To think there were people who would risk going to the old cities just for a few shiny objects baffled her.

"It's true." The man spoke as though she had expressed her doubt verbally. "These all come from the old cities. The men who brought them to me are long dead of course."

He had lifted his head and brayed laughter. "Foolish buggers. As soon as the first sores appeared, they were driven away to the outskirts, they were."

Bree had shuddered. The outskirts were filled with faeries and leeches, and the gods only knew what other types of creatures. She had not objected when Sophia appeared and pulled her away from the display case.

Now, she shook her head again as Sophia showed her the boots she picked out.

"I do not have the money for them, Sophia," she said quietly. "And I have gone nearly my entire life without shoes. I will be fine without them."

"Do you believe you can walk all the way to Vanden without shoes?" Sophia raised her eyebrow at her.

"What's wrong?" Avery had joined them.

"I found the perfect pair of boots for Bree," Sophia said. "But she is insisting she does not need them."

"I do not have the money for them." Bree scowled at Sophia. "Drop it, Sophia."

Sophia grinned. "She shows some spirit. I was beginning to think she would be a scared, creeping mouse forever."

"Sophia, enough, my love," Avery said. "Bree, you can't go without boots."

"I can and I will," Bree replied.

"Tristan will not let you learn to use a sword without wearing boots," Avery said.

Bree sighed and looked at the floor before repeating, "I do not have money for them."

"How will you travel to Vanden if you have no money?" Sophia asked suddenly.

Bree flushed. "I thought I might see if there is a family in town who is looking to hire a housekeeper."

Sophia frowned. "This is not the city, Bree. People here still use slaves." Her nose wrinkled with distaste. "You will not find a family who will pay you to work for them."

Bree could feel the tears threatening to fall. She had come up with her plan on the ride to town and had been proud of herself for devising a way to make some money. She was anxious to return to Draken's home and save her brother, but after some time to think on it she had realized she could not make the journey without money. Although she was worried for her brother, she knew that Draken would not kill him. By now Kaden would know she had escaped the Lycans during the hunt.

She sniffed and blinked rapidly. She suddenly missed Kaden so much it was a physical ache in her belly. She wished there was a way she could tell him she was safe. He would know she had escaped the beasts, but he would not know if she had survived beyond that.

"Bree?" Avery's arm was suddenly around her. Without thinking about it, Bree turned and hugged the redhead. She buried her face in Avery's neck and breathed deeply. Avery rubbed her back and kissed the side of her head.

"What is wrong, my love?"

"Nothing," Bree whispered. "I just – I miss my aunt very much."

"Of course, you do," Avery answered, stroking her hair. "We will hire you to work in our household. A few months and you will have the money you need to visit your aunt."

Bree leaned into Avery. Warmth was radiating through her entire body and she already felt better. "You said you had no need for more workers."

Avery put a hand under her chin and tipped her head up gently. "Aye, but I bet Marian will disagree with me. She will be more than happy to have help with laundry and cooking, and other house duties."

"Mama," Sophia began but Avery gave her a look that quieted her instantly.

"Now," Avery wiped away the tears on Bree's cheeks with her thumbs, "you must go and pick out some clothes that fit. Pick out some pairs of pants, and a few shirts and a dress or two. We will take these boots and find you a pair of shoes as well."

Bree opened her mouth to object and Avery pressed her hand gently over her lips. "You can pay me back with your first week's wages. Deal?"

"Deal." Bree smiled happily at her before crossing the store to the shelves piled high with clothing.

"Mama, you said earlier that you don't believe she has an aunt in Vanden. Why are you pretending otherwise?" Sophia asked once Bree was out of earshot.

"She obviously needs money for something. And there must be a reason she has asked to learn how to fight with a sword. Perhaps with time she will trust us enough to tell us the truth, and allow us to help her," Avery replied.

"James likes her," Sophia said suddenly.

"Aye, he does." Avery smiled fondly at Sophia. "Do me a favour, my sweet Sophia, and do not tease him about her."

Sophia grinned at her. "Will you ask Nicky the same favour?"

Avery returned her grin. "I already have. He has promised to be on his best behaviour."

"BREE! LOOK AT WHAT I CAN DO!"

Bree turned from where she was hanging the bed sheets on the line and watched as Leta did a cartwheel. She clapped and the girl bowed deeply.

"Well done, Leta!"

"Thanks. Sophia showed me how to do it last week, and I've been practicing every day."

The little girl watched as Bree continued to hang the sheets on the line.

"Do you like it here, Bree?"

"I do." Bree smiled. "Your family is very kind."

"Do you like me?"

"Very much so." She winked at the little girl.

She pinned the sheet carefully to the clothesline and began to hang the next one. Over the last four weeks she had grown very fond of Leta and the rest of her family. She snorted softly. Fond was an understatement for how she felt about Avery. She was fooling herself if she tried to pretend that she didn't love the Red.

She had never been in a household like Avery's and Tristan's. The humans who worked in their home were treated as equals to the family, and most nights there would be at least three or four of them in the common room. They played games and shared stories with the family, and no one seemed to think it odd.

Bree had tried to hide her affection for Avery, but she feared she was doing a poor job of it. Avery was the mother she had always dreamed of having, and she found it difficult to stay away from her. Avery was very kind and would often invite her to sit next to her on the couch in the evenings. She would cuddle Leta on one side and Bree on the other, and Bree soaked in her gentle touch and sweet words like a flower in the rain.

"I like you too. My brother has a crush on you."

Bree's heart sped up. James had been teaching her to ride for the last three weeks, and the first few days she could hardly concentrate on what he was teaching her. Every time she looked at him, she remembered the way it had felt to kiss him, how warm his mouth had been on her breast and how gentle his touch was.

She would end each riding lesson with trembling limbs and butterflies in her stomach. Although there was nothing in James' infrequent touches that suggested he even remembered that morning in the common room, she often pretended that he wanted to kiss her. Pretended that he had touched her and kissed her not to heal her, but because he wanted her.

She wasn't afraid of him anymore. In fact, she wasn't afraid of any of them. A month of living with them, of seeing how kind they were to each other and to humans, had gone a long way in showing her that not all Lycans were like Draken and his pack.

A twinge of guilt went through her. Although James and his family were not like Draken, she still felt like she was betraying Kaden by loving Avery and lusting after James. Even before they were captured by the cruel Lycan, her brother had cautioned her to stay away from creatures that were not like them.

She gave Leta a small smile. "Does he now? Did he tell you this?"

"Nah." Leta tugged on one of the wet sheets and then wiped her damp hand on her pants. "But I found one of his drawings of you."

Bree frowned. "Drawings?"

"Aye." Leta grinned at her. "Evan spends most of his time reading or drawing. Look."

She pulled a folded-up piece of paper from her pocket and handed it to Bree. She carefully unfolded it and stared at the surprisingly good portrait of her face.

"Evan has the crush on me?" she asked as she handed the paper back to Leta.

"He does! He's always mooning over you when he thinks you're not looking!" Leta said gleefully.

Bree ignored the disappointment in her belly. Of course, Leta wasn't talking about James. She spent two hours alone with the Lycan every day, and he treated her no differently than he treated Sophia or Leta.

This hope that he wanted her the way she wanted him was

ridiculous. Besides, it didn't matter. In another month or two she would have enough money to leave their home and go after Kaden. Even if she was successful in rescuing him without being captured, tortured and killed, she would still never see James or his family again. Kaden would never agree to work for Lycans, and she would not leave her brother. No matter how good the Lycans were to her.

"Where's Tia?" Leta asked suddenly.

"She's around here somewhere. Whistle for her," Bree replied.

Leta whistled piercingly and after a moment, Tia came darting around the corner of the house. She leaped at Leta who caught her and giggled loudly when Tia licked at her face, her entire body wiggling happily.

"Tia loves me."

"Yes, she does." Bree smiled at her. "Who are those men with your father?"

"I dunno." Leta shrugged disinterestedly. "I think they're here to purchase some horses from Papa. They're human." Her nose wrinkled. "They smell bad."

Bree laughed. "Not everyone has access to running water like we do, Leta."

"I'd rather bathe in the lake. Do you know how to swim, Bree?"

"No."

"I could teach you!" Leta said excitedly. "Mama taught all of us how to swim. She even tried to teach Papa to swim better. It's so funny to see him trying to swim. He's terrible at it."

"It's too cold to swim, Leta." Bree shivered. "We'd freeze to death."

"I'll teach you next summer. After Mama, I'm the best swimmer," she boasted.

"That would be nice of you," Bree said.

"I bet we – "

"Well, hello there."

Both Bree and Leta whipped around as Tia growled deep in her throat. A man, he was tall and lean with dark brown hair, was leaning against the corner of the house.

Leta took a step back. Her head was up, and she was inhaling deeply as she stared mistrustfully at the man in front of them. Her brown eyes were starting to lighten, and she was squeezing Tia so tightly the little dog made a whimper of discomfort.

"Don't fear me, little half-breed. I wish you no harm." The man smiled and held his hands up.

"Who are you?" Bree asked bluntly.

"I'm here to buy horses from the half-breed's father."

"Don't call her that," Bree snapped at him. "Go into the house, Leta."

When the girl didn't move, she gave her a gentle push. "Go on now."

Leta turned and ran to the house with Tia as Bree went back to pinning up the sheets. Her stomach was churning, and her palms were sweating. There was something about the man that made her anxious, but she was determined not to let him see her nervousness. She wished for a brief moment that she had a sword but scoffed inwardly at herself. Although she trained with Nicky nearly every day, she was nowhere close to being able to use a sword effectively.

"Tell me, pretty one – are you a Lycan or a human?"

"Human," she said.

"Like me!" The man gave her a delighted grin and moved closer, ducking around one of the sheets flapping gently in the cold breeze.

He looked her up and down. "I'm not surprised you're

human. The Lycans would never allow one of their own kind to be a slave."

She didn't reply and took a few steps backward under the pretense of straightening the already straight sheet on the line.

The man looked around, taking in the large house behind Bree. "These Lycans have done very well for themselves. Everywhere I look there are human slaves. They seem to have a great amount of them."

He reached for Bree's arm and she took another step backward, glaring at him.

"Come here, girl. I wish to take a better look at you."

"No," she replied.

He laughed. "You dare to deny me? A slave? The Lycans allow their slaves too much freedom I think."

He stroked one of the sheets with a rough and dirty finger. "Do you think the Lycans would consider selling something to me other than a horse? I am in need of a slave to clean my house and warm my bed."

She gave him a look of disgust and he frowned. "What? Do you not find me pleasing to the eye? I've not had any complaints before."

He crooked his hand at her. "Come here, girl. I grow tired of your games. If the Lycan's consent to selling you to me, you will learn quickly that I am not to be disobeyed. My last slave found herself abandoned at the outskirts when she defied me."

When she didn't move, he shot forward with terrifying quickness and grabbed her upper arm through her sweater. "Would you like to live with me, sweet one?"

She tried to pull her arm free and his hand tightened harshly. Her breath hissed out between her teeth at the pain, and she raised her free hand and slapped him hard across the face.

He stared in disbelief at her as his tanned cheek started to redden. "You did not just do that, you silly little bitch."

He raised his hand but before he could strike her, a soft voice spoke behind them.

"Let her go."

Relief coursed through Bree at the sound of James' voice. The man dropped her arm and she stumbled backward toward James. He put his arm around her waist and pulled her back until her body was pressed firmly against his. His hand cupped her hip and when he spoke, she could feel the vibration in her back.

"Go back and join your friends."

"Now hold on, half-breed." The man smiled at him. "I wish to purchase this slave from you. How much for her?"

"She is not for sale."

"Come now, everything is for sale." The man crossed his arms across his chest. "You have more than enough slaves. Sell this one to me – I'll give you a fair price for her."

James, his nostrils flaring, said, "She is not a slave."

The man arched his eyebrows. "Well then, she is free to make her own decision." He winked at Bree. "My home is not as large as the half-breed's but that isn't a bad thing is it? You will spend less time cleaning and more time warming my bed."

There was another vibration against her back as James growled low in his chest and his hand tightened on her hip. "The woman belongs to me."

A look of disgust passed over the man's face. "Keep her then. I wouldn't take her into my bed knowing she has spread her legs for a half-breed Red."

James growled again. Bree could feel his chest expanding against her back and she glanced upward, her heart constricting with fear. His eyes were green and glowing, and she tried to step away from him, but his arm tightened around her waist.

"Say one more word about her and I'll kill you where you stand, human." James' voice was thick and inhuman, and fear flooded the man's face.

He backed up a few steps. "I meant no disrespect."

James grunted. "I know exactly what you meant, human. Scurry back to your friends and finish your business with my father before I lose my patience completely."

The man backed away until he disappeared behind the house. Bree waited a few moments, her heart thumping loudly, and then looked up at James. His eyes were back to their normal brown and he was staring down at her. She sagged against him and he turned her around, keeping one arm around her waist.

"Did he hurt you, little one?"

"No. He grabbed my arm but it's fine," Bree said.

"Let me see." James tugged on the bottom of her sweater, and she raised her arms so he could pull it over her head. She stood in front of him, shivering lightly in her thin sleeveless shirt.

———

JAMES STUDIED BREE. FOUR WEEKS WITH A STEADY SUPPLY of food had done her a world of good. Her previous thin frame had filled out, and her cheeks glowed with health. He had been careful to touch her as little as possible in the last month, and today was the first time he had allowed himself to touch her on purpose. Even as he had been talking with the stranger, his hand was registering the new fullness of her hip, and now he raised the hem of her shirt to the bottom of her breasts and examined her belly.

She blushed and pushed his hands away. She tugged her shirt down nervously as he smiled to himself. Her ribs were no longer visible, and her hip bones didn't jut out nearly as much as before. His eyes dropped to her breasts. They were still small, not more than a handful really, and he could see the outline of her nipples against her shirt as they hardened in the cold air.

A thread of lust went through him and he tamped it down. Skinny little Bree had gotten into his head in a way that no other woman ever had. The last four weeks, his mind had constantly returned to the morning in the common room when she had kissed him. Her mouth had been so soft, and the way she had timidly kissed him had set his body on fire.

Each riding lesson he gave her was a lesson in torture for him. He had to force himself to touch her as little as possible. She was more comfortable around him then she used to be, although he would freely admit that had more to do with his mother than him, but he was afraid of doing anything that would frighten her again.

She had wanted him that morning in the common room. It was obvious in the way she'd kissed him and in the way she responded to his touch, but the look of fear that had crossed her face when he spoke of joining her in his bed had been heartbreakingly real.

He frowned as his gaze fell on her arm. There was a red mark in the shape of the man's fingers, and fresh anger filled his body.

He thought briefly of killing the man for touching her, but Bree's face was tightening, and she gave him a worried look. "My lord, have I done something wrong?"

He took a deep breath. "No, Bree. Of course, you haven't." His fingers traced the red mark on her arm. "This will be a bruise by tomorrow."

She glanced at her arm dismissively. "It's fine."

"Close your eyes."

She gave him a nervous look but did what he asked. He leaned down and pressed his mouth against the red marks on her arm. She inhaled sharply, trembling against him as he placed a series of small, light kisses against her arm.

"James," she moaned softly.

"Yes, Bree?" His other hand slid up her back to cup her neck under her mass of blonde hair.

"What – what are you doing?"

"Healing you," he whispered.

She moaned again as he let his mouth drift up her arm to her shoulder. He kissed the top of it, and then pressed his lips against her flesh where her neck became her shoulder. He knew he should stop. He had told himself he wouldn't touch her this way again, but his mouth seemed to have a mind of his own.

He pulled gently on the back of her neck and she tipped her head to the side, giving him access to her throat. Her eyes were still closed, and she was panting harshly as he traced her skin with his tongue. She gripped his arms with her small hands and stepped closer to him. He kissed the curve of her jaw and then nuzzled his way to her ear. His tongue dipped into it and she shuddered, breathing his name lightly as he kissed her cheekbone and the tip of her nose.

She tilted her head up, her lips parting invitingly, and he groaned and dropped his mouth to hers. He thrust his tongue deep into her mouth. Her soft moans were driving him crazy and he cupped her breast in his hand. Her nipple was hard against his palm and he pressed his pelvis experimentally against her. His cock was hard and throbbing, and he felt her tense as it brushed her stomach.

He threaded his fingers in her hair and held her head as he

increased the pressure of his mouth on hers and stroked her tongue. She relaxed against him and he squeezed her breast, making her groan, before he moved his hand around to her ass. He kneaded it lightly and pressed her up against his hard body.

He released her mouth and was just starting to lift her up, he wanted to press his cock directly against her warm center, when Tia barked loudly. Bree pulled away and looked behind him, her cheeks turning pink. He turned to see Leta staring at them, holding Tia in her arms.

"Gross," she announced. "I'm telling Mama you were touching Bree's butt."

"Leta," James said warningly. "What did mom tell you about spying on people?"

"I wasn't spying!" she protested.

"I told you to stay in the house."

She gave him a defiant look. "I wanted to make sure Bree was okay."

"She's fine. Go back in the house." Beside him Bree was slipping her sweater over her head, and he had just enough time to see that the red marks were gone from her arm before it was covered by the fabric.

"Evan's going to be mad when he finds out you were kissing Bree. He likes her," Leta said saucily.

"Leta," James sighed impatiently. "You need to" -

Bree brushed past him and crouched next to Leta. "Honey, James was just helping me heal. The man grabbed my arm and bruised it, so your brother was kind enough to hug me and help my arm to stop hurting."

Leta giggled. "He touched your butt, Bree."

Bree grinned at her. "Yeah, I know. Will you do me a favour and not tell anyone he did that?"

"Aye. Sometimes I see Papa patting Mama's butt when

she walks by him. She laughs and smacks him." Leta stared at her older brother. "You should have smacked him."

"I'll remember that." Bree put her arm around Leta's shoulders. "Come, it's too cold out here." Without looking at him, she led the little girl into the house.

CHAPTER 9

"Stop being so timid and strike at me, Bree."

"I'm trying!" Bree panted and lunged at Nicholas. He dodged her easily and struck her sword with his own. It tumbled from her hand, and she cursed and picked it up.

Nicholas grinned at her. "You're doing better."

She rolled her eyes. "No, I'm not."

"Aye, you are. Two weeks ago, you couldn't even hold the sword up for more than ten minutes at a time."

"At this rate I'll be a great swordsman by the time I'm eighty," Bree said.

Nicholas laughed. "You don't need to be a great swordsman, Bree. You just need to be proficient at defending yourself."

Bree lowered the sword and rubbed her aching arm. She didn't want to tell Nicholas this but if it wasn't for sitting with Avery every night, she wasn't sure she'd be able to train as much as she was. She left every training session with her arms and shoulders aching and throbbing from holding up the sword, and only Avery's healing powers allowed her to pick up the sword the next day.

"Let's try again," Nicholas urged her.

She shrugged out of her sweater, it was cold out but the exercise had warmed her, and flexed her shoulders experimentally.

"Remember to try and think of the sword as an extension of your hand. Shoulders back, head up and -"

Movement caught her eye and she groaned when she saw James, Tristan and Leta come out of the barn. It had been two days since she had kissed James behind the house, and she'd avoided him since then. Her cheeks burned with embarrassment. She wanted him very much, but she wasn't sure he felt the same way. She suddenly wished bitterly that she had more experience with men. She thought James wanted her – that hardness pressing against her belly two days ago had been a good indication he did – but she had been here a month, and he only touched her when she was hurt and needed healing.

If he truly did want her would he not go out of his way to touch her like Tristan did with Avery, she wondered. The large Lycan was always holding the Red's hand or stroking her hair. Last week Bree had caught them in the kitchen making out like they were teenagers. Tristan's love and affection for Avery was obvious, and it made Bree's heart happy to watch them together. Perhaps one day she would find someone who would look at her the way Tristan looked at Avery.

"Bree? Pay attention." Nicholas tapped her leg with the flat side of his sword.

"Sorry." She risked another glance at James and the others, and Nicholas followed her gaze.

It was obvious they were going to stop to watch, and she gave Nicholas a hopeful look. "Could we go somewhere else to train?"

He shook his head. "No. It's good to have others around.

You have to learn to not be so distracted by your surroundings."

She sighed as he raised his sword. "Raise your sword, little one."

———

JAMES WATCHED AS NICHOLAS AND BREE FOUGHT. His stomach was rolling, and his fists were clenched tightly at his sides. Leta was chattering beside him but he didn't hear a word. Every nerve in his body was screaming at him to shift and protect Bree from harm.

His heart was pounding in his chest, and he growled lightly when Nicholas knocked Bree to the ground and held his sword to her throat.

"He won't hurt her, James," Tristan said.

James didn't reply. A surge of jealousy went through him when Nicholas took Bree's hand and pulled her to her feet. He picked some dried leaves from her hair and then ruffled her hair. She gave him a mock scowl that made him laugh before he kissed her roughly on the forehead.

James took a step forward. His instinct had swung from wanting to protect, to showing his impudent brother that Bree was his. How dare he touch her. How dare he try and take what belonged to him. He would show Nicholas that he would be wise not to –

"Papa? Why is James shifting?" Leta's voice was thin with alarm and she looked around warily.

"Control it, James."

His father's low growl demanded obedience, and James immediately looked away from Nicholas and Bree. He took a few deep breaths as Tristan lifted Leta into his arms and kissed her smooth cheek.

"What's wrong, Papa?" Leta was still looking around in alarm and her eyes had lightened.

"Nothing is wrong, my sweet." Tristan tugged on her braid. "Your brother is tired that's all."

"Oh," Leta replied doubtfully. She stared at her brother's back for a moment before watching Nicholas and Bree again.

"She's not very good at this," she said.

"Hush, Leta. She will improve," Tristan replied.

"She's too small. The sword is too heavy for her," Leta pointed out. "She can barely lift it and she's been practicing for weeks. I will be much better at it than she is."

"Leta, you're being rude. Do you remember when your mama and I talked to you about not saying everything that you think?" Tristan gave her a stern look. "If Bree heard what you were saying, it would hurt her feelings. Is that what you want?"

"No, Papa," Leta said. "But Mama says I should always be truthful. Bree isn't very big, and she's not very good with the sword."

"That may be true, but you must be more tactful with your words," Tristan said.

James could hear the laughter in his father's voice.

"What does tactful mean?"

"It means that you -"

Bree made a sharp cry and Leta gasped as James whipped around. Nicholas dropped his sword and stepped toward Bree, staring horrified at the long, deep cut on her forearm.

THE BLOOD FLOWED FROM HER ARM AND BREE STARED IN disbelief at the slice on her arm. The pain kicked in and she blinked back the tears as Nicholas moved toward her and stared at her arm.

"Bree, I'm so sorry!" Nicholas' face was as pale as her own, and she gave him a shaky smile as she clamped her hand down on the cut. Blood was pouring out of it at an alarming rate.

"It's fine, Nicky. It was an accident," she said.

Nicholas ran his hand through his hair and gave her a decidedly panicked look before reaching out for her. "Come with me, little one. We'll find Mama right now. She can -"

Bree's eyes widened as James grabbed his brother and tore him away from her. He dragged Nicholas to the ground and leaned over him, his fists twisting in Nicholas' shirt. "Do not touch her again!"

Nicholas' face flushed and he shoved angrily at his brother. "Get off me!"

When James didn't move, Nicholas punched him hard in the stomach and shoved him to the ground. He climbed to his feet as James stood. James' body was swelling, and a reddish-brown beard was appearing on his face. His eyes glowed brightly and when he snarled at his brother, his teeth had both lengthened and sharpened.

"It was an accident, baby brother." Nicholas' body was swelling as well as he stared cautiously at James. "I did not mean to -"

"If you hurt her again, I will hurt you. Do you understand?" James said softly.

"You mean you will try." Nicholas' eyes turned yellow and he scowled at James. "Do not make me embarrass you in front of her. Do you really want your woman to watch me hand your ass to you?"

Bree watched in horror as James roared with anger and dove at his brother. Nicholas grunted loudly as James' shoulder drove into his stomach. They fell to the ground, punching at each other as they growled and snarled like rabid dogs.

"Stop it!" she cried. Blood was still pouring from her arm and she felt shaky and faint. She looked at Tristan who was setting Leta on the ground. The little girl was actually grinning as she watched her brothers fight.

"Tristan, they'll kill each other!" Bree said.

He rolled his eyes. "They've been fighting like this since they were pups, Bree. Come, we will take you to Avery while they work things out. You're losing too much blood."

She shook her head and backed away from him. "No! Please, Tristan – stop them."

"Aye, little one, if that will make you feel better." Tristan clapped his hands sharply. "Enough!"

When the two brothers ignored him, he waded between them. Although his sons were large and powerful, he grabbed each of them by the scruff of the neck and pulled them apart easily.

"I said enough." He shook them lightly before letting them go.

James and Nicholas snarled at each other as they both climbed to their feet, and Tristan growled a warning. "It was an accident, James. Nicky would never purposely hurt her, and you know it."

"I told him not to teach her the sword!" James said hotly. "If he had done what I asked, this would never have happened. She is too little to learn the sword and we all know it. I will keep her safe."

"Will you? Because your woman stands there bleeding while you fight like a spoiled little pup with your brother," Tristan said.

James froze and then strode toward Bree. She stumbled

back as he approached her, but already his eyes were darkening to their usual brown and the beard had thinned to scruff. He took off his shirt and wrapped it around her arm before picking her up. He started toward the house without speaking.

She glanced back at Tristan and the others. Blood was trickling from Nicholas' nose, and bruising and swelling were starting to appear on his face. Tristan clapped him on the back. "Let's find your mother, Nicky. You can sit with her for a bit."

JAMES CARRIED BREE THROUGH THE HOUSE AND TO HIS bedroom. He shut the door behind them, and Bree's breath caught in her throat. At Avery's and James' insistence, she had been staying in James' room. There were no empty rooms in the servant's quarters, and James refused to let her move into any of the guest rooms.

"It is too cold in the guest rooms for you. You are to stay in my room." He had spoken with a finality that she hadn't dared argue with.

Just over a month ago he had carried her to this very room, and she had been terrified he would make her join him in his bed. Now her pulse was speeding up with anticipation, and she felt a twinge of disappointment when he carried her to the armchair by the fireplace instead of the bed.

He sat down with a soft grunt and gathered her against his body. She was facing away from him, and he pulled her back against his chest and wrapped his arms around her slender body. He was careful not to touch her arm as she turned her face and tucked it into the curve of his neck. He was deliciously warm, and she melted against him with a soft sigh.

Already the pain in her arm was gone, and the now-familiar fluttering was starting in her belly. His heart was thudding solidly against her back and she asked, "Are you hurt?"

He laughed. "No. My brother and I have had worse fights."

"It was an accident. Nicky didn't mean to hurt me."

He shifted further back into the chair. "Aye, I know. But he should have been more careful."

He cleared his throat and seemed to choose his words carefully. "I fear you are too small to learn the sword, Bree."

"I'm not," she insisted. "I just need to practice more."

"Why are you so anxious to learn how to use a sword?" he asked.

"It's smart for a woman to know how to defend herself when she travels alone. It's a long way to Vanden."

He didn't reply but his arms tightened around her and he tensed underneath her.

"Are you all right, my lord?"

"Aye," he grunted. One of his hands slid down and began to rub the top of her thigh through her pants while the other stroked her side lightly.

Deep within her belly, little flames of desire flickered into life. She closed her eyes and tried to ignore the feel of his hands touching her, the warmth of his breath on her cheek and the hardness of his chest against her back.

It was useless. She wanted him to kiss her, wanted him to touch her the way he had touched her earlier. Her nipples hardened into twin points, and she squirmed as the ache between her thighs appeared.

"Does your arm still hurt?" he murmured.

It didn't hurt but she was hit with sudden inspiration. She stared up at him and nodded shyly. "Aye my lord, it does.

Perhaps," she paused, her face reddening, "perhaps a kiss would help."

A smile crossed his face and he reached up and cupped her cheek, tilting her face toward his. "Perhaps it would."

He pressed his mouth against hers and she kissed him eagerly, pushing her tongue at his lips until he parted them, and she could slip it into his mouth. He kissed her deeply, holding her head as he explored and teased her warm mouth until she was wiggling against him.

He sucked on her upper lip before releasing her mouth. She made a soft moan of need and arched upwards, trying to take his mouth again. He pulled her head back and tugged on her braided hair.

"How does your arm feel now, little one?"

"It's very sore, my lord. I can hardly stand the pain," she whispered.

"Hmm, it seems that a kiss is not enough. Perhaps we should try something else."

"Aye, perhaps," she responded eagerly.

His hands reached for the buttons on her shirt and he undid them quickly before sweeping the thin fabric down her arms, carefully easing it over the makeshift bandage on her arm.

He reached around her and cupped both of her breasts, his thumbs rubbing against her nipples as she arched her back and moaned. The back of her skull pressed into his shoulder, and he groaned as her small ass ground against his pelvis. She was squeezing the arms of the chair compulsively as he kissed the top of one bare shoulder, before tugging on both her nipples.

"Ohhh," she breathed, her back arching again. She turned her head and kissed him hard on the mouth. He returned her kisses as his fingers pulled and teased her nipples.

Bree moaned into James' mouth. Every time his fingers pulled on her nipples, it sent a throb of pleasure straight to the area between her thighs. She rubbed against him as he continued to torment her nipples until they had darkened to a deep red and were swollen and rock hard.

"Oh please!" she cried. "It aches so much."

"Spread your legs, honey," he whispered into her ear.

She parted her legs as he slipped his hand into the waistband of her pants. She leaned against him and moved restlessly. His shirt slipped from her arm, revealing smears of blood and her smooth skin. No trace of the cut remained, but neither of them noticed as his fingers circled the curls between her thighs before slipping further down.

She moaned, her pelvis arching into his hand at the first feel of his warm fingers against her skin. He parted the lips of her pussy and found her clit. He rubbed the swollen button as he licked and kissed her throat. He rubbed her clit more firmly as her hands dropped to his large thighs, and her fingers dug into the fabric of his pants.

"Does that help with the ache?" he whispered into her ear.

"Aye! No! I don't know," she moaned.

His other hand cupped her left breast, squeezing the firm flesh as he circled her clit with his fingers.

Bree moaned again. Her eyes were clamped shut, and all she could feel was James' rough fingers against her clit and his warm mouth on the sensitive skin of her throat. Her breath was coming in harsh pants and her hips were thrusting against his hand frantically.

She suddenly grew silent, and then her body was arching up off his lap as her first ever orgasm rushed through her. She twisted and writhed, and he wrapped one arm around her waist to prevent her from falling off his lap.

She collapsed against him and he slipped his hand from

her pants and stroked her flat stomach. Her ass was against his cock and he rubbed it lightly against her. When she didn't object, he shifted her until she was sitting on his lap sideways. She kept her eyes closed as he kissed her swollen mouth. She could hear and feel him unbuttoning his pants, and he took her hand and guided it to his cock.

"Touch me, Bree," he whispered.

Her cheeks flushed brightly. She bit at her lower lip before wrapping her slender fingers around him and moved her hand hesitantly back and forth. He groaned loudly and, without opening her eyes, she whispered, "Does that hurt?"

"No," he bit out. "It definitely doesn't hurt."

She took a deep breath and bent her head before opening her eyes. Her mouth opened slightly, and her hand squeezed involuntarily around his cock as she studied it. She ran her thumb over the top of it, frowning a little at the moisture she felt.

Bree couldn't stop staring at his cock. Touching James' cock was like nothing she had ever imagined. She was fascinated by how soft and smooth the skin was. It moved in her hand, a hard bar of steel that throbbed and pulsed.

She looked up at him. His eyes were glowing green and the beard was thick on his face. She had a fleeting image of Draken, his eyes glowing like James', and she shrieked with fear and scrambled off of his lap.

He stood, tucking his cock back into his pants, and took a few steps towards her. "Bree, my love? What's wrong?"

"Stay away from me," she moaned. She covered her naked breasts with her arms and backed away from him.

James smiled at her reassuringly as he moved slowly towards her. "It's all right, Bree. Just relax."

"I'm sorry," she whimpered. "I'm so sorry but I can't – I shouldn't do this with someone like you."

He recoiled as if she had slapped him. A look of hurt crossed his face and she gave a small cry of dismay.

"I'm sorry, James. I -"

"It's fine, Bree," he said dismissively before walking toward the door of his bedroom. "How's your arm?" He reached for the handle on the door.

"I – I'm sorry what?"

He looked at her, his face cold and distant, and she blinked back the sudden tears. "Your arm? Is it healed?"

She had completely forgotten about her arm and she glanced quickly at it. "Aye, it's fine."

He nodded and opened the door.

"James, wait!"

"What is it?" He gave her an impatient look.

"I'm very sorry. I didn't mean for it to come out the way it sounded. It's not that I don't -"

He cut her off. "I said it was fine, Bree. Apology accepted and don't worry – I won't touch you again."

He slipped out of the room and closed the door behind him. Bree started to cry in earnest as she sank to the floor and buried her head in her hands. She was an idiot. She had only been frightened for a moment. In her heart she knew that James was nothing like Draken and scrambling away from him had been an involuntary reaction. Her fear had dissipated by the time she was standing across the room from him. In its place was shame.

If Kaden knew what she was doing, he would be disgusted and angry with her. Lycans had kept them prisoners. They had tortured them and starved them and used them for sport. It wouldn't matter to Kaden that James and his family were different. His hatred for the Lycans ran deep and if he knew that she trusted them, if he knew she had almost had sex with one, he would never forgive her.

She crept to James' bed and climbed into it, burying herself completely under the covers as she sobbed quietly. She had hurt James' badly, she had seen it in his face, and knowing that she had hurt him and that he would never touch her again made her chest ache.

She closed her eyes. The look on James' face flickered through her mind again, and she curled into a tight ball and continued to cry. She deserved his anger.

CHAPTER 10

B ree stiffened and cocked her head to the side as adrenaline rushed through her body. She listened intently and when there was only silence, she relaxed and continued to stuff her clothes into the large leather bag. Tia stared at her curiously from the bed, obviously wondering why she was up when it was still dark.

The last four days had been horrible. She'd expected James to be angry with her, but he'd shown no anger at all. Instead, he had looked at her with a terrible coldness that chilled her to the core. The first day she had tried to engage him in hesitant conversation. He spoke to her but in an oddly disconnected manner. She hadn't tried again. She would have preferred anger over the cold calmness that radiated from him.

It was as though she meant nothing to him at all which, Bree decided, she didn't. She was really nothing more than a roll in the hay for him. When she had turned him down and insulted him, he had simply lost interest.

She didn't blame him for his coldness. What had happened between them was completely her fault. She had asked him to kiss her, to touch her, and when he did, she freaked out and basically called him a monster to his face.

He had stopped teaching her to ride. The day after she had rejected him, he hadn't shown up at the barn for their morning lesson. She had waited for nearly half an hour, pacing nervously back and forth until she admitted the truth to herself. He wasn't going to show up.

She sighed and buckled the leather bag shut. Her conversation with Sophia this morning had helped a little. She'd been lugging a basket of wet and heavy laundry out to hang on the line when she had literally run into James. Struggling to carry the heavy basket, stumbling a little on the frozen ground, she had run straight into him as she rounded the corner of the house. She'd fallen backward, landing on her tailbone with a hard thud, as the basket tipped out of her hands and the wet laundry spilled on to the ground.

"I'm so sorry!" she'd gasped.

He'd grunted in reply and continued on his way without helping her up. She was kneeling on the cold ground, gathering the spilled laundry up and blinking back hot tears, when Sophia knelt beside her.

"Are you okay, Bree?" She asked kindly.

"Aye. I tripped over my own feet. I'm so clumsy," Bree said.

"No, you didn't. I saw my brother run into you," Sophia replied.

"I ran into him. It was my fault entirely."

She stood and lugged the basket to the clothesline. Sophia followed her and took her arm.

"Bree, will you tell me what happened between you and my brother? You're obviously upset, and everyone can see his coldness toward you."

Tired and upset and desperately needing someone to

confide in, she told Sophia everything that happened, her words spilling out in short bursts in between bouts of crying. Sophia comforted her and offered to speak to her brother, but Bree begged her not to.

"I hurt him badly," she sighed miserably. "I said an awful thing to him that I didn't really mean, and now I don't know how to make it better."

"Why did you say it, if you didn't mean it?" Sophia asked.

Without thinking, she blurted out, "Because if Kaden knew -"

She'd stopped and given Sophia a cautious look. "I was just frightened. His eyes were glowing, and it scared me, and I wasn't thinking. But I swear I didn't mean it."

Now, she slipped the leather bag across her chest and adjusted it against her hip. She reached for the sword that was leaning against the wall. She had insisted that Nicky continue to train her on the sword and yesterday, under the pretense of practicing later on her own, she had taken it to her room.

She slipped it into the leather sheath belted around her waist, and then glanced around the room. She had moved out of James' room and into one of the empty guest rooms the night she hurt him. There was nothing left in the room that belonged to her, and she took a deep breath and smiled at the small dog sitting on the bed.

"Be a good girl, Tia," she whispered as she buried her face against the dog's small body. "I love you so much."

The dog whined a little and she kissed the top of her head. "I'm sorry but I can't stay here anymore. I can't stand that I've hurt him so much, and I miss the way he used to look at me. Besides, I need to rescue Kaden."

The dog cocked its head at her, and she sighed softly. "Don't look at me like that, Tia. I might be back for you someday. And if I am, I'll have Kaden with me. You'd like that, girl. I know you miss him."

The dog rolled onto her back and, tears slipping down her cheeks, Bree rubbed her belly for a few minutes before standing. The dog jumped to her feet, her tail wagging hopefully, and Bree wiped the tears from her cheeks and said, "No. Stay, Tia. It's not long until morning and Leta will come looking for you."

She walked to the door of the bedroom and, without looking back, slipped out of the room.

———

SHE HAD BEEN WALKING FOR NEARLY TWO HOURS WHEN SHE realized she was being followed. She continued to walk, her ears straining to hear the light rustling coming from her left as her hand dropped to her sword and tightened on it.

She took a deep breath and whirled around, pulling her sword free and holding it in front of her. With a bravery she didn't feel, she called out loudly, "I know you're there. Come out right now."

There was nothing but silence in reply, and as the seconds spun into minutes, she began to feel a little foolish. The noise had probably been nothing more than a deer. She searched through the trees, squinting in the dim light, and adrenaline flooded through her veins when she saw the figure duck out from behind a large tree. It stepped forward and she raised her sword threateningly.

"Bree, it's me."

Her mouth dropped open and she stared in shock at the young boy emerging from the trees. "Gods be damned! Evan, what are you doing here?"

He regarded her solemnly. "I was in the common room and I saw you leave. I decided to follow you."

"What were you doing up at that hour?" She frowned.

"Why are you walking in the opposite direction of Vanden?" he countered.

She groaned. "Evan, do you know how stupid it was to follow me?"

He shrugged. "I want to know where you're going. Why did you leave without saying goodbye?"

"Evan! This is madness! You need to turn around and go home right now." She glared at him.

He looked around. "It's dangerous in the woods, Bree. You can't go alone.

She wanted to scream with frustration. Evan was right – it was dangerous in the woods. He might be a Lycan, but he was only fifteen and she'd never forgive herself if something happened to him.

"Come on." She grabbed his arm and pulled him back toward his home.

"Where are we going?"

"I'm going to take you back until we're a few miles from your home, and then you're going the rest of your way by yourself," she snapped. "Your family will be worried sick about you by now."

"I'm not going back without you," he said stubbornly.

"Evan! This is not a joke. Do you understand me? I have somewhere I need to go, and I can't stay at your home any longer. Someone needs me and it's very important that I help him. Okay?"

"We can help you. Just tell us what you need us to do," Evan replied.

"No! You don't -"

She stopped as he suddenly stiffened and lifted his head

into the air. He inhaled deeply and she looked around the forest. "What is it?"

He looked at her and her stomach dropped at the look of panic on his young face. "Faeries. I can smell them."

Her hand tightened on her sword and she lifted it in front of her as she stepped in front of Evan. "How close are they?"

"I – I do not know. We need to go, Bree. Right now." His voice was shaking with fear, and she gripped his arm tightly.

"Evan, listen carefully. I want you to shift and run toward your home. I'll hold the faeries off. Run as fast as you can and do not look back, do you hear me?" She muttered fiercely.

"I can't leave you," he whispered.

"You can and you will!" She shook him lightly. "Shift, Evan. Right now."

A low and ugly laugh drifted through the trees. "Too late, my pretty."

Bree turned, herding Evan behind her as four fairies flew out from the trees. She held her sword in front of her and willed her hand not to shake.

"If you do not want to die today, you would be wise to fly away right now." She could hear the tremor in her voice. Evidently the faeries could too because they grinned at each other and landed on the ground in front of them.

"Ooh, you're a brave one then, aren't you, my pretty?" One of the faeries, his face pierced in multiple places with bits of human bones, grinned at her. His teeth were covered with dirt and moss, and his large leathery wings flapped gently as he rose a few inches into the air.

Another of the faeries moved a little closer, she could barely make out his features through all the markings on his face, and she stepped back. She dropped her bag on the ground and pushed Evan back toward the trees.

"We don't care much for the taste of dog," the faerie sneered, "but since you're too tiny for the four of us to share we'll have to roast him up as well."

The others grinned, and one of them raised the sharp spear he was holding into the air and hooted loudly. "I get dibs on tasting her first!"

Behind her, Evan was growling softly and continuously, and she could feel his arm swelling under her hand. She dropped his arm and took a quick look at him. His eyes had switched from their normal light green to a glowing, brilliant shade of emerald. As his clothes exploded from his body and he shifted into a brown wolf, she screamed at him to run and charged at the faeries.

They weren't expecting her to attack them and as she ran forward, slashing at the closest one with her sword, they scrambled backward in surprise. She stabbed one in the leg, and he howled with pain as she sprinted past him and threw herself at the largest of the faeries. She hit him hard and he tumbled to the ground, pulling her down on top of him.

Panting with fear and adrenaline, she raised her sword and thrust it into his side. He screamed with surprise and pain, and she gave her own short howl of pain when she felt the sharp blade of a spear pierce through her skin.

She twisted away quickly, rolling off the faerie and wincing as she landed on the frozen ground. One of the faeries had stabbed her in the back just below her right shoulder blade, but the adrenaline in her body made the pain insignificant.

The faerie fell on her, his hands reaching for her throat. They tightened around her and he leaned down until his face was inches from hers and inhaled. A feeling of heaviness overtook her and before she could succumb to it, she reached up and jammed her thumbs into both of its eyes.

He screamed in agony as her thumbs punctured his eyeballs and she yanked viciously. His eyes popped out with a gruesome sucking sound and he released her and staggered away, clapping his hands over his eyes. Thick, black blood was pouring from between his fingers, and he made inarticulate grunts of pain as he thrashed blindly through the trees.

Crying and panting, she snatched her sword up and staggered to her feet. She could hear Evan barking as he launched himself at one of the faeries. He landed with a hard thud on its back and it fell to the ground. Howling, Evan bit into one of its leathery wings and pulled. There was a wet ripping sound as Evan tore half its wing off. He backed away, the wing hanging from his teeth, as the faerie screamed in agony and crawled toward its brothers.

The faerie she had stabbed in the thigh flew toward Evan. He dropped on top of him and Bree screamed when he stabbed his spear deep into the young Lycan's side. Evan shrieked with pain as the largest faerie, his side bleeding from her sword, landed beside them and stabbed his spear into his flank.

Bree looked down. The faerie she had blinded had dropped his spear, and she reached down and grabbed it. She couldn't defeat both, but if she could get the largest one away from Evan, he might be able to kill the other and escape. She knew she was going to die but as she sprinted toward Evan and the faeries, the knowledge of her own imminent death brought no fear. Instead, she felt only a cold acceptance.

She took in a deep, gasping breath of air and shrieked her final war cry to the forest before throwing herself at the large faerie. She landed with a heavy thud on his back. The feel of his smooth leathery wing beating against her face made her gag, and she shoved the faerie's spear deep into one wing.

He screamed in agony and bucked like a wild beast under

her. She stabbed at him with her sword, but he twisted and turned before hurling his body backward. He slammed her into a tree. Her breath exploded from her lungs in a hard, hot rush, and she lost her grip on her sword and slithered to the ground.

He turned and glared at her, his lips curling back, and reached behind his broad body. He tore the spear from his wing and splintered it in half before snapping his teeth at her like a dog.

"I'm not going to take your essence, you stupid little girl. I want you alive and conscious when I roast you like a pig," he spat. "You will suffer more than any human has ever suffered before."

A loud howl cut through the cold air, and a large red wolf came bounding through the trees. He leaped at the faerie. His jaws opened wide and his large white teeth snapped viciously as he landed on the hideous creature. The wolf wrapped his mouth around the faerie's head and with a quick violent jerk, ripped the faerie's head from its body.

He raised his snout to the sky and howled piercingly. Behind him, two other wolves, one grey and one white, were tearing into one of the remaining faeries. Its guts poured out of it in a slippery slide of blood, and they turned away from its dying body. The faerie Evan had injured raised its hand in supplication and tried to crawl away.

"No," it whispered as the white wolf stalked toward it. The wolf knocked it onto its back, and the faerie's scream turned to a gurgling moan as the wolf ripped its throat out. The faerie she had blinded had collapsed against a tree, and the white wolf loped almost casually to it and tore a gaping hole in its chest.

The red wolf was standing over her and she stared up into its jade-coloured eyes. "James," she whispered.

It whined softly and then ran toward his brother as Sophia's voice rang out. She had shifted back to human form, and she was kneeling naked next to Evan.

"James! He needs you!"

James shifted back to human and quickly lifted the brown wolf into his arms. He held Evan against his chest as the wolf whimpered with pain. Sophia stroked his head lightly.

"You're okay, Evan. You're okay, honey," she soothed.

Bee staggered to her feet as Nicholas, naked and panting loudly, appeared beside her. "Are you all right, Bree?"

"I'm fine. Evan - is Evan okay?"

"We need to get him home." James gathered Evan closer and strode through the trees. Without looking at Bree, Sophia followed.

"Can you walk, Bree?" Nicholas asked.

"Aye." Her entire body was aching from being slammed into the tree, and the wound on her back where she had been stabbed with the faerie's spear was burning and itching. Ignoring it, she picked up her bag and gave Nicholas a grim smile as he took her hand. They hurried after James and Sophia.

CHAPTER 11

B ree looked up as the door to the bedroom swung open and James and Nicholas entered. When they had arrived home, James had carried Evan to Avery and the three of them had disappeared into Avery's and Tristan's room. Nicholas had led her to her room and given her curt instructions to stay in the room before leaving.

That had been three hours ago, and she'd been pacing the room ever since. She'd nearly left the room a few times, but the memory of the look on Nicky's face when he told her to stay kept her in the room.

"Is he all right?" she whispered.

Nicky nodded. "Aye. He's with Mama."

"Thank the gods." Relief flooded through her and she gave the brothers a weak smile.

James stared grimly at her as Nicholas sighed. "How do you feel, Bree? Were you injured?"

"No, I'm all right." She had used one of her shirts to stem the bleeding from the wound on her back. It had oozed some yellow liquid at first, and she had rinsed it carefully until it appeared clean. It was burning and itching fiercely but the wound looked shallow to her. After what happened, she didn't have the courage to ask James to heal it. It would have to heal on its own.

"I'm so sorry," she said. "I didn't know Evan was following me. If I had, I would never have let him -"

"Where were you going? You weren't heading toward Vanden." James' voice was curt.

"I um -"

She swallowed nervously as James gave her an impatient look.

"I knew I didn't have enough money to get to Vanden and I um, I was going to a friend's house. I thought I could stay with them while I earned more money before going to my aunt's."

"Stop lying!" James suddenly roared and she shrank back from his hot gaze.

He stalked toward her. "Stop lying and tell me the truth for once!" He glared angrily at her, and she straightened her spine and returned his gaze defiantly.

"Yelling at me isn't going to make me tell you anything," she snapped.

"My brother almost died because of you, Bree. We saved your life, took you in and fed you, and gave you a place to stay. You owe us the truth!" he shouted.

"I didn't mean for Evan to get hurt. I told you if I had known he was following me, I -"

"You're a foolish little girl and I should have left you to die in the forest!" he shouted again.

"James!" Nicholas grabbed his arm and shoved him backwards. "Leave! Leave right now!"

James growled at him and Nicholas shoved him again. "I mean it, James. Leave. If you don't, I will drag you out of here like a small pup. I swear to the gods I will."

James stared at him for a long moment before stalking from the room. He slammed the door behind him as Nicky stared quietly at Bree. She knew she was pale, and she could feel her mouth trembling, but she took a deep breath and faced him squarely.

"He didn't mean that, Bree. He's just upset about Evan and about you. When we discovered you were both gone, he went crazy," Nicholas said.

She sighed. "He meant what he said, Nicky. We both know it."

He shook his head. "No, he didn't. We were following yours and Evan's scent and when he – when he heard you scream, the look on his face..."

Nicholas gave her a strained smile. "He cares for you, little one."

"No, he doesn't. It doesn't matter anyway. I just want to see Evan and tell him I'm sorry, and then I'll be leaving. Your brother is right – you've done so much for me and I've done nothing but bring trouble to your family. It's better for everyone if I go."

"You're not going anywhere, Bree."

She stiffened. "Do you mean to keep me as a prisoner, Nicky?"

He sighed. "Evan almost died. We don't blame you for that, but -"

"He does," she whispered.

Nicholas scrubbed his hand through his hair. "We don't blame you, but you owe us an explanation and until you give us one, you're not leaving."

He hesitated. "We can't trust you right now, Bree. You know that don't you?"

She nodded as he walked towards the door. "I'll have Marian bring you some food." He stepped out of the room and she heard the click of the lock as he shut the door firmly.

SHE WAS SO HOT SHE COULDN'T STAND IT. ALTHOUGH THERE was no fireplace, the room was curiously warm, and she had stripped down to her shirt. The food Marian had given to her earlier lay untouched on the side table. She had no appetite, and the wound on her back was throbbing with a deep pulsing pain she had never felt before.

She scratched at the skin on her arms. The burning and itching from the wound had spread through her entire body over the last few hours, and she had shallow bloody scrapes on her torso and thighs where she had scratched them raw.

Using the mirror on the wall she had examined the wound, sucking in her breath at the sight of it. Her entire back was bright red and the area around the wound had swollen into a hard, hot ball of flesh. Just touching it sent a bolt of agony through her entire back. The bleeding had stopped but it was oozing a dark, thick yellow fluid that smelled like rotting meat.

She had tried to sleep but the itching and pain would not allow it. In the middle of the night she had climbed out of bed, dismayed at how weak her legs were, and stumbled to the water pitcher. She drank deeply and then poured water over her burning skin. It throbbed like fire against her wound, and she'd rushed to the basin next to the bed and thrown up bile and blood.

Now, she stared at her reflection in the mirror. Her face was pale, and her eyes were sunken into her head. The fever raging through her had drawn every last bit of moisture from her body, and she licked her chapped lips and smiled weakly at Tia.

"Poison, Tia. The spear must have had poison on it. I think – I think I'm dying." The dog trembled in her view, and she blinked rapidly and ran a shaking hand over her face. When she looked again the dog had disappeared and she stared around the room in confusion.

"Pull yourself together, Bree," she moaned. "Tia isn't here."

She shook herself, wincing at the pain that radiated through her. The fever was making her delirious. She had not seen anyone since Marian had brought her food earlier. For all she knew, the Lycans had killed her little dog by now.

They wouldn't. You know they wouldn't. Don't be ridiculous. It's the fever that's all. Pound on the door - hell, pound on the wall - until someone comes. You need help.

"He was right you know, Tia," she croaked. The little dog was back, staring gravely at her, and it followed her as she staggered to the water pitcher. "He should have left me to die in the forest."

She tipped the water pitcher to her mouth, moaning softly when only a few drops of water dripped into her mouth. She tossed it aside and stumbled toward the bed. The world wavered alarmingly, and she sunk slowly to her knees beside the bed, resting her forehead on the mattress.

She scratched at her neck, tearing at the soft skin until blood appeared. She examined the blood on her fingers with disinterest before turning to look at Tia.

"I wish I had told him the truth," she told the dog. "I wish I had told him that I think I love him, and that I was scared Kaden would hate me for it."

She coughed harshly, not noticing the fine spray of blood

that flew out of her mouth and covered the quilt, and then dragged in a few shallow breaths.

"You have to tell him for me okay, Tia?" She smiled when the little dog licked her hand. "That's my good girl."

Her eyes slipped shut and she drifted.

IN HER DREAM SHE WAS A RED. SHE TILTED HER HEAD, staring fascinated at the bright red strands that slipped across her vision. She tried to reach up to touch them, and her heart quickened with fear when she realized her arms were tied behind her. She looked around, her eyes widening with dismay and confusion. She was tied to a large wooden pole in the back yard of the Lycan's home. Branches and leaves were piled around her legs and feet and Leta, wearing a crown of flowers and carrying Tia, was dancing in a circle around her, singing softly.

"Leta," she whispered. "Help me."

The little girl ignored her and continued to dance and sing. There was movement to her left and she craned her neck, fascinated all over again by the fiery strands that swung about her head. Sophia was standing next to the clothesline. Instead of clothes, she was draping the skinned flesh of the faeries over the line. Their skin flapped in the breeze, carrying the scent of death to her, and she moaned with fear.

"Sophia…please," she whispered.

Sophia turned toward her, and Bree shrieked with horror. The Lycan's eyes were missing and blood ran in thin lines down her smooth cheeks. "He should have let you die, Bree."

"I'm so sorry, I'm so sorry," Bree cried repeatedly as Avery and Tristan appeared in front of her. In Tristan's arms was the limp body of Evan.

"You killed my baby boy," Avery said. "I took you into my home, and you killed my baby boy."

"The Red must burn," Tristan growled.

"I'm sorry!" Bree cried again. There was a low growling to her right as James in his wolf form approached her. He carried a burning torch in his mouth, and she moaned with fear.

"Please, James. I love you. Please don't do this."

He jerked his large shaggy head and tossed the burning torch into the branches at her feet. As the leaves and branches caught fire and the flames grew, she squinted through the smoke.

James had shifted back into his human form and he was staring silently at her. Nicky appeared beside him and he gave Bree a look of sorrow. "You should have told us the truth, little one."

"I will!" she screamed. "Please let me go! I'll tell you everything!"

"It's too late," James intoned as large leathery wings sprouted from his back. "The Red must burn."

As her skin burned, Bree shrieked shrilly. She writhed in pain as the flames licked at her flesh. She deserved to die. She –

Bree jerked herself awake. Her head slipped from the bed and she fell sideways, whacking her skull on the floor so hard she saw stars. Moaning and crying, she grabbed on to the bed and pulled herself into a sitting position.

She turned and leaned against the bed, barely noticing when the pressure of the bed split open the wound, and blood and foul-smelling pus dripped down her back. She ran her tongue over her lips, feeling the dry and cracked flesh, and cackled.

She had burned to death in her dream, and now the fever

would burn her to death from the inside out. She squinted out the window. It was dawn. She could see the sun rising over the horizon.

She wished she was outside. It would be better to die feeling the sun on her face.

The door to the bedroom opened and she stared blearily at the figures in the doorway.

"Hello, Sophia. Hello, Nicky." She coughed harshly. Blood dripped down her chin and she wiped it away wearily.

"Are you here to kill me?" she asked dully.

"Gods be damned." Nicholas gave Sophia a look of horror and the two of them ran to Bree. Sophia touched her forehead and her eyes widened.

"Nicky, she's burning up!"

Nicholas squatted beside Bree and brushed her damp, lank hair away from her face. "Can you hear me, little one?"

"I'm dying. I deserve to die," she sang in a hoarse voice.

"What's wrong with her?" Sophia said

Nicholas sniffed at Bree's skin. "Bree, were you stabbed by the faeries?"

"Kaden!" Bree suddenly shrieked. "Where are you? I can't find you! Where are you?"

Nicholas grabbed her shoulders and tilted her forward. The back of her shirt was covered in blood and a foul-smelling liquid, and he grimaced. "She must have been stabbed. The poison from the spear is killing her."

"Kaden," Bree moaned. "Please help me."

"Go and get James," Nicholas said to Sophia.

Sophia was staring at Bree with wide, frightened eyes, and Nicholas reached out and shook her roughly. "Sophia! She's dying. We need James. Go quickly."

Sophia sprinted from the room, shouting James' name.

CHAPTER 12

"How is she?" Avery sat down on the bed.

"Better." James, lying on his back with Bree stretched across his body, gave his mother a thin smile. "She's not coughing up blood anymore."

Avery turned down the covers to Bree's waist and studied her naked back. The swelling was still there but the puncture from the spear wasn't quite as large. She stroked Bree's back with both hands for nearly ten minutes before leaning down and kissing her pale cheek.

She touched her forehead and then rested her hands on Bree's back. "The fever is completely gone."

"Aye."

"Has she woken?"

He shook his head. "No. She's been muttering in her sleep, but she hasn't opened her eyes."

"She will wake soon, my love. Do not worry."

"I said horrible things to her, Mama," James said miserably. "I told her it was her fault Evan almost died, and that I – I should have left her to die in the forest."

Avery squeezed his arm. "We all say things in anger that

we do not mean. When she wakes, tell her you're sorry. Bree is a sweet girl and she'll forgive you."

"I would neither forgive nor speak to her when, out of fear, she said she could never be with someone like me. Why should she forgive me for my deliberate cruelty?"

Avery squeezed his arm again. "She will forgive you when she wakes. I know it."

"What if she doesn't wake?" he whispered.

"She will. She is healing nicely. I imagine she'll be awake before -"

Bree suddenly thrashed against him. "Kaden! I'm sorry! Please don't leave me."

Avery frowned as James tightened his arms around Bree's slender waist. "Shh, little one. You're safe."

"Kaden, where are you?" Bree moaned. Her back arched and she gave a short cry of pain before slumping against James. Avery rubbed her back soothingly as she stared at James.

"Who is Kaden?"

"I don't know. She's been calling his name off and on, all day," James replied. Jealousy coloured his words, and Avery patted his arm in sympathy before standing.

"You've been lying with her for hours. Why don't you go and have something to eat? I'll stay with Bree for a bit."

He shook his head. "No, Mama. I won't leave her again."

Avery bent and kissed his forehead. "I'll have Laura bring you a plate of food."

He shifted to his side as Avery left his bedroom, pulling Bree close until her entire body was pressed against his. He studied her face, brushing her hair away from her cheeks and tracing her smooth skin with his fingertips.

He hesitated and then pressed his mouth against her lips.

She didn't stir and he kissed her twice more before laying his head next to hers.

When he had ran into the guest room and seen her dying body, a howl of panic and sorrow had burst from his chest. His shock had been so great he had nearly shifted. Only Nicky's voice had kept him in his human form.

"Help her, James! Keep it together so you can help her!"

He had collapsed on the floor beside her and pulled her into his lap. Afraid that even moving would kill her, he'd stayed on the floor of the guest room for nearly two hours. The smell of death permeated the room and once she was in his arms, the poison had run out in a steady stream from the swollen, pulsing wound on her back. It hadn't taken long before they were both covered in the foul-smelling liquid. Bree was burning up in his arms, and Avery had helped him strip off her clothes and suggested he climb into a cool bath with her.

"She is not going to die, my sweet," his mother said reassuringly as she examined Bree's back. "Her wound is no longer dripping the poison, and I believe it will not be long before the fever breaks. But the cool water will help, and you should wash the blood and the poison from her skin."

He sighed heavily and rubbed her back. He wished she would wake. He was surprisingly hurt by what she said the day she was cut by the sword, and his hurt and anger had made him cold with her. He could see it upset her but had continued to ignore her. She'd run away because of his anger and was forced to defend herself and his brother from the faeries. She had nearly died because he was a fool.

He sighed again and kissed her bare shoulder. Gods, he wanted her. What had started off as a physical need had quickly turned into an emotional one as well. She had only been in their home for a few weeks, but he was fascinated by her. He wasn't the only one - both his mother and Leta had grown very fond of her.

Bree loved his mother. He could see it in her eyes every time she looked at Avery, but even that love was not enough for her to share her secrets. Even after a moon, they barely knew anything about her. She was kind and sweet, but she grew nervous and clammed up the moment anyone asked her a question about herself.

He had argued with his mother about allowing Bree to work but she had insisted, reminding him that if they didn't let her work in their home to earn money, she would leave. He knew his mother was right but doing chores around the house had kept Bree too busy to get to know him better.

Not that it mattered. Bree might be attracted to him, but she had made it perfectly clear she wouldn't sleep with a Lycan. And even if he had been able to change her mind before, it was too late now. She had left his home because of his cruelty to her, and she had chosen to die from the faerie's spear instead of asking him to heal her.

What if she hated him when she finally woke? What if she tried to leave again? He pulled her closer and buried his face in her neck. He couldn't let that happen. He would convince her to stay with his family even if it meant never touching her again.

Feeling tired and depressed, he burrowed closer to her warm body and closed his eyes. The warmth of her skin and the steady rise and fall of her chest comforted him, and he slipped into a light sleep.

WHEN HE OPENED HIS EYES, SHE WAS STARING AT HIM. HER light blue eyes regarded him solemnly, and he blinked and gave her a tentative smile. "Hello, little one."

"Is Evan okay?" Her voice was hoarse.

"Aye. He's fully healed."

Her eyes slipped closed and he stroked her long hair. "Bree?"

"What?" She didn't open her eyes.

"Why did you not ask me to heal you from the faerie's spear?"

She sighed. "I wanted you to stay with Evan. He was hurt so badly and the wound on my back was shallow. I did not know the spear carried poison on it and by the time I did..."

"You should have called for me," he said. "It was almost too late when Sophia and Nicky found you."

She opened her eyes and stared steadily at him. "You made it clear that you thought I should die."

He winced and tightened his arms around her. "I should not have said that, little one. I was angry and worried, and I did not mean it. Truly I did not. Please forgive me for saying it."

"You were right," she whispered. "You should have left me to die that day. I nearly got Evan killed."

"No!" He shook her lightly, his face paling when she flinched. "I'm sorry, honey. Evan told us what happened. He told us how he followed you without you knowing. He said that you told him to shift and run while you fought with the faeries."

He stopped and swallowed hard. "He – he told us how you attacked them to try and give him time to escape."

He stroked her back. "You were so brave, little one."

She laughed bitterly. "No, I wasn't. I was desperate and scared to death. I was terrified that Evan would die."

131

"He didn't."

"He almost did, and you hate me for it. I can't stand that you hate me now." She closed her eyes as tears dripped down her face.

"I don't hate you, Bree," he said.

"You do. I know you do," she replied.

"I swear I do not. I'm so sorry. Please forgive me." He could feel panic rising in his chest and, not knowing what else to do, he pressed his mouth against hers in a soft and gentle kiss.

She immediately kissed him back, and he cupped her face and kissed away the tears on her cheeks. "I'm sorry. Will you forgive me?"

"Aye," she whispered. He wanted to kiss her again, but she licked her lips and struggled to sit up. "I'm very thirsty."

"Stay here. I'll get it for you." He threw back the covers and tugged on his pants before crossing the room. He brought back a glass of water for her and helped her sit up, tucking the pillow behind her.

She inhaled sharply at the pressure on her back, and he gave her a worried look. "How do you feel, Bree?"

She took a drink of water. "Tired mostly. My back hurts a little."

"Are you hungry?" Before she could reply, he had left the bed and come back with the tray of food Laura had left while they were sleeping.

"I am not very hungry, my lord." She looked out the window. The sun was setting, and she felt a weary sort of gladness that she would live to see another sunrise.

"Eat just a little," he urged. "Some bread and cheese at least. It will help you regain your strength."

Too tired to argue, she nibbled at the bread and the cheese he handed to her. "You should eat as well, my lord."

"James." He frowned at her. "You're to call me James."

"Eat, *James*."

He grinned a little at her cheeky tone and picked up a piece of bread.

―――――――――

BREE LEANED HER HEAD AGAINST JAMES' SHOULDER. AFTER eating, he had wrapped the quilt around her and carried her to the bathroom. Ye could hear his family talking and laughing as they ate dinner, and she gave him a timid look as he carried her back to his room.

"You should take me to the guest room and then go be with your family. I'm just tired now. I'm sure I'll feel better in the morning."

He shook his head as he opened the door to his bedroom. "No, little one. You're staying in my room tonight."

She gave him a cautious look. "I will not leave in the night, James. I promise."

"I know you won't. But you're not fully healed yet, Bree. You need to sleep with me tonight."

She blushed as he slipped her under the sheet and took off his pants before joining her.

He smiled reassuringly. "I'm just going to hold you. I promise I won't do anything else. Turn to your side so I can look at your back."

She turned to her side obediently and James inspected her back.

"How does it look?" she asked.

"Better. Much better." He kissed her back and she shivered. "Sorry, little one."

He laid down beside her and spooned her, pulling her body tightly against his. He put his arm around her waist and rubbed her abdomen in small circles. He wanted to cup one small breast, but he had promised her he would do nothing but hold her. His cock was already starting to stir from being so close to her, and he groaned inwardly. He would not be able to hold her like this much longer. He cursed his weakness and casually moved his pelvis away from her.

"Are you tired?"

She nodded and he rubbed her thigh in what he hoped was a soothing manner. "Go to sleep, my love," he whispered as he moved his pelvis further away.

She was starting to tremble, and he moved his hand up and rubbed her upper chest, being careful to avoid her breasts. "Are you cold, Bree?"

"Aye," she whispered. She shifted backward. Her soft ass pressed snugly against his cock and he groaned.

"What's wrong?" she asked

"Nothing." He cleared his throat roughly and willed his cock to behave itself. It was useless. As though it had a mind of its own, his cock stiffened and pressed against her ass. She inhaled sharply and made a soft noise in the back of her throat.

"I'm sorry," he groaned.

"Don't be," she whispered. "I – I like it."

His hand drifted down to her hip and squeezed tightly. She squirmed against him, and they both gasped when his cock pressed between her ass cheeks.

"James, please," she moaned softly.

She didn't want him to take her virginity and he wouldn't. He could just make her come. It would help her heal and sleep he rationalized, as his cock swelled and throbbed against her.

She was moving restlessly against him and he cupped her

breast. She groaned and arched her back, and he pulled lightly on her nipple.

"I'm going to make you feel good, my love," he whispered into her ear. "It will help you heal."

He slid his hand between her thighs and cupped her warm sex. His fingers rubbed gently at her clit she moaned loudly. She didn't stop him when he took her thigh and lifted it over his hip. She was completely open to him now and he explored her leisurely, his fingers running through the soft blonde curls before stroking the lips of her pussy.

"Oh," she sighed as his other hand slid under her and cupped her breast. He placed warm, open-mouth kisses on her neck and shoulder as he rubbed her clit until she was wet and slippery.

"Does that feel good, honey?" he whispered into her ear.

"Aye, so good," she panted.

His fingers pulled and tweaked her nipple, as he rubbed his cock against her ass and his thumb against her clit. He slipped one finger into her tight opening. She moaned and thrust her hips at him, and he hurriedly removed his finger. She was warm and deliciously tight. If he continued to touch her like that, he wouldn't be able to stop himself from taking her, despite his promise not to.

She turned her face to him, and he kissed her full mouth. She slipped her tongue hesitantly into his mouth and he sucked hard on it. She shuddered and clutched at his forearm as he pinched her clit lightly before rubbing it again.

She was getting close. Her entire body was trembling and heaving against him, and her pale face had flushed with pleasure. He rubbed harder, watching her sweet face as she closed her eyes and arched her body. She bit at her bottom lip as her body first tensed and then bucked wildly against him. He continued to rub her clit until she collapsed against his hard body, and then he slid his hand up and cupped her breast.

"Gods," she muttered weakly.

"How do you feel?" he murmured.

"Good," she sighed. "I feel so good." Already her eyes were slipping shut and her body relaxing as she drifted toward sleep.

He smiled a little and ignored his throbbing cock. "Go to sleep, honey."

"Aye," she agreed sleepily.

"Bree?" he whispered into her ear.

"Hmm?"

"Who's Kaden?" He held his breath, hoping she would be too sleepy and relaxed to lie to him.

"My brother." She closed her eyes and slept.

CHAPTER 13

S he was underneath him, her soft thighs spread wide and her tiny hands gripping his waist tightly. He was deep inside of her and she was as wet and tight as he had dreamed she would be. Her soft cries and moans of excitement were making his cock twitch and he groaned and cupped her breast, squeezing it roughly.

She whispered his name and he leaned down to kiss her. Her hair was in her face and he tried to brush it away, frowning when more appeared. Her hair was everywhere, wrapped around his throat and plastered against his face and he frowned again. What was happening?

She said his name again. This time there was a thread of alarm in it.

"Don't be afraid," he tried to whisper but her hair was in his mouth, choking him and he couldn't –

His eyes flew open and he jerked in the bed. He inhaled sharply when he realized he was holding Bree against him. She was curled up on her side with her back to him, and he had pressed his large body against her until he was nearly flattening her into the bed. His face was buried in her long, blonde hair, and his hand was squeezing her breast. He groaned with dismay - his cock was between her legs and he was pushing the head of it against her tight opening.

Shame flooded through him and he rolled away from her, clenching his hands into fists as he stared across the room. He had groped her like an animal in his sleep. Gods, he had almost taken her virginity. Another minute and he would have –

His stomach rolled with guilt as his cock softened. He had told her he would never hurt her, and she had trusted him. She was right to be afraid of him.

"James?"

He twitched violently at the feel of her soft hand on his back.

"Did I – did I do something wrong? Why did you stop?" She patted his back hesitantly.

"I'm sorry. I'm so sorry," he whispered hoarsely. "I was sleeping - dreaming - and I know that it isn't an excuse, but I swear to you I did not mean to -"

She pulled her hand away. "What do you mean you were sleeping?"

He turned to face her. "I – Bree, what -"

It was dark in his room. The fire had died down to embers and it was still a few hours until dawn. Still, his Lycan abilities meant he had no problem seeing how red her cheeks were or the look of confusion on her face.

"I woke up and you were touching me and kissing my neck. You spoke to me. You asked me how I felt. I said fine and that I thought I was fully healed. Then you said that you wanted me, and I could feel your – you against me and I thought…"

She trailed off with a small moan of embarrassment. "You were dreaming. Gods, I'm so stupid. I should have known once I said I was healed you wouldn't touch me, but it felt so good and I -"

"Bree, I thought I had attacked you in my sleep." He spoke over her. The panic at what he had almost done was still buzzing in his head, and he had barely heard half of what she said. "I've never lost control like that."

He suddenly grabbed her arms and rubbed them roughly. "Did I hurt you? Are you bruised or hurt in anyway?"

She shook her head. "No, I swear to you I am not, James."

BREE WASN'T LYING TO JAMES, BUT SHE ALSO WASN'T BEING entirely truthful

She was hurting but it wasn't the type of pain he was worried about. She wanted him so much her entire body was aching. He had been so close to taking her. She had felt his cock pushing against her opening, and in that moment, she had forgotten every single reason why she shouldn't let him take her. Why it would be a mistake to let him give her the relief that her body was aching for. She'd forgotten her fear over his size and his strength, and she felt nearly mad with desire for him.

"Are you sure I haven't hurt you?" The worry in his voice made her smile a little.

"Aye, I'm fine." She gasped and trembled as he ran his hands up and down her naked body searching for what, she didn't know. "James -"

"I don't see any bruises," he mumbled to himself. "But I've scared you and I'm sorry, little one."

Her body throbbing for release, she could feel her irritation growing. He might be able to turn his desire on and off like a faucet, but she certainly couldn't, and the way he was touching her was setting her skin on fire with need.

"James!" she snapped. His hands paused in their exploration of her ribs. "I am not frightened, and you didn't hurt me."

"Thank the gods," he said.

She snorted in frustration. "I'm going back to the guest room."

He shook his head immediately. "No, you're not, little one."

"I am." She couldn't stay in his bed next to him for the rest of the night without throwing herself at him. She scowled and pushed him on the arm.

"Bree, it's only a few more hours until dawn. Stay in the bed and let me heal you completely."

"No." He was on the outside of the bed, his large body blocking her way out, but she could be quick when she wanted to be. He gave a grunt of surprise when she suddenly clambered over his broad body. He caught her about the waist just before she slid off his broad body.

She smacked him hard on the chest. "Let go of me."

He shook his head. "No. I'm sorry, honey. I know you're frightened of me but I -"

"Gods be damned! I am not frightened of you!" she snapped again at him.

She wiggled and squirmed against him, pushing against his chest and squeezing her knees into his hips. "I swear to the gods, if you do not let me go, I will punch you -"

She stopped, the breath squeezing from her lungs in a hot, surprised rush. She could feel his cock, hot and hard against her core, and she looked down at him. The look of lust on his face made her knees weak.

He groaned and released her. "You're right, little one. You should go."

"Aye," she agreed breathlessly. "I should."

She braced her hands on his chest and rubbed herself against his cock. He made a choking sound and his hands grabbed the bed sheets.

"The gods help me – do not do that. Please, Bree," he muttered.

"Do not do what?" She pressed herself against him and slid upward in a slow, smooth motion. His cock dragged across her clit and she moaned softly at the exquisite pleasure.

"Bree…"

His voice was tight, and she could see the way he was fighting for control. An unfamiliar ripple of power went through her. He was so big and powerful compared to her, yet she had the strangest idea that at this moment he would do whatever she asked of him.

She ran her fingers through the hair on his chest and decided to test her theory. "That feels so good, my lord. Please, may I do it just once more?"

His cock twitched against her and he closed his eyes.

"Just once more, little one. Then I will leave you and go to the guest room," he rasped out.

"Of course, my lord," she agreed sweetly.

She leaned over him and gently pulled at his hands. He resisted and she tugged harder until he let go of the sheets. She placed his hands on her breasts and moaned when he squeezed them roughly.

She rubbed herself back and forth over his hard cock. The head of it bumped against her clit, and she wiggled back and forth against it as bursts of pure pleasure shot through her lower body. His eyes were squeezed shut and she ran her fingers across the thick beard on his face.

"Open your eyes," she whispered.

He hesitated and she smoothed her fingers over his mouth. "Please, James."

His eyelids fluttered open. They were still mostly brown, but she could see flecks of green growing in them, and her body stilled against him. She watched as his eyes lightened and the flecks widened.

He growled and closed his eyes, panting harshly under her. "Don't be afraid."

"I'm not," she whispered. She pressed her finger lightly at his lips and when he opened them, she slipped her finger between them. He sucked her finger deep into his mouth and a spasm of such intense pleasure went through her that she bucked her hips against him.

He groaned as his cock slipped towards her warm entrance. "Time for me to go, Bree."

"Aye." She leaned over him and rubbed her breast against his mouth. His eyes popped open and he stared up at her before sucking her nipple into his mouth. She cried out at the feel of his firm lips tugging on her sensitive nipple. He bit down lightly on it before abrading it with his tongue and she cried out again, rubbing herself frantically against him.

His hands moved to her hips and he positioned her over his cock. The head of him slipped into her and they both moaned with pleasure. He was shaking violently under her, and with a low moan he pushed her body up until he slipped out.

"No!" She reached between them, grasped his cock and tried to push him back into her.

"Please don't, honey," he groaned. "I'm sorry but I won't be able to stop if you keep doing that."

"I don't want you to stop," she whispered.

He froze beneath her and gave her a cautious look. "Bree, are you sure about this?"

She nodded and kissed him hard on the mouth. "Aye, I want you. Do you – do you want me?"

"Gods yes," he groaned. With a quickness that startled her, he rolled over and flipped her onto her back. He nudged her thighs apart and settled himself between them.

She arched her hips against him eagerly, but he hesitated. "Bree…"

She kissed him again and he moaned at the feel of her tongue stroking his lips. "Don't stop, James. I'll go mad if you do."

He nodded and reached between their bodies. He rubbed her clit and she twisted under him. "I want you inside of me."

"I know," he whispered. "But I want you to come first. It will make it easier."

He rubbed her clit and sucked on first one nipple and then the other until she was crying out loudly. He pushed his finger into her just as she came, and he groaned at the way her inner muscles clamped down around his finger. As she collapsed against the bed, he slid a second finger into her and stretched her lightly.

"James?" She gave him a questioning look and he kissed her.

"I just want to make it easier for you."

"I can't wait." She smacked him lightly on the chest, flushing when he grinned at the impatience in her voice. She squeezed his shoulders. "I thought you wanted me."

"I do," he groaned. "I don't want to hurt you, little one."

"It's going to hurt. It cannot be helped," she whispered.

He stared down at her, his eyes glowing a soft emerald,

143

and she rubbed her hand across his beard. "I want this, James. Truly."

He lifted one creamy thigh in his hand. He hooked it around his hips, and she raised her other thigh and clasped it gently around him. His cock probed at her wet opening, and they both groaned when he pushed the head of it into her.

"Relax, Bree," he whispered and kissed her softly on the mouth. She kissed him back, relishing the taste of his lips.

Heat was pulsing in her belly and she barely heard him when he whispered against her mouth, "I'm sorry, honey."

He thrust into her with one smooth motion and she cried out. She tore her mouth from his as her thighs clamped around his hips and her nails dug into his back. He gritted his teeth and stayed completely still as she bit her bottom lip and whimpered softly.

"I'm so sorry." He kissed her repeatedly, stroking her bottom lip with his tongue as she stretched around him.

"Better?" he asked anxiously.

"Aye." To her surprise, the pain had faded completely after only a few seconds. In its place was a warmth and tingling that made her entire body shudder with pleasure. She moved experimentally under him, and he groaned under his breath.

She smiled up at him and traced his mouth with her fingers. "Does it feel good, James?"

"Gods yes," he muttered.

She smiled again and pushed her hips against his. His breath hissed out and she ran her fingers over his back. "It feels good to me too."

"Honey, I need to move," he groaned.

"Aye," she agreed.

"Brace your feet on the bed," he rasped.

She did as he asked, curling her toes into the sheets as he

propped himself above her and moved with slow and steady strokes. She watched his face, tracing his wide cheekbones with the tips of her fingers as his breathing started to quicken.

There was a curious feeling of warmth growing in her belly as he pushed and retreated in a smooth gliding motion. She watched fascinated as a drop of sweat slid down the side of his neck. She lifted her head and licked it away with her tongue, smiling at his loud groan.

He was moving faster now, and she put her hands around his waist and lifted her pelvis to meet each stroke. He groaned again, and she jerked in surprise when he slipped his hand between them and rubbed her clit.

Immediately, the warmth turned into a fiery pulsing heat that had her thrusting her pelvis at him in hard, short bursts. He cried out and surged into her, filling her completely. Her thighs widened to accept him, and her hands tightened around his waist as he rubbed her clit in hard, firm circles. He was plunging in and out of her now, the motion of his body rocking her into the bed as he thrust back and forth.

"James, oh James," she moaned before her entire body stiffened under him and she came around his pulsating cock. He planted his hands on either side of her head and drove deep into her as her pussy tightened around him. With a harsh cry of pleasure, he threw his head back and came deep inside of her.

He collapsed on top of her, panting harshly into her ear and she stroked his wide back for a moment before he rolled off of her. She curled up on her side as he turned to face her. He had a look of worry on his face, and the green in his eyes faded and became the warm chocolate brown they normally were. She blinked and the beard on his face was gone. She touched his cheeks, feeling the rough stubble under her fingers as he moved closer to her.

"Are you all right, Bree?" he asked anxiously.

"Aye."

"Does it still hurt?" He rubbed her hip.

"No, my lord. It does not. It only hurt for a moment. I," she hesitated, "I believe your powers helped me heal almost immediately."

A look of relief crossed his face. "Aye, perhaps. I had not thought of that."

He looked like he wanted to say something else and she stifled a yawn. She wanted to curl into him and go to sleep. The orgasms he had given her had made her sleepy, and her entire body was tingling pleasantly. He must have sensed it because he tugged her against his body.

"Go to sleep, little one." He smoothed her hair back, and she threw her arm around his waist and buried her face into his warm skin.

CHAPTER 14

Bree took a deep breath and walked down the hallway toward the common room. She had woken late this morning to find herself alone in the bed. Her palms were sweaty, and her stomach churned. James was not angry with her, but she hadn't seen anyone else in his family. What if they hated her? What if Avery hated her?

For one horrible moment she thought she might throw up. Losing Avery's love would be as bad as if she lost Kaden's. She realized that she had begun to think of Avery almost as her mother, and she cursed her stupidity.

She had nearly killed Avery's child. The Red was kind, but her kindness would not extend to someone who had put her own child in danger. If she was lucky, the worse they would do is kick her out of their home. A snippet of her dream came back to her and she shuddered. James would not let them hurt her. She was almost positive of it.

Anticipating they would banish her from their home, she had slipped to the guest room and grabbed her bag. It was still packed with her things, and she hesitated before taking the sword as well. They might insist she leave the sword behind, it belonged to them after all, and she would not fight them on it, but she sent a silent prayer to the gods that they would allow her to keep it.

She realized she had stopped walking and was standing trembling in the middle of the hallway. She took a deep breath, closed her eyes, and muttered softly to herself, "Courage, Bree. Courage."

"Bree?"

Her eyes popped open and she stared at Evan.

He smiled tentatively at her. "Hi."

"Hi, Evan." She wanted to hug the young boy but crossed her arms nervously over her chest instead.

He stared at the bag and sword in her hand but didn't comment on them. "Thank you for saving my life," he said.

"Evan, I didn't save your life. If it hadn't been for me, you wouldn't have -"

He shook his head. "I decided to follow you, Bree. It's not your fault."

Before she could protest again, he stepped forward and gave her an awkward hug. "Thank you."

"Oh, Evan. I'm so glad you're okay." She hugged him fiercely and kissed him on the cheek. He blushed brightly and backed away, looking down at the floor.

"Dad is looking for you. He's in the common room."

"Aye. I will go see him now." She smiled sweetly at him. "Good bye, Evan. Take care of yourself."

He stared oddly at her. "I will. I'll see you later, all right?"

She smiled and squeezed his arm again before making her way to the common room. She dropped her bag on the floor and leaned her sword against the wall, before knocking on the closed door and entering the room. Tristan was standing next to the fireplace and Sophia, Nicky and James were clustered together against the far wall. The only one missing was Avery and Bree's heart dropped into her stomach.

"How do you feel, Bree?" Tristan asked.

"Good." She gave James a brief, nervous look. He was staring solemnly at her, and her legs began to shake. Even Nicky, usually so happy and quick to joke, had a serious look on his face and she gripped the back of the armchair in front of her for support.

"We need to talk about what happened." Tristan folded his arms across his chest. "What you did was very dangerous, Bree."

"I know." She made herself look him in the eye. "I'm sorry. I didn't mean for any of this to happen."

The door opened behind her and Avery swept into the room. "Sorry, Leta needed me to -"

She stopped and stared first at Bree and then at her husband and children. "Gods," she grumbled, "are you trying to frighten her to death?"

She crossed to Bree and smiled kindly at her. "How are you feeling, my sweet Bree? Did James heal you completely last night?"

When Bree only stared at her, her mouth trembling and tears shining in her eyes, Avery frowned at the others. "What did you say to her?"

She gathered the small blonde against her and stroked her back as Bree choked back a sob.

"Don't cry, my love." Avery gave the others another disappointed look. "We agreed we would be gentle with her."

"We've barely started." Tristan gave the others a sheepish look. "I swear we haven't -"

"Why don't you hate me?" Bree whispered.

"Hate you? Why would I hate you?" Avery stared at her in confusion.

"Because I nearly killed Evan," Bree said miserably.

"No, you tried to save him, and I will always be grateful to you," Avery said. "Now, let's have our talk in the kitchen. I imagine you haven't eaten yet?"

Bree shook her head and followed Avery numbly out of the common room as the others followed them.

BREE STARED DOWN AT THE FOOD IN FRONT OF HER. HER throat was a tiny pinhole and despite what Avery had said in the common room, she still felt sick. She wouldn't be able to eat, no matter what.

Avery sighed and glanced at Tristan. He shrugged and she sat down beside Bree, taking one cold hand in her own. "My love, what we want to talk to you about is not what happened with Evan. We want you to tell us the truth about where you were going. You need to trust us."

Bree continued to stare at her plate, and she jumped a little when she felt James' hand rub her back. "Tell us, little one."

"I was going back to Draken's pack."

"What? Why would you do that?" Sophia nearly shouted.

"I – I have a brother. His name is Kaden and he's still being held prisoner by Draken. I was going to rescue him."

She looked up at Nicky. "It's why I wanted you to train me on the sword."

Tristan sat down beside Avery. "Bree, going back to Draken's on your own is a very foolish idea."

"You'll die if you go back there," Nicholas said.

"I won't leave Kaden there!" She gave them both a furious look as Avery squeezed her hand. "He has spent most of his life protecting me, keeping me safe from all sorts of awful things, and I will not leave him to be tortured by Draken and his pack."

"We're not saying you should," Nicky said patiently. "We're saying that trying to do it alone isn't going to work."

Bree shook off Avery's hand and stood up. She paced the large kitchen as the others watched silently. "What would you suggest I do then? My parents are dead, and we have no other relatives. It has always been just Kaden and me. If I do not rescue him, who will?"

"Bree -" James began and she cut him off with a loud snort.

"You would do anything for your family, James." She stared at all of them. "Every one of you would be at Draken's door in a heartbeat if he had Leta or Evan. Kaden raised me, risked his life to keep me safe, and I have to at least try to save him."

She rubbed her forehead wearily. "I can't thank you enough for everything you've done, and I'm sorry that I've brought so much trouble to your family. I know you're going to ask me to leave, and I understand why. It was wrong of me to try and sneak away, and it put Evan in danger. I should have told you the truth and I'm sorry that I didn't."

She stopped in front of James and smiled up at him. "You've done so much for me already, but I need to ask you for one more thing. Will you look after Tia for me? After I save Kaden, I'll come back for her. I promise."

He looked at her gravely. "You'll die trying to save him. You know you will."

"He would do the same for me."

She wanted to kiss him goodbye, but she was acutely aware of the rest of his family staring at them. She settled for taking his hand and squeezing it. "Thank you so much, James. I – I'm so glad I met you."

She turned away before he could reply. She started toward Avery, wanting to hug her goodbye, but James put his hand on her arm and tugged her to a stop. "You're not going back to Draken's."

Unexpected anger flared inside of her and she shook his hand off. "Do you think you can stop me? Will you keep me a prisoner in your home like Draken did?"

He shook his head. "No. But I'll go to Draken's, find your brother, and bring him back to you."

Her mouth dropped open and she stared at him in shock.

"Well if you're going to this Draken's house, then I'm going as well," Nicholas said cheerfully. "There's no way I'm letting you have all the fun."

Sophia rolled her eyes. "You call breaking into the house of a mad Lycan fun, Nicky?"

He grinned at her. "You don't?"

When she didn't reply, he reached out and ruffled her hair. "Aww, is itty-bitty Sophia afraid of the big bad wolf?"

She slapped his hand away. "I kick your ass on a regular basis. I can handle Draken and his wolves."

"We'll wait until after the full moon. We might be stronger during the moon cycle but so will Draken and his pack," James said thoughtfully. "We should come up with a plan to sneak in and take Kaden. We'll take a few days to study his home and his land. We need to find out if -"

"Boring," Nicholas said. "I say we knock on the front door and introduce ourselves. Let him know we've come for Kaden and demand his release. If he doesn't want to give him up, we'll take Kaden by force."

James frowned. "I know you love a good fight, but I think it's best if we -"

"Stop this!" Bree suddenly shouted.

"None of you are going anywhere near Draken!" She

said. "You have no idea how – how dangerous he is. I would never forgive myself if something happened to one of you. I appreciate your willingness to help but I can't ask you to do this."

"You're not asking. We're offering to help," Nicholas replied.

Bree looked at Avery and Tristan. "Tell them they cannot go with me."

Tristan shrugged. "They're adults, Bree."

She snorted with anger and knelt beside Avery, taking her hand and squeezing it. "Please, my lady. Your children will die if you let them go to Draken's. You can't be okay with that."

Avery rested her hand on the top of Bree's head. "But you want me to be okay with you going alone and dying at the hand of this Draken?"

Bree flushed. "I am not your child. You barely know me."

Avery smiled at her. "Aye, and you barely know me. But it doesn't mean that I, or anyone else in my family, will allow you to just go to your death. If Sophia, Nicky, and James want to help you, I won't stop them."

Bree tore away from her and stomped to the far end of the kitchen. She glared at all of them. "I won't let you go with me. Do you understand?"

"You can't stop us, little one," James said.

She scowled at him. "I'll sneak away again. I swear to the gods I will."

Leta burst through the doorway of the kitchen, her tanned face glowing happily. She jumped into Tristan's lap and hugged him excitedly. "They're here, Papa! They're here!"

Tristan laughed and stood up, dangling Leta under his arm and swinging her back and forth before smiling at Avery. "They made good time."

Avery stood and held her hand out to Bree. "My sister is here, Bree. Come, I want you to meet her."

Bree stared at her. "I – we have to – I mean…"

Avery put her hand up. "We'll discuss this more later. I promise. Do you believe that Draken will kill Kaden in the next few days?"

Bree shook her head slowly. "No. He is big and strong, and they value him as a slave. They tend to hunt the weaker ones."

James made a snort of disgust as Avery took Bree's hand. "Then give us a few more days. I promise you we will think about the possibility of letting you go alone."

James opened his mouth to protest and Avery gave him a hard look. "James, Nicky – go and build up the fire in your grandmother's room. It is a cold day and she will appreciate a warm room."

She led Bree toward the door. "Come, my sweet. I am excited for Maya to meet you."

CHAPTER 15

"Avery!" A slender blonde woman and a woman with grey hair were standing in the front yard.

Avery dropped Bree's hand and embraced the smaller woman. "Hello, Maya."

Bree watched as the sisters hugged before Avery led Maya to her. "Maya, this is Bree. She's staying with us for a while."

"Hello, Bree. It's nice to meet you." Maya smiled and held out her hand.

Bree shook it briefly. Although Maya was smaller and had blonde hair instead of red, she smiled exactly like Avery smiled and Bree could feel herself wanting to like the woman immediately. She gave Maya a nervous smile as Sophia brushed past her.

"Welcome home, Grandmamma. I missed you." Sophia hugged the grey-haired woman hard, and she winced before returning her hug.

"Gently, Sophia. I'm old remember?" The woman's shoulders were stooped with age, but her dark brown eyes danced with laughter as Leta barrelled into her and wrapped her arms around the woman's waist.

"Grandmamma! I have a dog now! Well, actually she's Bree's dog but Tia loves me just as much, and she's been sleeping on my bed and playing with me."

"A dog?" The woman raised her eyebrow at Tristan who hugged her gently.

"Hello, Mother."

"Hello, Tristan. Where are the boys?"

"They're just -"

He paused as Nicholas and James, followed closely by Evan, came out of the house.

"My sweet Nicky." The woman held her arms out and Nicholas embraced her gently. She stroked his blond hair and kissed his cheek before turning to James and Evan.

"Here are my handsome boys." She smiled at them and kissed James before putting her arm around Evan. "I swear, you've grown a foot in the moon I've been gone, Evan."

Bree was surprised when James approached her and took her hand in his large one. He smiled comfortingly at her as he pulled her forward.

"Grandmamma, I want you to meet someone. This is Bree. Bree, this is my grandmother Vivian."

"Hello," Bree whispered.

James' grandmother gave her a cool and appraising look. The woman bore a striking resemblance to Sophia, and Bree was immediately intimidated by the older woman. She could feel herself wanting to shrink into the ground as Vivian stared at hers and James' clasped hands for a moment.

"Hello, Bree. It's nice to meet you," she finally said.

"It's lovely to meet you as well," Bree squeaked out. She was barely able to contain her sudden and wildly inappropriate urge to curtsey.

"Where are Marshall and the children?" Avery asked.

"They dropped Vivian and me at the house, and then drove the wagon straight to the barn." Maya shivered delicately.

"Come, let's go inside. It's freezing out here," Avery said as Tristan took Vivian's arm and led her toward the house.

"Hi, Vivian." Avery hugged her mother-in-law and Vivian kissed her loudly on the cheek.

"Hello, darling."

"TELL ME, CHILD. HOW DID YOU MEET JAMES?"

Bree gave Vivian a nervous smile. Tristan's mother had cornered her by the fireplace in the common room almost immediately, and she had no idea if she should tell her the truth or not.

She breathed a sigh of relief when Avery appeared beside her. "James and Nicky found her in the woods, about a day and a half from here. She had been attacked by Lycans and was close to death."

"What?" Vivian gave Avery a startled look. "Attacked by Lycans?"

Avery nodded. "Aye. Apparently, there is a Lycan named Draken who is collecting humans and using them for hunting purposes."

"Gods be damned," Vivian breathed. "I thought that had died out years ago."

Avery scowled. "So did we."

She put her arm companionably around Vivian's and leaned her head against her shoulder. "James healed her, and he and Nicky brought her back home. Bree has agreed to stay with us for a while and we're so glad she did. She's lovely."

Bree flushed with embarrassment as the door to the common room opened and a dark-haired man, followed by a young woman and man, entered the room.

"That's Marshall, Tristan's brother," Avery said as Tristan and Marshall embraced. She pointed to the young woman who resembled Maya from her slender figure to her pale, blonde hair. "That's Maya and Marshall's daughter, Danielle."

She laughed as a young blond man picked up Leta and tossed her high into the air. "And that's Doran, their son. Doran and Danielle are twins and only a few weeks younger than James."

Another young woman, this one dark haired and full-breasted, entered the common room. She searched the room and gave a shriek of delight when she saw James. Bree watched as she sprinted across the room and launched herself at him.

He caught her, his eyes widening with surprise as she kissed him fully on the mouth. She clung to him, kissing him deeply and running her hands up and down his back as Bree sucked in her breath and turned to face the fire. Her hands were icy cold, but her face felt like it was on fire.

"What is Martine doing here?" She heard Avery ask.

"She was visiting Dani and when she found out we were traveling here, she asked to join us. You know how fond she is of James," Vivian replied.

"Aye." Avery's hand was on her back, rubbing softly, and Bree blinked back the tears that were threatening.

"Bree? Are – "

"I should go, my lady." Bree gave her a large false smile. "I imagine Marian needs help in the kitchen."

Before Avery could respond, Bree pulled away from her and bolted for the door. Vaguely, she could hear Vivian asking Avery why she was helping in the kitchen, but she didn't hear Avery's response as she ran out of the room.

"MARIAN, LET ME TAKE THOSE FOR YOU." BREE HURRIED over to the older woman and took the pile of laundry out of her hands.

"You're a sweet girl, Bree." Marian smiled at her. "It's all my own clothes anyway. I was just going to run them back to my room before I start on supper."

"I'll take them back there for you."

"That's very kind of you. It's the last room on the right," Marian called as Bree walked down the hallway of the servant quarters.

She hesitated at the end. Had Marian said right or left? She shrugged and chose left, turning the knob and peering into the room. It was a small room and the layer of dust suggested no one had been in it for a very long time.

Leaving the door open, she crossed the hallway and entered Marian's room, placing the clothes on the bed before leaving. After a moment's hesitation, she entered the small, unused room. The bed was covered with a dust sheet and there was a plain wooden chair in one corner. The room had no fireplace and it was chilly. She slipped past the bed and rubbed a clean spot on the window. It faced into the back yard, and she could see Tristan and Marshall standing at the entrance to the barn.

"This used to be my room."

She turned and smiled at Avery. "Really?"

"Aye."

"Why did you stay in the servant's quarters?" Bree asked.

Avery joined her at the window. "Tristan bought both

Maya and me from a slave house. Maya was Sophia and Nicky's nanny and I – well, if I am completely truthful – I was bought only because Sophia wanted me."

Bree stared flabbergasted at her. "Tristan bought you as slaves?"

Avery laughed softly. "Aye, little one. He did."

"But – but, you don't have slaves here."

"We don't now," Avery said. "At that time, Tristan did own slaves. He didn't treat them cruelly, but he didn't pay them. Shortly after he purchased Maya and me, he realized his error and started paying the people who worked for him."

"Did it have something to do with you?"

Avery grinned a little. "Perhaps. I have always felt very strongly on the subject of slavery. I may have helped him to see the light."

Avery stared around the small room. "I haven't been in this room for many years."

"So, you and Tristan fell in love?"

"We did." Avery smiled at her. "We were attracted to each other from the beginning, but it took a while for us to confess our feelings. There were some obstacles in our path."

"Because you're a human and he's a Lycan?" Bree asked.

"Well, in a way. It didn't bother me that Tristan was Lycan, nor did it bother him that I was human. But Vivian did not approve of our love. She wanted Tristan to marry a Lycan, and she believed it would be best if Sophia was raised by a mother who was Lycan."

"What changed her mind?"

"I saved Sophia's life." Avery stared out the window for a few moments until Bree touched her arm hesitantly.

"I'd like to stay in this room if I could."

Avery frowned. "It's much too cold, Bree."

"With your sister and her family visiting, the guest rooms are full. I'll just use a lot of blankets."

Avery hesitated. "Are you not going to stay with James in his room?"

Bree blushed to the roots of her hair, and Avery patted her arm. "I'm sorry, my love. I did not mean to embarrass you."

"It's fine," Bree mumbled. She looked at the floor. "I – I would prefer to stay in this room."

Avery stared at her for a long moment and then sighed. "Very well. You can stay here. If you promise that you will not sneak away in the night."

She tipped Bree's head up and gave her a searching look. "Do you promise, Bree?"

Bree nodded. "Aye."

"I know you are worried for your brother and I understand that. I could not imagine how I would feel if Maya was in danger and I couldn't do anything about it. But I promise you, we will come up with a plan to save your brother."

Bree nodded again and Avery kissed her forehead. "I am trusting you to not run away, little Bree. I won't lie – the others won't trust you and James, in particular, will not want you to stay in this room by yourself. I'll support your request and help convince him because I know in my heart you won't leave again without telling us. But do not turn me into a liar."

"I won't. I promise you, Avery." Bree was on the verge of tears again and Avery drew her into a hug.

"I know you won't, my love. Now, if you're going to sleep in this room, you'll have to ask Laura to show you the rock trick."

"Rock trick?"

Avery laughed. "Come, little one. Let's find Laura and she can explain."

"PLEASE DON'T STAY IN THIS ROOM, BREE."

James deep voice startled her, and she dropped the stack of blankets she was holding, onto the bed. She turned and smiled weakly at him. It was after dinner and she had just finished cleaning the tiny room of the dust and changing the sheets on the bed.

She didn't sit with the family for dinner. She'd ducked out to the barn as soon as she finished helping Marian with the food, and helped Ian clean out some of the stalls. If he found it odd that she was there, he didn't mention it. When Marian showed up with plates of food for both of them, Bree sat on a bale of hay and visited with Ian while they ate. She didn't know him very well, but he spoke kindly to her and his admiration for Tristan and his family were clear.

"Have you worked for Tristan for a long time?" She asked between bites of smooth potatoes and warm venison.

"Oh aye, years and years. I wasn't a slave. My father and Tristan's father were friends and after my wife died, Tristan asked me to stay with him. Said he needed help with the horses."

Ian had looked with distaste at the cooked carrots on his plate before pushing them from his plate onto Bree's. "Marian's always trying to get me to eat vegetables. I'm a Lycan for the gods sake – we're not supposed to eat vegetables."

Bree suppressed a smile as Ian continued. "Tristan didn't really need help. He just knew how much I was missing my Anna. He gave me a purpose and a place to call home when I thought I would go mad with loneliness. And he paid me a fair wage for it."

He grinned at Bree. "Of course, then the lady Avery came along and suddenly everyone was getting paid. She changed him for the better she did. Tristan loved her from the start, I think. Why, she used to help me in the barn from time to time and more than once, Tristan felt the need to remind me that she was off limits."

"So, you never married again?"

"No. I never found another Lycan who caught my fancy the way my Anna did."

He finished eating and stood. "I'm just about finished in here. You best be heading back to the house before James shows up and feels the need to remind me that you're off limits."

She'd blushed brightly, and he laughed before shooing her out of the barn.

Now, she took a deep breath and smiled at James. "Did your mother not tell you she gave me permission to stay here?"

"Aye. But I would prefer if you joined me in my bed."

Her stomach gave a funny little lurch and warmth flooded through her pelvis. Just the way James was looking at her was heating her up. She pushed the image of being under his hard body out of her head and made herself remember the way Martine had kissed him in the common room.

"I can't, James. I don't regret what happened between us last night, but it's not something we should do again."

"Why not?"

She blinked at his bluntness. "It's complicated."

"Explain it to me then." He leaned against the wall and folded his arms across his chest.

She sighed. "My brother hates the Lycans. If he found out I was sleeping with one, he would be angry with me. Worse – he would be disappointed and hurt."

"You're a grown woman, Bree. You should stop letting people tell you what to do."

That made her laugh. "You try and tell me what to do all the time, James."

"I don't," he protested. "I just – I want to keep you safe."

"Aye, and so does my brother. What is the difference?"

"The difference is that I do it because…"

She watched as redness crept into his cheeks. "Because what?"

He didn't answer her. Instead he gave her a look of frustration. "If you won't join me in my bed then at least sleep in my room. You'll freeze to death in here."

"I won't. I have plenty of blankets and rocks." She grinned at him.

He scowled at her. "Rocks? I have no idea what the hell you're talking about but please, stay in my room. I'll sleep in another room."

"All the other rooms are full," she pointed out.

He grunted in frustration and stalked across the room. He pulled her up against him and cupped her face, rubbing his thumb across her mouth. "Then stay with me, Bree."

He kissed the tip of her nose and gave her a hopeful smile. "It's lonely in my bed without you."

She was so close to giving in. His voice and warm hands were breaking down her defenses. As he tilted his head down to kiss her, she closed her eyes and parted her lips. Immediately, the image of Martine kissing him invaded her mind, and she opened her eyes and pushed free of his arms.

He looked at her with barely-concealed frustration, and she could feel anger seeping into her. After years of fear and anxiety, she welcomed the foreign feeling. It felt so good to feel something other than fear. She folded her arms across her chest and glared at him. "I'm sure you can find someone else to warm your bed."

"What are you talking about?" he said.

She raised her eyebrows at him. "I was in the common room when Martine kissed you, James."

He actually blushed. "We are old friends. I've known her since I was a pup. She's just a very friendly girl."

She snorted and rolled her eyes. "Aye, very friendly."

"Bree, I swear there isn't anything going on between us. I haven't even seen her in nearly a year."

"Really? Because she kissed you like something was going on between you."

"If I had known she -"

"Have you slept with her?" she asked.

He gave her a hesitant, cautious look and her heart plummeted to her feet. He had slept with her - it was written all over his face. The question had popped out of her mouth before she could stop it, and now she wished bitterly that she had kept her big mouth shut.

"I have," he said. "But it was only once, and I didn't mean to do it."

"Didn't mean to? How exactly do you accidentally have sex with someone?"

He flushed. "It was three years ago. Martine was visiting and it was during the moon cycle. I was young and impulsive, and it's harder for Lycans to resist the urge to mate when the moon is full."

When she only stared at him, he sighed and rubbed his hand through his hair. "Martine has always had a crush on me. I should not have slept with her that night, but I was weak."

He gave her a pleading look. "I knew it was a mistake immediately. The next morning, I apologized to Martine for what had happened, and told her it could never happen again. She said it was fine, but she does have a tendency to be um, over-exuberant in her greetings."

When she didn't say anything, he gave her a tentative look. "It was only once."

"She wants it to happen again," Bree said.

"But I don't," James said. "I want you."

He reached for her and she backed away. "I can't, James. Once I rescue my brother, the sex between us would have to end anyway. I've already betrayed him once by sleeping with you. I can't keep betraying him."

"Bree -"

"Please go," she whispered. Her anger and jealousy had faded, leaving her feeling tired and depressed, and she wanted to be left alone.

"How do I know you won't sneak away in the night?" he suddenly asked.

"I promised your mother I wouldn't." She gave him a weary smile. "Good night, James. I'll see you in the morning."

He hesitated in the doorway, giving her one last look of longing mixed with frustration. "If you get too cold in the night, come to my room. You can sleep in my bed and I'll sleep in this room, all right?"

She nodded. "Aye, thank you."

CHAPTER 16

"Bree, come sit with us." Dani waved at her from across the room, and Bree smoothed her skirt down before sitting on the couch next to the young blonde woman.

Dani put her arm around her and grinned at her. "The skirt fits."

"Aye. Thank you. It's very lovely," Bree said.

"You're welcome. It looks way better on you than me anyway. Don't you think, Martine?"

The brunette gave a short nod and a strained smile. She was looking out the window, and Bree knew just from the look on her face that James was outside.

Dani rolled her eyes at Bree. "Martine is obsessed with my cousin. They have sex once and she thinks they're betrothed."

"Shut up, Dani," Martine said without tearing her gaze from the window.

"Martine, you know he only had sex with you because it was the full moon." Dani turned to Bree and snorted disdainfully. "The Lycans are ridiculous during the full moon."

"It's more than that. He's just distracted right now."

Martine gave her a hurt look. "Besides, it is almost the full moon. He won't be able to resist me. You know he won't." A small pleased grin crossed her face, and she hugged herself happily before looking out the window once more.

Bree swallowed down the surge of jealousy that went through her. She studied Martine. The girl was pretty in a soft and curvy kind of way. Her dark hair and dark eyes complimented her tanned skin nicely, and she had full breasts and hips.

She stared down at her own thin body. Her breasts were small and even after nearly two months of regular meals, she would never have hips or a full bottom. She looked like a boy compared to Martine and she sighed softly.

Martine was right – James wouldn't be able to resist her during the full moon. And now that he knew there was no future with Bree, why should he resist Martine. She was beautiful and seemed nice. She was also a Lycan and she certainly wasn't afraid of her own shadow like Bree was. She could probably lift a sword easily.

"Bree? What's wrong?" Dani asked.

"Nothing. I'm so glad I've met you, Dani," Bree said. She meant it. She had bonded quickly with the young woman over the last three days. Of course, it was nearly impossible not to like her. Dani was sweet like Maya but with a wicked sense of humour like Marshall's, and she had a carefree attitude that Bree both admired and coveted.

"I'm glad we've become friends too, Bree." Dani kissed her on the cheek with a loud smacking sound. "I've already asked Mama if you can come to our house and stay with us for a while."

"Oh, I – that's very nice of you," Bree said. She didn't know how to tell Dani that once she rescued her brother, he would take her away from the Lycans and she would never

168

see any of them again. It wasn't something she could share with her anyway. Dani was sweet and kind, but she had lived a sheltered life. She had no idea of the hardships that others had faced. Bree hoped she never would.

She frowned as something Dani said earlier sunk in. "Dani? What do you mean 'the Lycans'? Are you – are you not a Lycan?"

Dani shook her head. "Nope, I'm as human as you and Mama. I didn't get any of the Lycan genes. Mama says it's probably because Dad is only half-Lycan himself. Of course, Doran can shift, and we shared her womb for the gods sake."

"Really?"

"Aye. Doran started shifting when he was two, but I never did."

"Does it bother you that he can shift, and you can't?" Bree asked curiously.

"No. I like being just like Mama. I never have any trouble controlling my emotions during the full moon or wrecking my clothes when I shift."

Bree giggled. "I never really thought about the clothes being ruined."

Dani grinned at her. "Dad said it nearly drove Mama crazy when Doran was a toddler. For a while there she just let him run around naked because he was constantly shifting and tearing his clothes apart."

"Is that normal?" Bree asked.

Martine turned around. "No. Doran had a harder time learning to control the shift because he is only a quarter Lycan."

There was a thin note of condescension in her voice, and Dani immediately rose to her brother's defense. "He controls the shift just fine now, Martine. Besides, if you get your wish and marry my cousin, none of your children will be full Lycans. James is half-human remember."

When Martine just sniffed in reply, Dani turned back to Bree. "Aunt Avery said your parents died?"

"Aye. They were robbed and murdered while they were traveling home one night."

"I'm sorry," Dani said. "Do you have any siblings?"

Bree was saved from answering when Martine stood and paced back and forth in the common room. "This is so boring. I'm going out to talk with the boys."

"Talk with James you mean," Dani snickered. "And see how many times you can touch him before he runs away."

"Shut up, Dani!" Martine snapped. Her eyes glowed a deep yellow, and she bared her teeth and growled at Dani before flouncing from the room.

Bree gave Dani a look of wide-eyed fear. Dani patted her knee. "Don't be afraid, Bree. She's just grumpy because there are only two days until the full moon. The Lycans always get," she paused and giggled, "horny and kind of grumpy before the full moon. I guarantee you that Mama and Dad, and Aunt Avery and Uncle Tristan will spend most of tomorrow in their beds."

She made a face. "Which is kind of gross but that's what happens when you live with Lycans. All of the Lycans will be moody as hell tomorrow. Mark my words. Well, maybe not James if Martine gets her way. Which she might. She got her way three years ago."

Dani rolled her eyes. "I am seriously so happy to be a human. Imagine not being able to control yourself just because the moon is going to be full. Ugh."

"How long does it last?" Bree asked.

"Just until after the hunt," Dani said. "They'll come back

worn out and sleep the day away, and then they'll be back to normal. Mama and I always – Bree what's wrong?"

"They go hunting?" Bree whispered. Her body was trembling, and she could feel the blood draining from her face.

Dani nodded. "Aye. Every full moon. All Lycans hunt during the full moon, Bree. Did you not know that?"

Bree stood up on legs that felt like they were made of wood. "No, I didn't know. Excuse me, I – I have to go," she whispered through numb lips.

She turned and lurched from the room as Dani stared in confusion at her.

"Bree, wait! What's wrong?" Dani chased after her, but Bree hurried into the kitchen and down the servant's quarters, disappearing into her room and slamming the door behind her.

JAMES GRABBED DANI'S ARM WHEN SHE RAN OUT OF THE kitchen. His cousin looked upset and he gave her a curious look. "Dani? What's wrong?"

"I don't know. Do you know where your mom is? I think I said something that upset Bree."

"What did you say?" James shook her roughly, his voice harsh, and she frowned up at him.

"You're hurting my arms, James."

"I'm sorry." He let go of her and gave her a contrite look. "What were you and Bree talking about?"

"We were talking about Lycans and how you're all so damn moody before the full moon. I said you would be fine after the hunt and that -"

James groaned. "Gods be damned. Where is she, Dani?"

"She ran to her room. Should I go and find Aunt Avery?"

James hesitated. "Aye, you'd better. I'll go and talk to Bree now, but I think she'll feel better if Mom is there."

Dani ran off and he walked quickly to Bree's room. He knocked gently on her door and then opened it. "Bree? Can I come in?"

She looked up from where she was hurriedly packing her bag. "Get out of here, James."

He shook his head and entered the room, leaving the door open to try and ease her fear. "Listen to me, honey. What Dani said -"

She stepped back and reached for her sword. She held it in front of her and pointed it at his chest. "I'm leaving and you can't stop me. Dani told me about the hunt."

"It's deer, Bree."

"I thought you were different. I thought that – wait what?"

"We hunt deer. Not humans – deer."

She stared at him for a moment, her entire body tense, and then suddenly dropped the sword and collapsed on the bed. She buried her face in her hands and rocked back and forth as he approached her gingerly and sat down beside her.

"I'm sorry, honey. I should have told you we hunt during the full moon. It was foolish of me to forget. I promise you that we only hunt for deer and only during the full moon."

He rubbed her back tentatively, and she surprised him by dropping her hands from her face and leaning against him.

"I'm sorry," she whispered. "I should have known better than to think that you would... I'm so sorry."

"You have nothing to be sorry about." He smiled at her and wiped away the tears that were visible on her cheeks. "With your history, it's not surprising that learning that we hunt would frighten you."

Bree's relief was tinged with shame. She felt terrible that she'd even thought for a moment that James would be like Draken and his pack.

"How – how are you feeling?" she asked. This was the closest she'd been to him in three days, and she was finding it difficult not to throw herself at him.

"Fine, why?" he asked.

She stared at his mouth. Dani had said the Lycans would be horny. She wondered if he was, wondered if he was anxious to kiss her and touch her and strip her naked. Her eyes dropped to his chest. She could see just a hint of his chest hair, and she clenched her hands into tight fists to stop herself from touching it.

"Bree?" James' voice was worried, and she raised her eyes to his. "Are you all right?"

"Fine." She licked her lips as she returned to staring at his mouth.

He has such nice lips, she thought dimly. Her nipples hardened against her shirt as she pictured his mouth pulling gently on them. His tongue would be warm and would –

"Bree, stop looking at me like that, for the gods sake," James said.

She dragged her gaze from his mouth and back to his eyes. A soft moan escaped her throat. They were completely green, and she could almost see the beard growing on his cheeks.

"James," she whispered, nearly pleaded, and he groaned and cupped the back of her skull.

He bent and placed a soft kiss at the corner of her mouth. "You smell good, Bree."

He sucked her lower lip into his mouth and traced it with his tongue, as her hands pressed against his chest.

"I've missed you," he breathed before covering her mouth completely with his. Bree moaned and kissed him back. He gripped the back of her neck and massaged it gently as one big hand rested on her thigh. He rubbed her leg through her skirt, and she didn't protest when he slipped his hand under her skirt and traced the bare skin of her thigh.

He pushed his hand between her thighs and stroked her through her panties. Her soft gasp was swallowed by his mouth, and she pressed herself closer to him as he traced the edge of her panties and then worked his fingers under them.

He touched her, and she moaned with eager anticipation when his finger parted her wet lips and rubbed at her clit. She was soaking wet and he nipped her lip before whispering, "You've missed me as well, little one."

"Aye," she moaned. "I have."

"Good." He kissed her hard, stroking her tongue with his as he circled her clit with his rough fingers.

He was starting to press her backward onto the bed when Avery came hurrying into the room, followed by Maya and Vivian.

"Bree, do not be frightened. They don't -"

She stopped abruptly, staggering forward when Maya ran into her back, before giving James and Bree a look of embarrassment. "Oh, I'm so sorry."

Bree, her face flaming, pushed James' hand out from under her skirt and stood up. "Avery -"

Avery, her own face red, turned and pushed both Maya and Vivian from the room before following them out.

As their footsteps echoed down the hall, Bree covered her face with her hands. She was utterly mortified.

"Little one?" James voice carried a hint of laughter, and she lowered her hands and glared at him.

"Stop laughing, James."

He pressed his lips together in an effort to hide his grin. "I'm not."

"Your mother and your aunt and your *grandmother* just caught us with your hand up my skirt!" She said.

"It could have been worse. They could have caught me fucking you," he said blithely.

Her mouth dropped open and she blinked in astonishment at him.

"What?"

"You – you've never spoken like that in front of me before," she said.

"Does it bother you?" he asked.

She studied him carefully, wondering if she should tell him the truth. Fuck was a coarse word, a word that described the act of lovemaking in a crude way, and she felt like she should be offended by it. Instead, her pelvis was throbbing with renewed lust and she wanted him to say it again. The way it sounded coming from his mouth brought forth delicious images of his large body between her thighs, of his rough hands manipulating her body into the positions he wanted her in.

"Does it, little one? Tell me the truth," he said.

"No. I – I like it."

He grinned at her, his eyes lightening to green, and she took a nervous step back as he started toward her. "Good. I like fucking you. I've missed fucking you."

"James…"

"Have you missed fucking me?" He reached out and gathered a strand of her long blonde hair between his fingers. He tugged on it gently. "Have you, Bree?"

"Aye."

"Say it."

"I've missed fucking you," she said hoarsely.

He growled low in his throat and reached for her waist.

"James?"

His face tightened with anger at the woman's voice and he dropped his hands to his sides. "Aye, Martine?"

"Is everything okay?"

"It's fine. Leave us please."

"Bree, I'm sorry I frightened you." Dani's voice, low and hesitant, drifted into the room and Bree gave James a small smile before hurrying forward.

Martine and Dani were standing in the doorway. Dani was staring at her anxiously, but Martine was giving her a suspicious look.

"It's fine, Dani." Bree smiled at her. "You didn't mean to and honestly, everything seems to frighten me."

Dani hooked her arm around Bree's. "Martine and I were going to go for a ride. Would you like to join us?"

She nodded. "Aye."

James cleared his throat. "Put Bree on Rosie. She's the gentlest."

"Okay," Dani said. She led Bree from the room as Martine gave James a hard look before following them.

CHAPTER 17

B ree sighed and stared out the window of her bedroom into the darkness. Tia whined softly from the bed and Bree made a soft cooing noise. "Go to sleep, Tia. Everything's fine."

It was the night before the full moon and today had been strange and a bit stressful. She rubbed her arms briskly and then stripped out of her clothes, leaving her thick woolen socks on. She pulled James' shirt over her head and wrapped herself in a blanket before standing at the window again.

She had continued to keep his shirt, hiding it under her other clothes piled neatly in the dresser, and only wearing it when she was alone. He hadn't asked her to return it, but she didn't know if he had forgotten she had it or just didn't care. She sighed and stared blankly into the darkness.

James had avoided her all day, and she was confused and a little hurt by it. He had spent most of the day either in his room or in the barn with Nicky and Sophia. She reminded herself that it was for the best and pulled the blanket closer. Just like Dani said, the Lycans were moody and out-of-sorts today. Even Nicky, normally so cheerful, had snapped at her when she accidentally bumped into him. He had apologized immediately but his tanned face was strained and distracted.

Leta was whiny and temperamental. Not even Tia could cheer her and finally, just after dinner, Avery had gathered her into her lap. She sat down in the rocking chair next to the fireplace and rocked her for several hours, singing softly to her.

Bree hadn't even had the chance to apologize to Avery for what she had walked in on yesterday. Dani was right when she said that Avery and Tristan would spend most of the day in their bedroom.

Bree rested her forehead on the cold glass. Tomorrow would be the full moon, and James would undoubtedly mate with Martine either before or after the hunt. Strong and unpleasant jealousy flowed through her as she pictured Martine in James' bed. He may regret it later, but at the time he would be more than willing to give Martine the same type of pleasure that he had given her.

She rapped her forehead sharply against the glass, relishing the sting, as she tried to shove the images of Martine and James wrapped around each other out of her head. She banged her head again and then froze when he spoke softly.

"Is there a reason you're trying to break the glass with your forehead, little one?"

Tia woofed softly in greeting. Bree didn't need to look at the dog to know that her entire body would be vibrating with excitement. Her heartbeat sped up, and she stared into the darkness as she heard the soft click of the door shutting. Her ears strained to hear him. Unfortunately, he could be as quiet as a cat when he wanted to be. He was standing directly behind her, his hot breath blowing on her neck, before she realized he had crossed the room.

"Why are you here, James?" she asked.

"To ask a favour of you."

"What?"

"I want you to stay in your room all day tomorrow. Do not come out until we have left for the hunt."

She frowned into the darkness. "Why?"

He gave a grunt of frustration and stepped closer to her. "Please, will you do as I ask?"

"Tell me why and I'll consider it," she replied.

"Gods be damned, Bree!" he snapped. "I'm asking you to stay in your room. It's safer for you."

"You told me I have nothing to fear from you, James."

"You don't. It's just…"

He gave her a pleading look. "Please, Bree. Just stay in your room until I am gone."

"No. Not until you tell me why," she said stubbornly.

She gasped when he abruptly pushed her up against the window. She could feel the cold creeping through her blanket as he held her against the window. He knotted his fingers into her hair and forced her head to the side so he could place his mouth at her ear.

"You should stay in your room because if I see you, I won't be able to stop myself from fucking you," he muttered hoarsely.

There was a hardness pressing against her ass that sent a heavy thrill of excitement through her, and a flood of wetness between her legs. She pictured James carrying her to his room, pictured him pushing her legs apart and taking her like she belonged to him, and she couldn't keep her ass from rubbing against his cock.

He growled and yanked her away from the window. He tugged the blanket away and cupped her breasts through her shirt. She moaned when he tugged hard on her erect nipples and she pressed her ass against his cock again.

His hand left her breast and slipped under her shirt. She parted her legs willingly, and her hips arched when he plunged two fingers deep inside of her.

"Your pussy is so wet," he moaned.

She made a soft noise of need and pressed her pelvis against his hand, driving his fingers deeper into her.

He inhaled sharply and pressed his mouth against her neck. "I want you so much."

"Fuck me, James," she whispered, her face reddening.

He stiffened against her. "What did you say?"

She stared into the darkness. "Fuck me right now. I want you just as much."

He pulled away and she moaned with disappointment. He was rejecting her. Before she could turn to face him, his hands were reaching for the hem of her shirt. He yanked it over her head and dropped it to the floor. He pressed against her and she realized he had only backed away to remove his shirt. She sighed with delight at the feel of his chest hair against her smooth back.

He pulled her away from the window, and she could feel his hand at the small of her back as he unbuttoned his pants. He pushed them down impatiently before sitting down on the wooden chair in the corner of the small room.

"James?"

"Straddle me, Bree," he demanded.

"What? Backwards?" She gave him a bewildered look, her eyes widening at the look of dark lust on his face.

"Aye," he said impatiently. He pulled her backward, steadying her when she stumbled a little, and waited as she awkwardly spread her legs around his. She stood there for a moment, feeling uncertain and shy, before looking down. His cock was standing straight up, and he was gripping the base of it with one hand.

"Sit down, Bree." He cupped the back of her neck and pressed her downward.

"James, I don't think I'm flexible enough for…"

Her protest turned into a long, drawn-out moan when he guided his cock into her wet and ready core. He impaled her fully, stretching her tightness around his thick length as she moaned again. His thighs were shaking beneath her, but he waited patiently as she adjusted to his size.

Bree, her legs stretched wide around James' thighs and her sock-covered feet dangling, looked down between her legs as James gripped her hips and lifted her easily up and down. A stab of desire went through her at the sight of his thick cock sliding in and out of her.

"Put your hands on my legs," he rasped.

She did as he asked, gripping his legs firmly and rocking against him. He groaned, his breath stirring her hair, and reached upward to cup her breasts. He stroked and kneaded them, pinching and tweaking her nipples as she moaned.

He thrust back and forth, the chair creaking loudly beneath them, as Bree held on to his thighs and arched her back. He leaned forward and licked a slow, meandering path up her spine with his warm wet tongue.

"Gods, she moaned. Her nails were digging into his thighs, leaving moon-shaped crescents, but if it hurt, he made no indication. He nipped at her shoulder blades and she shivered with delight. His right hand left her breast and moved downwards to her soft curls.

"Watch," he demanded.

She watched as his fingers made tiny circles in her soft blonde curls before sliding to her clit. She cried out when he rubbed it firmly, and little sparks of liquid need ignited in her belly.

She arched her back again as he circled her waist with one

arm and bounced her on his cock. His fingers never stopped their circling and rubbing, and she cried out his name as her orgasm rushed through her. She shook and shuddered around his thick cock before collapsing against him.

He growled in her ear, his beard rough against her cheek, and thrust rapidly in and out before his pelvis arched and he drove his cock deep into her. Warm wetness flooded through her as he climaxed.

They stayed that way for a few minutes until Bree began to shiver in the chilly room. He stood, she felt a fleeting sense of loss when his cock slipped out of her, and carried her to her small bed. Tia wagged her tail excitedly and he dropped one of the blankets onto the floor before placing the small dog gently on it.

She smiled when he tucked the blanket around Tia, before he climbed into the bed beside her and curled his large body around hers. His hand brushed against something hard, and he pulled the flannel-covered rock out from the under the covers and looked at it curiously.

She smiled at him. "It helps warm the bed."

He tossed it to the floor with a loud thud. "Using rocks to keep you warm when you have a Lycan very able and very willing to keep you warm," he snorted.

He cupped her breast and kissed the back of her neck and she smiled happily to herself. Tomorrow she might have her regrets, but for now she had never been happier.

THEY LAID IN THE DARKNESS FOR NEARLY AN HOUR. BREE was on the verge of sleep when his hand started to squeeze her breast. He rubbed her nipple, teasing it into a hard point, before switching to the other one. When both nipples were hard and throbbing, he turned her on her back and bent his mouth to her right breast. He spent long minutes sucking and licking at both of her nipples, until she was gasping and arching under the thick stack of blankets that covered them.

His hand moved downward, and he pushed her legs roughly apart, cupping her pussy and sliding his fingers against her sensitive skin. He rubbed her clit as his mouth nibbled on the small swells of her breasts. He lifted his head and kissed her deeply, his tongue exploring her warm mouth with renewed urgency, as he teased her clit until it was swollen and hard beneath his fingers.

She was close to coming when he suddenly stopped, and she pushed at his hard chest in frustration. He gave a low laugh and turned her to face him, bringing her leg up and over his hip. As his hard cock probed at her pussy, she gasped out, "Again?"

"Aye." He pushed into her and she bit her lip with pleasure. He rocked back and forth, his hand slipping between their bodies to cup her breasts. They kissed until Bree was breathless. She kissed his neck, trailing her tongue down his throat and then kissing his broad chest. She tasted his warm skin, nipping at his collarbone as his cock moved in her in a smooth, slide and retreat motion.

Their soft moans and gasps filled the tiny room as they touched and kissed and rocked against each other. Finally, when they were both shaking with need, he reached between them and rubbed her clit, bringing her to another explosive orgasm. Her pussy tightened around his cock as she came, and he groaned her name and gave in to the sweet release that his body was screaming for.

Panting harshly, she buried her face in his neck and wrapped her thin arms around him.

"How do you feel, little one?"

"I feel super," she muttered sleepily, making him grin into the darkness.

He stroked her hair as her breathing slowed and she relaxed against him. He would let her sleep for a couple of hours and then wake her again. He had no idea if she would allow him into her bed again after tonight, and he planned on taking advantage of her willingness.

He pulled her closer and buried his face in her soft hair. Gods, he had fallen for her, and fallen for her hard. The thought of her leaving him, of never seeing her again, filled him with a wordless horror and his arms tightened involuntarily around her. She squirmed against him in her sleep and he loosened his grip.

He would rescue her brother even if it meant losing her. He stared into the darkness. Perhaps he could speak with her brother, convince him how much Bree meant to him and that he would never hurt her. He sighed softly. He couldn't let her leave him. She needed him and he needed her.

CHAPTER 18

E arly the next morning, he nuzzled his face into her hair and kissed the side of her neck until she woke.

"James?"

"Were you expecting someone else?" He arched his eyebrow at her, and she giggled.

He smiled at her. "I have to go, honey. It's not a good idea for me to stay in your bed any longer."

"Are you afraid you'll bite me?" she asked. She knew full well that a Lycan's bite during the full moon would turn a human.

He hesitated. "I would never hurt you, Bree. But it's harder to control certain urges during the full moon." His eyes took on a strange shine as he said the word moon, and she shivered.

He hugged her. "I won't hurt you."

"I know. Do you still want me to stay in my room?"

He traced the curve of her naked hip with one rough finger and winked at her. "No. I think I can control my urge to fuck you now."

She blushed a little. He had taken her three more times in

the night, and she wondered if his stamina was always like this or if the cycle of the moon had something to do with it.

"What are you thinking about, little one?" he asked.

"I…" Her blush deepened and he kissed her forehead.

"Tell me."

"I just wondered if you always had this much, um, energy or if it's the moon."

He grinned at her. "My ego is begging me to tell you it's all me, but in honesty the full moon does play a small part."

She wiggled her eyebrows at him. "Just a small part?"

He growled playfully. "Aye, just a small part. I'll prove it to you later."

The smile fell from her face. "You will be with Martine later."

He shook his head immediately. "No, I won't be."

"You won't be able to help yourself. Before you -"

"I told you before, Bree. I was young and impulsive. It was a mistake and it won't happen again."

"Have you been around her during a full moon since then?" she asked.

"No," he admitted. "But I want you, not her. I won't do anything but hunt with her tonight. I promise you."

He stroked her bare side. "You don't need to stay in your room, but I want you to keep your distance from me today, all right? Don't get too close to me or my siblings."

"I won't."

He kissed her a final time. "Go back to sleep, honey."

"GODS, MY THIGHS HURT." MAYA GROANED AS SHE SAT DOWN on the couch next to Avery. "I swear, every full moon Marshall comes up with new and inventive ways to -"

She stopped as Dani entered the room and Avery grinned before putting her arm around Maya's slender shoulders. "I feel great."

"Of course, you do." Maya laughed. "It's just one of the many benefits of being a healer."

Bree flexed the muscles in her thighs. Nothing on her body hurt. In fact, after sleeping a few more hours she had woken up feeling amazing. Despite her lack of sleep, she had tons of energy and her whole body had been tingling pleasantly for the entire day.

She should be sore. After what she did with James last night, every muscle in her body should be screaming at her. She smiled a little. The aches and pains that should have plagued her were healed by lying against James' warm body. Maya was right. There were benefits to being a healer – or at least sleeping with one.

"What are you smiling about?" Dani poked her in a friendly manner, and Bree gave her a guilty look.

"Nothing. I was just, um, thinking about something."

Avery and Maya were looking at her with matching grins and Bree blushed. She had sought Avery out first thing this morning and, blushing and stammering like a fool, had blurted out an apology.

Avery smiled sweetly and patted her shoulder comfortingly. "It's fine, little Bree. Remind me someday to tell you the story of the first time I met Vivian."

When Bree gave her a curious look, she laughed again before leading her toward the kitchen. "Let's just say it involved me being naked and in her son's bed. Not my finest moment."

Avery squeezed her arm. "In all seriousness, we're happy that you and James are together. I know we've only known you for a little while, but you've become part of our family and we love you very much."

Bree had started to cry, and Avery gave her a worried look. "I'm sorry. I didn't mean to upset you."

"You haven't," Bree said. "I – I love you too, Avery."

Avery had hugged her in the hallway and then wiped the tears from her face. "Let's go to the kitchen. I believe Vivian and Maya are waiting for us to have tea with them."

"Vivian as well?" Bree had been surprised. She hadn't seen a single one of the Lycans since she'd woken, and Dani had said they were all outside together.

Avery had nodded. "Aye. She rarely goes on the hunts anymore. She says her bones are too old for that sort of thing."

She'd given Bree a reassuring look. "Vivian won't hurt you. I promise. She has excellent control."

"I'm not afraid of her hurting me," Bree replied. "But I'm not so sure she'll want to be around me after... I don't think Vivian likes me very much."

"She likes you just fine. She hasn't said a word to me about you, which is a good sign. If she didn't like you, I'd know." Avery had laughed. "And once she gets to know you better, she'll love you like the rest of us do. I guarantee it."

Now, Bree stared out the window into the darkness. The Lycans had left half an hour ago, and she was trying hard not to think about James and Martine hunting together. He had promised her he wouldn't mate with Martine and she trusted him. Still, it was a small gnawing in her stomach that wouldn't go away. She sighed. It would be a long night.

She looked up as Vivian, followed by Laura, Nadine, Marian and Renee, entered the room. Laura and Marian had trays laden with food, and Renee and Nadine were carrying trays with delicate glasses and bottles of wine. Avery jumped up from the couch.

"Are you ready ladies?" she asked.

"What's going on?" Bree whispered to Dani.

"It's tradition," Dani replied. "They have their hunt every full moon and we have this."

Bree watched as Avery flipped a switch on the wall. The ceiling, which had tiny lights strung across it, lit up in a muted soft glow. Bree gasped with delight. She stared mesmerized at the ceiling as Renee and Nadine handed out glasses of wine.

Maya was standing next to a bookshelf fiddling with something, and Bree nearly fell off the chair when music began to play. Dani was grinning happily.

"Isn't it beautiful?" she whispered to Bree.

"Aye." Bree couldn't stop staring at the lights on the ceiling. She had never been in a home that had electricity, and she thought she would never grow tired of looking at them.

"Come on, Bree." Dani was tugging on her hand. "Dance with me."

"I don't know how to dance," Bree protested.

"I'll teach you." Dani dragged her to the middle of the room and after a few initial moments of self-consciousness, Bree forgot about the other women and concentrated on learning the steps Dani was teaching her.

At one point she looked up and laughed with delight. Most of the women were up and dancing, either with each other or just twirling alone to the music. Even Vivian was sitting on the couch with a glass of wine, tapping her feet to the beat of the music and smiling contently.

BREE LAID IN HER SMALL BED, SHIVERING A LITTLE DESPITE the blankets. It was almost dawn and the Lycans would be home soon. Dani had told her that they came back around dawn and went to bed for most of the day. She squirmed into a more comfortable position. She'd barely slept the entire night, and she was tired and a little out of sorts. Although he'd spent only one night in her bed, she missed James' warmth. She wondered if he would come to her when he came home.

She didn't want to admit it, but she was hoping he would. She sighed and turned on her side, staring at her closed door. He most likely wouldn't. He would be tired from his night of hunting and her bed, although comfortable, was too small for just him, let alone the two of them.

She bit her lip, her brow furrowing with indecision, before she suddenly threw back the covers. She wanted to be with him and once she rescued Kaden, what was happening between her and James would end. For now, she would enjoy it while it lasted. Shivering in the cold air, she left her room and crept quietly down the hall.

JAMES HESITATED AT THE ENTRANCE TO THE KITCHEN. HE WAS tired and cold, and he wanted to go to Bree's room, but they hadn't spoken about what would happen when he returned from the hunt. He paused for a few moments longer and then, with a heavy sigh, headed to his own room. As much as he wanted to join her in her small bed, he didn't want to frighten her. He had taken her multiple times last night. His need for her had been a steadily beating drum that he couldn't, nor wanted to, ignore. Although she responded enthusiastically each time, he still wasn't entirely sure how she felt about him.

He closed the door of his room and slipped out of his shirt. Someone had thoughtfully built up the fire in the fireplace and he stood close to the dancing flames, holding his hands out to warm them up. He didn't get chilled very often, but it was an especially cold night, and all the Lycans were feeling the bite of the wind as they loped back home.

He inhaled deeply. Oddly enough, he could smell Bree's scent in the room, and it made his chest ache with loneliness. Perhaps he should have gone to her room. He pushed the thought out of his head.

He stretched, his spine cracking, and smiled as he remembered the hunt. The thrill of the chase, the way the pack had worked together, always made him feel happy and content. It had been a good night and he –

He turned as his door opened and Martine slipped into the room.

"Hello, James."

He sighed. "Hello, Martine."

"It was a good hunt, was it not?" She was wearing a thin white nightshirt and she crossed her arms over her waist, pulling the material tightly against her ample breasts. She lifted her head and inhaled, wrinkling her nose a little as she stared suspiciously around the room.

"Aye, it was." He gave her a guarded look. "Why are you here?"

"I was cold." She pouted prettily at him. "I thought you could warm me up."

"No. You need to go back to your own room. I told you last night before the hunt started that I wouldn't mate with you."

She pouted again and moved a little closer to him. "It's because of Bree, isn't it?"

When he didn't reply, she gave him a wounded look. "What does she have that I do not, James? We had a pleasant time together three years ago."

"I've told you before, that was a mistake. I'm sorry, I don't mean to hurt your feelings but -"

"Just give me a chance," Martine said. "The human is too small and fragile. You'll break her bones just trying to take her to your bed."

"Martine." James tried to keep the impatience out of his voice. "You're not listening to me. I have no interest in you."

"My lord?"

Both he and Martine jumped at the sound of the soft voice coming from his bed. Bree had apparently been burrowed deep under the covers, and he couldn't stop the smile of delight from crossing his face when she stuck her blonde head out from under them.

"Are you coming to bed soon? It is lonely without you," she said sweetly.

"Aye, little one. I'll be there in a minute," he replied.

Martine, her mouth open and her gaze shocked, stared at Bree for a full minute before closing her mouth with a snap.

"Unbelievable," she huffed and stomped from the room, slamming the door behind her.

Bree flushed prettily at the look James was giving her. "What?"

"Nothing." He smiled. "I am glad you're here."

He shed his pants quickly and climbed into the bed, molding his body against hers. Her skin was warm and fragrant, and she shivered lightly at his cold touch.

"You are cold, my lord."

"It is cold outside."

"Aye, but you've never felt cold to me before," she replied.

"Perhaps you should help me warm up." He cupped her breast in his hand.

"I don't know. I'm so little – you might break my bones," she said.

He laughed and pinched her nipple, making her gasp. "Luckily for you, I have a talent for healing."

Boldly, she reached down and grasped his cock. It was already half-hard, and it stiffened and grew in her hand as she stroked him.

She gave him a questioning look. "Tell me, my lord. Are you bigger than most men?"

He could feel his cheeks reddening and she grinned at him. "You're blushing."

"No, I'm not," he said.

"You are," she said.

He groaned when her small hand squeezed him firmly. "Tell me the truth. Are you considered bigger than most?"

"Bree -"

"Tell me. Or will I be forced to find another to make my own comparison?" she teased.

He was immediately upset, and she made a small squeak of alarm when he pushed her to her back and hovered over her. "I will kill any man who touches you. You belong to me. Do you understand that?"

BREE STARED INTO JAMES' EYES. THEY WERE GLOWING bright green, not with lust, but something else. Jealousy, maybe. She swallowed hard. "James, I -"

"Do you understand?" He spoke slowly and deliberately. All trace of his usual good nature and humour had faded from his face, and she reached up and stroked his cheek hesitantly.

"Aye. I was only teasing you, my lord," she said.

"Do not tease me in such a manner," he replied. "The

thought of you in another man's bed is not one I will ever find amusing."

"All right," she said.

He reached down and pulled her thighs apart, wedging his large body between them and grinding his pelvis against hers. "Promise me you will never take another man into your bed. Promise me you won't sleep with anyone but me."

"I won't," she said immediately.

"Say it," he demanded.

"I promise I won't sleep with anyone else."

He stared at her, his nostrils flaring and his eyes glowing, and she rubbed one broad shoulder. He closed his eyes and when he opened them, the anger had been replaced with a mixture of shame and regret.

He rolled off of her and stared at the ceiling. "I'm sorry, Bree. I shouldn't have made you promise that. I have no right to tell you what to do."

He rubbed his hand across the stubble on his cheek. "Lycans are, well, territorial about their women but that's not an excuse for my behaviour. I overreacted and I should not have scared you into saying something you did not want to say. I'm sorry."

She cupped his face and made him look at her. "You didn't scare me, and I would not have said it if I didn't want to."

"Truly?"

"Aye." She lifted her head and planted small kisses on his throat. "I don't want to be in anyone's bed but yours."

She sat up and pushed the covers to his waist. As many times as they had been in each other's beds, she had never really explored his body. It had always been him touching and stroking her soft skin until she thought she would go mad with need. She wondered if she could do the same to him.

"Bree?" He was starting to sit up and she pushed him gently on the chest.

"Lie still please."

He relaxed against the bed with his hands clasped behind his head, as she leaned over and traced her fingers across his broad chest. No scars or imperfections marred it and she quickly ran her fingers down his sides, looking for ticklish spots. He didn't squirm or twist away, and she pouted at him.

"Not ticklish?"

"No, little one." He grinned at her.

She skimmed her hands across his chest. When her finger grazed across one nipple, he inhaled sharply, and she gave him a shark-like grin. She leaned down and licked his flat nipple. He groaned and one large hand slipped under the sheet, cupped her bare ass and squeezed before he relaxed against the bed once more.

She scowled and he smiled at her. "What's wrong?"

"I want to make you crazy – like you make me."

His face softened. "You do make me crazy, Bree. All I think about is you and how much I want you."

She scooted forward, her hands planted firmly on either side of his head and stared solemnly at him. "Truly, my lord?"

"Aye. You have no idea how happy I was when you poked your little head out from under the covers of my bed."

She smiled. "It was cold in my room and I missed your soft bed."

He gave her a mock scowl. "Only my soft bed?"

She shrugged. "Perhaps I missed the bed warmer a little."

His big hands were squeezing her ass again as he growled lightly. "Is that all I am to you – a bed warmer?"

"You're definitely more comfortable to sleep against than a rock." She grinned saucily.

James laughed and squeezed Bree's ass again. He was secretly delighted by her teasing. She was always so quiet and nervous, and this playful, teasing side of her was a welcome change. He was confident that she was no longer afraid of him, but he wanted more than that. He wanted her love.

The smile dropped from his face. He loved Bree and he was a fool for it. She had made it perfectly clear that once she had her brother back, she would have nothing to do with the Lycans again.

He would help save Kaden because he loved her. And in doing so, he would lose any chance of her love forever.

"My lord?" Her voice was soft and tentative. "Are you all right?"

"Fine."

She gave him a worried look. "Have I done something wrong?"

"No, of course not." He forced himself to smile at her. "I was just thinking about something."

"What?"

"It's not important." He stroked her hair back from her face and then lifted his head to kiss her mouth. "Have I mentioned how cold I am?"

"You don't feel cold any longer, my lord," she said as she ran her hands over his flat abdomen.

"Parts of me are cold, and I believe you mentioned something about warming me up," he replied.

"Aye, I did say that, didn't I?" Her fingers still roaming over his abdomen, she leaned down and kissed him slowly and thoroughly.

"What parts of you are cold?" she whispered as she rubbed his abdomen in lazy circles.

"Lower," he replied.

She pulled the covers down and stared at his erect cock. She slid back until she was sitting next to his hips, then reached out and wrapped her small hand around him. He moaned and she smiled a little.

"It doesn't feel cold." She stroked him back and forth, watching as a small drop of liquid formed at the top.

He didn't reply and she glanced up at him. He gave her a strained smile and tried not to beg her to suck him. She watched his face as she squeezed him more tightly and moved her hand in a quick back and forth motion. He groaned and licked his lips as he moved his hand to cup one small breast. He tugged on her nipple and she pushed his hand away.

"You're distracting me," she chastised him.

She ran her thumb over the head of his cock and spread the moisture she found, across it. He arched his hips into her hand as a small delighted smile crossed her face. "I have found a way to make you squirm after all, my lord."

She bent and took the head of his cock into her mouth. He cried out at the feel of her warm, wet mouth and arched his hips up, sliding his cock deep into her mouth.

She made a muffled gasp of surprise, and he gripped the back of her head and pulled her away. She looked at him in confusion. "Do you not like that, James?"

"I like it very much," he rasped. "Just – just warn me before you do that."

"Why?"

He gave her a wry smile. "You have no idea how you affect me, Bree."

She reached out and grasped the base of his cock firmly. "Just hold still this time."

"Aye, just hold still. No problem," he muttered under his

breath. She stuck her tongue out at him, before wetting her lips and closing her mouth around his throbbing cock once more.

He dug his hands into the sheets and forced himself to stay still as Bree sucked and licked at his cock. He watched her pink lips sliding up and down for only a few seconds before he groaned and looked away.

For nearly fifteen minutes she explored his cock with her mouth and her hands. She licked and tasted, and squeezed his cock firmly then lightly.

"Gently," he croaked out when her soft hand cupped his balls.

She returned her hands to his cock. She stroked him back and forth before leaning over him and taking him into her mouth again. His hips were beginning to move with short little thrusts, he couldn't help it, and she released him and grinned up at him.

"No moving, remember?"

"Bree, please," he groaned as she rolled his cock between her warm hands.

"Please what?" she asked sweetly.

"Honey, I can't wait much longer," he whispered.

"Are you sure?" She smiled at him. "I think you can wait."

He watched as she slowly inched her mouth down over his cock again. He panted and moaned, thrusting his hips at her as she sucked hard. Finally, his cock throbbing and his entire body shaking, he reached down and yanked her small body upward.

"James?" She frowned at him. "Why are you making me stop?"

"I wasn't going to last much longer," he groaned. The

combination of her eagerness and innocent exploration had made him feel like he was going to explode five minutes in.

"Oh." She leaned down and kissed him. At the taste of himself in her mouth, his hands squeezed painfully around her narrow hips. She pulled back a little and stroked his face.

"Can I try being on top?" she asked shyly.

"Aye." He watched as she eagerly straddled him. His cock rubbed against her wet heat, and they both groaned in response.

"Don't move, my lord," she whispered, and he gave a soft moan of assent as she rose up above him, took his cock in her tiny hand and guided it into her body. Slowly she sank down, taking him into her inch by torturous inch. When she was seated firmly on top of him, she braced her hands on his chest and bounced experimentally.

He thrust his hips upward in response, and she made a soft gasping cry of pleasure before slapping his chest lightly. "Don't move, remember?"

"Right," he choked out.

BREE STARED DOWN AT JAMES. EACH TIME THEY MADE LOVE in the past, he'd been the one to take control, to guide and manipulate her body into different positions and to make her come when he wanted. She wanted to be the one in control this time, and to her delight, he was submitting to her demands.

As the familiar warm tingling spread throughout her body, she lifted and lowered her body over his repeatedly. He groaned loudly at her slow and deliberate movements.

"Tighten your muscles around me, little one," he suddenly said.

"What do you mean?" She gave him a puzzled look.

Without speaking, he tickled her. Giggles burst from her mouth and she jerked against him, her inner muscles squeezing around his cock. He grabbed her hips and ground her pelvis against his.

Feeling a little self-conscious, she slid up and down and then concentrated on squeezing his cock again. Her lips curved into a smile when he gasped, and his fingers dug into the flesh of her hips.

"Do you like that, my lord?" she said.

"Aye," he ground out, his body jerking beneath her when she squeezed around him twice more.

She leaned over him, her breasts brushing against his chest and kissed his jaw. "Should I keep doing it?"

He moaned in reply, and she licked a slow path across his throat as she thrust her pelvis back and forth.

"Oh!" She suddenly shuddered above him and twitched to a stop.

"What's wrong?" He stroked her back.

"Nothing. That – that just felt really good," she said.

"Do it again," he encouraged.

She slid up and down his cock, her breasts brushing against her chest as her small hands clenched his shoulders. She closed her eyes. Her breath was quickening, and she had forgotten completely about teasing and tormenting James. Leaning her body forward was making his cock rub against her in a different way, and it was sending delicate bursts of pleasure out from her pelvis and down her legs. She had no idea what was happening, but she didn't want it to stop.

"Oh!" Another small gasping moan escaped her throat when James cupped her ass and helped her plunge up and down his cock. He moved her rapidly back and forth as she panted and moaned above him.

"It feels so good," she breathed.

The pleasure was igniting her senses, and she squirmed and writhed against him. James held her tightly and thrust back and forth inside of her. She made another breathless cry, and then her entire body was shuddering around him. Her core clenched down so tightly around his cock that he gave his own hoarse cry and climaxed.

She collapsed against his broad chest, and he stroked her back and kissed the top of her head before gently rolling her off of him. She curled up against him as he pulled the covers up and cocooned them in the blankets.

"Are you tired?" she asked.

"Aye," he muttered.

She kissed his shoulder and wrapped one thin arm around his waist. "Go to sleep, James."

"Good night, honey," he murmured.

"Good night, my love."

CHAPTER 19

"Have either of you seen Leta? Mama is looking for her," Sophia asked James and Nicholas.

It was three days after the full moon, and James and Nicky were standing in the yard discussing their plan to rescue Kaden.

"She was around earlier," Nicky replied. "I think she went to the barn with Ian."

Sophia frowned. "I already checked with Ian. He said he hasn't seen her all morning."

James shrugged. "She must be around here somewhere. You know how she is. She's always disappearing and coming back covered in dirt and -'

He paused and turned towards the trees, inhaling deeply. "Do you smell that?"

"Aye," Nicholas replied. "I do."

"Lycans," Sophia muttered.

"Find Leta now," Nicky said. "Find her and take her into the house before -"

"Are you looking for this one, my friends?"

The three of them turned as one and stared across the

yard. Sophia inhaled sharply. Leta, looking very pale and small, was standing with a group of Lycans at the edge of the woods.

Growling lightly, Nichola started forward and the biggest of the Lycans shook his head. He squeezed Leta's shoulder, and she whimpered in pain.

Sophia stared at the group. There were seven Lycans and a human. Despite the cold weather, the human was wearing only a pair of pants. He had a leather collar around his throat, and his hands were tied behind his back. Scars and bruises covered his bare upper chest, and he was tall and broad shouldered with dark hair. He stood silently as the Lycans around him twitched nervously.

"My name is Draken. And you have something that belongs to me." The biggest Lycan smiled benevolently at them.

Sophia walked a few feet forward and studied Draken carefully. He had long dark hair that hung loose around his shoulders, and cold blue eyes. He smiled at her, revealing straight white teeth.

"Well, you're a pretty one then, aren't you?" He looked her up and down, his eyes darkening with lust.

He inhaled deeply, sniffing at the air like a dog, before smiling at her again. "Oh, I do like your scent. It's been a long time since you mated. I would gladly take care of that for you, pretty one."

She didn't reply, and his nostrils flared as he took another deep breath. "I would consider taking you instead of the weak little human. I think you'd be much more fun."

She bared her teeth at him, and he chuckled before squeezing Leta's shoulder again. "Careful, I do have something that belongs to you after all."

"You're all right, Leta," Sophia called to her sister. "Everything will be fine."

Leta, tears dripping down her face, shuddered all over as the Lycan pulled her closer. "I wish to propose a simple exchange. The little half-breed for the woman. I know she is here. Bring her to me, and I'll let this one go."

"You're going to die today." James was suddenly standing next to Sophia, and she put a restraining hand on his arm.

"Wait," she murmured.

Draken laughed. "I don't think so, half-breed."

His smile brightened as he looked past Sophia and James. "Hello Bree!"

James snarled as Nicholas appeared beside him and grabbed his other arm. "Stop it, James."

James looked behind him. Bree was hurrying forward, and Tristan and Avery were close behind her. He took a deep breath. His need to shift was overwhelming. His fear for both Leta and Bree was making it hard to control. He needed to protect them both. He needed to kill the Lycan and -

"Enough, James," Tristan growled.

"Mama?" Leta whispered.

"I'm here, sweet one." Avery's voice was thin with fear, but she smiled reassuringly at her youngest. "Mama is right here. You'll be all right, my love."

"Kaden," Bree whispered. She stared helplessly at the dark-haired human standing with the Lycans. He gave her a small, sick smile but didn't say anything.

"James – control it!" Tristan roared.

Faintly, James could hear his father's harsh command, but he ignored it. He strained against Sophia's and Nicky's hands, as his body continued to swell and the hair on his body thickened. He growled and shook between his siblings as they laboured to hold him between them.

Bree was suddenly in front of him. Her thin face was pale, and her hands were cold as ice, but she smiled at him as she reached up and cupped his face.

"Stop, my love," she said.

He stared at her and willed himself to control it. After a few moments of staring into her calm, blue eyes, the urge to shift weakened and the red-hot rage within him subsided.

"Bree…"

She stood on her tiptoes and put her mouth to his ear. "He won't kill me right away. He'll torture me and draw it out for as long as he can. You'll have time to save me."

She kissed him. Her lips were cold, and he could taste fear on her mouth. She stepped back quickly and started toward Draken's pack. James called her name, and she looked over her shoulder at him as he stared helplessly at her.

"I love you, James," she said.

"I love you too, little one," he replied hoarsely.

She smiled, blinking back her tears, and walked toward Draken and the others without looking back.

She stopped a few feet in front of Draken. "Let her go."

Draken grinned. "Take my hand, and I'll let the little half-breed go."

He reached out, and without hesitating Bree closed the distance between them and took his hand. Draken let go of Leta, and the little girl whined softly and stopped beside Bree.

"Go, Leta." Bree stroked her hair without looking at her, and then gently pushed her toward her family.

As Leta ran to Tristan, Draken looked Bree up and down. "You look different." He touched the handle of the sword that was belted around her waist and then pulled it free, staring at the sharp blade with amusement.

"What have your new friends been teaching you?" He

laughed when she remained silent. "Silly me. I imagine you would like to say hello to your brother, would you not?"

He dragged her to where Kaden was standing silently. "I always admired your bond, you know. I thought only Lycans were capable of feeling such love for their pack, but you two humans certainly put us to shame. Your brother would die for you if he had to."

Draken put his arm around Bree and pulled her close. "I brought him with us in case you needed some convincing to come back. Now that I have you, I don't believe we need him anymore. Do you?"

"Draken, don't -"

Bree screamed in horror when Draken abruptly thrust her sword into Kaden's stomach. Just as quickly, he yanked the sword out. He smiled with delight at the blood streaking across it, before licking the flat of the blade with his tongue.

"Delicious!" He grinned at Bree and she threw herself at him, shrieking and screaming Kaden's name as her brother sunk to his knees. Blood was pouring out of his stomach and darkening the ground around him, and his tanned skin was rapidly paling.

One of Bree's flailing fists caught Draken on the jaw, and he snarled at her before waving one of the other Lycans over. "Take her!"

The Lycan picked her up and heaved her over his shoulder. Draken turned to James and the others standing in stunned silence in their front yard.

"Do not follow us. We'll smell you coming, and I'll rip the girl apart before you even get close," he snapped at them.

"He and his pack turned and strode deep into the forest.

"Save him, James! Save him!" Bree screamed as she and Draken's pack disappeared into the trees.

JAMES ROARED WITH RAGE, AND NICKY THREW HIS ARMS around his rapidly-swelling body.

"James!" Sophia was kneeling next to Kaden. "James! Get over here now!"

"Keep it together," Nicky shouted as James bucked and twisted against him. "Help her brother, and then we'll save her."

"He's dying, James!" Sophia shouted.

Tristan was suddenly standing in front of him and he took James by the shoulders, his large hands digging into his flesh. He spoke quietly, but his voice broke through James' haze of panic. "Look at me, James. Go and save her brother."

James stared at his father and then nodded. He followed Tristan and Nicky to Bree's brother. The panic was building inside of him, threatening to take him over, and his father must have sensed it because he squeezed his arm.

"We'll find her and bring her back, son. I promise you."

His father's calm manner soothed him, and he watched as Tristan, Nicky, and Sophia heaved Kaden to his feet. The man had passed out, and quickly James stepped behind him and wrapped his arms around Kaden's upper body. He held him tightly as Sophia pulled her jacket off and pressed it against the wound on Kaden's stomach.

After only a few minutes, she peeled it back cautiously. "I think it's healing," she said with relief. "The blood is starting to clot."

"Tristan?" Avery had approached with Leta in her arms, and she kissed the girl's smooth cheek before handing her to Tristan. She placed her hands against Kaden's bare chest. "Bring him into the house, James. I'll lie with him until he's fully healed."

"Where is Marshall?" Tristan asked. "I need to speak with him."

"He's still in the house with Maya and the others." Avery still touching Kaden's chest, reached out with one shaking hand and stroked James' face. "We'll get her back, my sweet James. Bring her brother into the house."

SOPHIA SAT ON THE SIDE OF THE BED AND STARED AT THE sleeping man. It was nearly impossible to guess that he was Bree's brother. He was as big, if not bigger, than her brothers and his body was thick with muscle. His skin was tanned, and he had dark hair. The covers were at his waist and there was no trace of the wound on his stomach. Her mother had left nearly half an hour ago, and Sophia had offered to stay with him until he woke.

He was still wearing the leather collar around his neck. She carefully unbuckled it and slid it free. There was a band of pale skin around his neck where the leather had protected his skin from the sun, and she frowned and fingered the metal loop at the front of the collar. They obviously made him wear it all the time.

She dropped the collar to the floor and studied his face closely. He wasn't traditionally handsome, she decided, but there was something about him that was very appealing to her. His nose had obviously been broken a few times, and most of his body was covered in scars. Lying with her mother had healed the bruises that covered him earlier, and she reached out and traced the wide scars that ran across his chest. The staggering number of scars on his chest and abdomen had made his chest hair grow in random tufts.

Lashes from a whip, she realized. She frowned as she ran

her fingers through the random patches of dark hair on his chest. The cruelty the Lycans had shown to these humans baffled and angered her. She let her fingers drift down his chest to stroke the muscles of his abdomen. What was the point? What had the humans done to deserve this treatment from the Lycans?

She gasped as her wrist was encircled in a hot, hard grip. She was yanked downward onto the bed. The human had her arms pinned above her head and one heavy thigh pressing across her legs, before she knew what was happening.

He was quick for a human. Powerful as well, she thought grudgingly. He placed one hand around her throat and slid it upward until it was stopped by the shelf of her jaw. He squeezed lightly and lowered his face until it was inches from hers.

"My sister. Where is she?" His voice was rough and deep. A shiver went through Sophia's body as something stirred within her. His eyes were the same blue as Bree's, but they were filled with anger and confusion.

She pulled at the hand holding her wrists. "Draken took her."

He cursed and then scanned her body with a slow, dark gaze that made her flush. His gaze lingered on her breasts before he stared at her face. "Where am I?"

"You're safe. My family gave your sister shelter. We're her friends. In fact, my brother -"

"I was stabbed," he said.

"Aye. My mother and brother saved your life." She pulled again at his hand. "Let me go."

"No. Not until -"

She shocked him by suddenly heaving her body upward. She was much stronger than she looked, and he could barely keep his grip on her. He grunted with surprise and used his weight to press her back down onto the bed. He was nearly lying across her now, his chest pushing against her breasts, as she struggled to free herself.

"Be still!" he demanded.

She growled at him and he jerked back when her eyes turned green.

"Lycan!" he snarled and squeezed her throat, cutting off her oxygen. "I hate your kind. I will not hesitate to kill you. Do you understand me, girl?"

She made a choking, growling noise and he leaned down again. "If you stay still, I'll -"

He roared with shock and pain when she headbutted him. His grip loosened around her throat and her wrists, and she grabbed his hair and yanked his head back as she wiggled out from under him. She slid off the bed, turning and punching him in the chest when he grabbed at her legs.

He fell back on the bed and she backed away, breathing heavily and snarling at him. He stood and took a couple of steps toward her. She snarled again, as her body rippled and her teeth began to lengthen.

"Stand back, human," her voice was a low growl. "Do not make me hurt you. Your sister loves you very much. When we bring her back from Draken, it would pain her greatly to see you missing body parts."

Her gaze drifted down his naked body and lingered at his crotch.

"Do you think I am frightened of you, Lycan?" he scoffed. "I've been tortured and enslaved by Lycans for nearly three years. There is no pain you can inflict on me that I haven't already experienced."

She took a deep breath and willed herself to calm down. "Kaden -"

"How do you know my name?" He gave her a startled look.

"I told you. Bree is my friend. She told us about you, and what Draken has been doing with the humans. We told her we would help rescue you. You need to relax. We're here to help you."

He snorted angrily. "There is no such thing as a helpful Lycan."

He looked down at his side, his brow darkening with confusion, and touched the spot where the sword had pierced him. "I do not understand."

"We can explain everything," Sophia said.

The door to the bedroom opened and Dani breezed into the room. She carried a bundle of clothing in her hands. "Sophia, is he awake? James is going crazy downstairs and Uncle Tristan sent me…"

She slowed to a stop, her eyes widening and her cheeks flushing brightly at the sight of Kaden standing naked next to the bed. Her eyes dropped to his penis and she bit at her bottom lip.

"The gods be damned," she breathed.

"Dani!" Sophia said.

The young woman tore her gaze from Kaden and gave Sophia a sheepish look. "Aye?"

"Go tell the others he's awake and I'll bring him downstairs."

"I'm not going anywhere with you, she-dog," Kaden spat.

Sophia's eyes flared green and a growl erupted from her throat at the insult. She took a step toward him and he grinned tightly at her. "I've killed your kind before. I can do it again."

"Whoa, whoa!" Dani held her hand up and stepped between them. "Have both of you forgotten that Bree is being held hostage? If we're going to save her, you need to stop fighting and start playing nicely together."

She took a step toward Kaden and smiled at him. "I'm a human, just like you. My name is Dani. And you are Kaden?"

He nodded and she took another step forward. "I know this is all very strange to you and I'm sorry we don't have more time to explain, but right now we need to save your sister. Once she is back with us, with her family, she can tell you everything."

"Her family? I'm her family," Kaden said.

"Aye, you are. And so are we." Dani glanced at Sophia. "Bree loves Sophia's brother James. He is a Lycan and he loves her. He is frantic to save her."

Kaden staggered back and collapsed into a sitting position on the bed. "Bree loves a Lycan?" he whispered. "No, she cannot."

Ignoring Sophia's warning growl, Dani sat down beside him and patted his shoulder. "Aye, she does."

He put his hand over his eyes and Dani patted his shoulder again. "I'm sorry, Kaden. I wish there was more time to explain but there is not. Right now, what is important is saving your sister from this Draken."

He stared at her. "You're a human? Are you a slave?"

"No, there are no slaves here. The Lycans will not hurt you," she said .

She glanced at Sophia. "Go and tell the others he's awake. I'll bring him downstairs in a moment."

"I'm not leaving you alone with him," Sophia said.

"He won't hurt me. Will you, Kaden?" Dani said to Kaden.

He shook his head and she smiled at Sophia. "We'll be right down."

Sophia hesitated and then slipped out of the room. She

closed the door and leaned against it for a moment. Anger at his insult, worry for Bree, and another emotion warred within her. She closed her eyes. She recognized the third emotion and she snorted angrily. Being jealous of her cousin's ability to win Kaden's trust was ridiculous.

He had tried to kill her for the gods sake. He might be Bree's brother, but he had none of her sweetness.

CHAPTER 20

"Draken, we should not be making camp so soon. We are only a few hours from their home." Terrence looked around nervously.

"I know. Do you believe me stupid? Do you believe that I can no longer tell time?" Draken said.

"No, my lord. But they will come for the woman. You saw how the Red looked at her," Terrence said.

"Aye, they probably will."

"We should keep going then."

Draken laughed. "You would have me run from other Lycans? Most of them are nothing but half-breeds. They helped the human escape from me, and now they must pay for it."

"My lord, what is your obsession with this human? We should kill her now and be done with it," Terrence said.

He made a single choking gasp as Draken turned on him and grabbed his throat. His eyes were a blazing, bright red and he growled as he forced Terrence to his knees. His fingernails lengthened, and he sunk them cruelly into the Lycan's neck as he leaned over him.

"Do you question my command? Would you like to be leader of this pack, Terrence? Is that it?"

Terrence shook his head as the other members of the pack watched uneasily.

"The others will come for the human – I'm counting on it. And when they do, we will kill all of them. I will make the little human watch as I rip the Red apart, limb by limb. She thinks she suffers now after watching me kill her brother? Wait until she sees what I do to the Lycan she loves," he snarled.

His sudden fit of temper ended as quickly as it started, and he released Terrence's throat. He patted the man almost gently on the top of the head as Terrence coughed and wheezed air into his lungs.

"She killed three of our brothers, Terrence. Have you forgotten that fact?" Draken asked. "Once we have killed the Lycans who will come for her, we will take her back home. Her escape from the hunt has given the other slaves hope. I can't allow that. We're taking her back home alive, and I will make an example of her to the other slaves."

He stared at Bree who was sitting on the ground, her hands and feet bound with rope. "She will be begging me for death before I am done with her."

He clapped his hands together briskly and, leaving Terrence on the ground, strode past the other Lycans who were setting up camp and crouched next to Bree.

"Hello, little Bree!" He reached out and petted her soft blonde hair. Instead of cringing away like he expected, she gave him a defiant look.

"Do not touch me," she warned.

He laughed and then slapped her hard across the face. The force of the blow knocked her to the ground. He grabbed her arm and yanked her upright, smiling with satisfaction at the bruise that was already beginning to form on her cheek.

"Your new Lycan friends have taught you bad habits," he said. "You used to be so sweet and timid."

She didn't reply and he gave her a gentle smile. "Do you know, Bree, that you are the first human who has ever escaped the hunt? It took us much longer than I anticipated to track you down. My brothers searched the forest for your scent for weeks. *Weeks,* little Bree. Of course, I would never have guessed that you would have found shelter with Lycans. My brothers told me they would not have found you if they had not stumbled upon your scent while you were fighting the faeries."

He grinned at her. "I'll admit when they came back and told me that you, weak little Bree, was fighting the faeries, I did not believe them. They would have taken you then except your Lycans showed up and rescued you. They were so distracted by their worry for you that it was easy for my brothers to follow them. Truthfully, I almost didn't bother to make the journey. My brothers told me how you were stabbed by the faerie's spear."

He cocked his head at her. "How did you survive their poison? A weak, pathetic human like yourself?"

She refused to answer, and he sat down beside her and folded his legs under him. "Of course, I would never have believed that a tiny little slip of a human like you could defeat three powerful Lycans."

He paused and gave her a considering look. "Mind you, that's not entirely true is it? The wounds on two of them suggested that you had help from Lycans. Tell me, did you kill any of them or did your new friends do your dirty work for you?"

"I killed Curtis. I pierced him through the heart with a tree branch. It was actually quite easy," she taunted.

His eyes flashed red and he raised his hand again. She flinched and he grinned, showing his sharp white fangs.

"They're going to come for you, human, and I'll make you watch as I kill the Lycan you love. He'll suffer and beg for death in front of you."

She surprised him by grinning fiercely. "I think you'll be surprised at who begs for death before this day is over."

"Aye, perhaps," he replied.

KADEN PAUSED OUTSIDE THE CLOSED DOOR. HE COULD HEAR loud voices and he glanced at the slender blonde woman standing next to him.

"I promise no one will harm you." She smiled and took his hand before opening the door and leading him into the room.

The room quieted. He kept his back straight and his head up as Dani squeezed his hand reassuringly. The room was large, and it was filled with people. He didn't know how many were Lycans and how many were humans, and his hand tightened unconsciously around the blonde woman's. All of the people were staring at him except for the large Red. He was standing next to the fireplace and staring into the flames. His body was noticeably vibrating, and his hands were clenched into tight fists.

"Danielle!" A dark-haired man spoke the girl's name sharply. He was standing beside a woman who looked so much like Dani that Kaden knew she was Dani's mother.

"Come over here," the man said.

"Dad, it's fine," Dani said.

"Now, Danielle."

Dani dropped his hand and crossed the room to her father. He put his arm around her as a redheaded woman and a tall, long-haired man approached him.

"Hello Kaden. My name is Avery. I'm a human and I'm married to Tristan." She glanced at the man beside her. "He is a Lycan."

When Kaden didn't reply, she took Tristan's hand and he linked their fingers together as she took a deep breath. "I know you have many questions, and I promise we will answer them later. Right now, we need to save your sister Bree. We care for and love her as much as you do."

"Doubtful," Kaden grunted.

Avery gave him a small smile. "We consider Bree to be a part of our family, and as her brother that means you are too. We hope you can set aside your hatred for Lycans for now, and trust that we want to save Bree just like you do."

Her speech finished she turned back to the others. "We need to decide who will go after her."

There was sudden high-pitched yipping and Tia skidded into the room. She ran straight for Kaden, barking and whining and wagging her tail excitedly. He bent and picked her up and she lunged at his face, licking his skin excitedly as he petted her with one large hand.

"Hello, hairball," Kaden said. "I've missed you."

As he petted Tia, Tristan squeezed Avery's hand. "The problem is that they'll smell us coming. We can't risk them hurting Bree before we can save her."

"We need to disguise our scent," Dani's father said.

"Aye Marshall, we do," Tristan replied.

An older man spoke. "We can use the horses. They'll help to disguise our scent."

"That's a good idea, Ian."

"What about human scent?" Avery said thoughtfully. "If they're busy smelling the humans, Lycans may be able to sneak up on them. Maya and I could walk with Kaden. Our smell may -"

"No." Tristan shook his head immediately. "You're not going, Avery."

She gave him a look of impatience. "You may need me if someone gets injured, Tristan."

"We have James. You're not going, and neither is Maya," Tristan said. "But we can use your scent to help disguise ours."

The Red by the fire spoke for the first time. "Neither human nor horse scent will be enough to fully disguise our own. You know that."

"True," Tristan said. "But it may help to confuse them a bit. It may give us the extra time we need to save her. We will -"

"Enough, Dad!" The Red shouted. He turned and glared at them, and even Kaden stepped back at the anger in his eyes. "It will not be enough! You know it won't! We're wasting time talking about plans when the only chance she has is if I go by myself."

"James, you are not going alone." A blond-haired man moved toward the Red.

"She is my mate, Nicky, and it is my responsibility to go after her. Not yours," James shouted again.

"You're my brother, James!" Nicky snarled at him. "You're crazy if you think I'm letting you go after this Draken alone."

James howled with rage but before he could shift, Avery was standing in front of him. Although he was nearly twice her size and shaking with anger, she reached out and took his arms without a hint of fear. "Calm, my love. You must be calm."

To Kaden's surprise, he seemed to shrink in front of her, and he gave her a look of utter despair before sinking to his knees and burying his face in her stomach. "I told her I would keep her safe, Mama."

"I know, my love," she soothed, her hands stroking his hair. "But you can't do this alone. You know you can't."

Kaden spoke to them for the first time. "The only chance my sister has, is if I go after her alone."

James climbed to his feet. "That's not going to happen."

Kaden stared at him in disdain. "Do you believe you'll stop me, Lycan? She is my sister. I will do whatever it takes to keep her safe."

"She is my mate," James said. "If anyone is going after her, it will be me. Do you understand, human?"

"I understand that for someone who keeps saying they love my sister, you've done a poor job of keeping her safe," Kaden replied.

James roared with anger and charged at him. His father shoved him back. "James! This isn't helping Bree!"

Breathing harshly, Tristan looked at Kaden. "If you want to see your sister again, you'll let us help you. Don't be a fool. If you go after them alone, they'll kill you. They nearly killed you once already."

Kaden's hand rubbed at his abdomen through the shirt Dani had given him. He still had no idea how he had survived the stabbing, or why there was no trace of the wound. He was opening his mouth to ask when Sophia's low voice drifted across the room.

"What we need is a distraction."

Marshall frowned. "What do you mean?"

Sophia stood next to Tristan. "Papa, the Lycan wanted

me. I could smell it on him and see it on his face. He even muttered something about taking me instead of Bree."

Tristan frowned. "You're not going with us, Sophia."

"Like hell I'm not," she immediately retorted. "I'm not a little girl."

He opened his mouth to protest again and she scowled. "Draken wants me. I may be able to distract him while the rest of you surround him. You can still use the human and horse scents to try and mask yours. The combination of both scents, as well as my presence, may be enough to allow you to at least get close."

"Sophia, do you really think he won't suspect something if you just come strolling up to Draken? He'll know we're planning an attack," Nicholas said.

Sophia stared at Kaden. "He'll go with me. He'll tell Draken that he's taken me as a hostage and brought me in exchange for his sister."

"No," Nicky said. "I don't trust the human." He stood next to his sister and put his arm around her.

Kaden snorted. "I don't trust you either."

"It's our best chance, Nicky. You know it is," Sophia said.

"Sophia -"

"Hush, Nicky." She squeezed his waist before moving past him to James. She cupped her brother's face and kissed his forehead.

"I can't ask you to do this, Sophia," James whispered.

"You're not asking me, baby brother. I'm offering because I love you and I love Bree."

James looked at his father and Tristan nodded. "It's the best idea we have."

CHAPTER 21

"Just do it already, Nicky." Sophia's voice held a note of impatience.

"Sophia, I can't," Nicky said miserably.

"You have to. It'll make it more real."

Kaden stood in the yard and watched as Sophia smacked Nicholas lightly on the chest. "You and James punch each other all the time. Pretend I'm James." She closed her eyes and lifted her chin.

"Sophia, is this really necessary? It could be healed by the time we even find Draken."

"Gods be damned, Nicky!" Sophia growled. She glanced over to where Kaden was standing and watching them silently. "I'll ask the human to do it then."

She started to stalk toward him. Nicholas grabbed her arm and pulled her back. "He's not touching you."

"Then just do it! Don't be such a chicken! Just -"

Her head flew back, and she fell to the ground as Nicholas' fist connected solidly with her face. Nicky immediately dropped to his knees beside her. "Sophia! I'm sorry! Are you all right?"

She rubbed her jaw. "I'm fine. Good job, Nicky."

Nicky helped her to her feet as Tristan led a large, black horse from the barn. Kaden could see the swelling starting on Sophia's face as Dani approached Nicky. She had what looked like a few of her dresses in her hand, and she rubbed the material all over Nicky's bare upper body before hugging him for a few minutes.

"There cousin, that should help a little." She wrinkled her nose. "You smell like horse as well."

"Good," Nicky replied.

Tristan smiled at Evan as the young boy approached him. "I'm going with you, Dad."

"No, Evan. You're staying here."

"No! Bree saved me from the faeries. I'm old enough to fight the Lycans. I'm going with you," Evan protested.

Tristan clapped his hand on Evan's shoulder. "I need you to stay here and protect your mother and the other humans."

"Ian and Doran and Leo are staying. They can protect them," Evan replied.

"Aye, but they will need your help." Tristan spoke with a finality that even Kaden could see would be useless to argue against. Evan apparently knew as well because he stopped arguing. Dani put her arm around his shoulder and drew him away.

"Marshall, promise me you'll be careful," Maya whispered as she rubbed his upper body with articles of clothing.

"I will, sweet Maya. You have nothing to fear." Marshall pulled her into his arms and kissed her deeply. "I will see you soon."

Kaden looked to his left. Avery was standing close to James, her hands on his chest and the Red gently pushed them away. "Enough, Mama. Both you and Aunt Maya have covered me with your scents."

She gave him a shaky smile as a dark-haired woman stood behind him. "James?"

"What is it, Martine?" He didn't turn around.

"I am sorry that Bree has been taken from you. I – I know you love her. I'll come with you, and help you save her if you'd like."

James turned to the woman. "Thank you, but there are more than enough of us."

She nodded and Kaden watched as Avery approached Sophia. She went to gather the young woman into her arms, and for some reason, Sophia backed away.

"No, Mama. I can't. I don't want to give Nicky an excuse to hit me again," she said with a small smile as she touched her swelling cheek.

Avery gave her a solemn look. "I love you, my Sophia. You know that, right?"

"I know, Mama. I love you too."

An older woman with greying hair had approached them as they were talking, and Sophia gave her a warm smile. "I love you, Grandmamma."

"I will see you soon, sweet Sophia," the woman replied before kissing her forehead.

"It's time to go." Tristan handed the reins of the horse to Sophia and kissed the top of her head roughly. "Are you ready, my sweet?"

Sophia nodded as Avery wrapped her arms around Tristan. They stood that way for long moments, his face buried in her neck as she whispered quietly into his ear.

Sophia led the horse to where Kaden was standing apart from the others. "Let's go."

Without replying, he followed her to the edge of the woods where Draken and his pack had stood. He watched as she closed her eyes and inhaled deeply. She handed him the reins and walked further into the woods, inhaling repeatedly. She circled slowly and then pointed to the left. "We go this way."

"Are you sure?"

She gave him a pained look. "Aye, I'm sure. Do you know how to ride a horse?"

"Aye."

Nicky had joined them and he boosted Sophia into the saddle. He squeezed her leg and gave her a brief smile before stepping back.

Kaden swung into the saddle behind her. He grunted and wrapped his arm around her waist, lifting her and pushing her forward a bit so he could wedge his large body into the seat of the saddle. He pulled her back against him, resting his hand against her flat stomach, and she stiffened at the feel of his pelvis against her ass.

Nicholas gave him a hard look. "Keep your hands off my sister, human."

"Stop it, Nicky," Sophia replied.

"The rope," Kaden said.

Nicky handed it to him with a scowl, and Kaden wrapped it around Sophia's wrists before securing it to the saddle horn. Nicky pulled a dagger from his boot but didn't hand it to Kaden.

"Nicky, give it to him," Sophia said.

"Sophia, it's silver. Are you sure you -"

"Aye," she said. "He would not be able to take me hostage without it. We need Draken to believe his story."

Nicholas hesitated a moment longer before handing the knife to Kaden. He took it and held it loosely in one large fist.

"The gods help you if you harm my sister," Nicky said.

"He won't. He needs me to find Bree," Sophia replied.

"Besides, you will not be far behind us. Stop worrying, Nicky."

"ARE YOU COLD?"

Sophia shook her head. "No. Why?"

"You're shivering," Kaden said.

She straightened her back. She was trembling, but it had nothing to do with the cold, and everything to do with the human behind her. She cursed herself for her weakness. Draken and the other's scents were strong, and she was having no problem following them, but her mind was constantly wandering back to Kaden.

She squirmed a little but instead of easing away from her, Kaden pulled her more firmly against him. She was attracted to the large, sullen human, and it was driving her crazy. Now was not the time to let her hormones get the best of her. She should be concentrating on finding Bree, and all she could think about was how warm his hand felt through the material of her shirt.

She was being ridiculous. He hated Lycans. She wasn't even sure that he wouldn't try and kill her at some point. Instead of being frightened by the thought, she thought about that moment in the bed. Thought about how he had looked when he was pinning her to the bed and staring at her breasts.

She closed her eyes at the tremor of lust she felt. She had never mated with a human before. She had never found one that she was attracted to and even if she had, it would be doubtful that they could handle her in bed. She did not approach mating in a shy or demure way like so many human women seemed to, and she suspected that a human male would find her demanding and rough. Although the Lycans she had mated with were more than capable of handling her demands, she did not believe a human would fare so well.

Kaden might. He's big for a human and he held you down easily enough.

She pushed the thought out of her head and squirmed against him again.

"Stop you're squirming," he said.

"You're holding me too tightly," she replied.

His hand tightened around her ribs almost painfully. "We need to make it look real, do we not?"

He reached up and swatted her long hair away from his face irritably. "Keep your hair out of my face, Lycan, or I'll cut it off."

"I have a name. It's Sophia, not Lycan, and if you even try and cut my hair, I'll rip your throat out."

"And how do you plan to do that with your hands tied so firmly to the saddle, *Sophia*?"

She tipped her head to look at him. "I have teeth, remember?"

His gaze dropped to her mouth, and she had to fight the urge to lick her lips. "Aye, I remember."

Was it just her imagination or did his gaze linger on her mouth? He gathered her hair in one hand, twisting it and pushing it over her shoulder.

"I'm surprised Draken even wants you," he said suddenly. "He hates half-breeds almost as much as he hates humans. He's even kept them as slaves."

"I'm not a half-breed," she replied.

"How is that possible? Your mother is a human." He paused. "She is not your mother."

"She's my step-mother," Sophia said.

"Were you angry when your father took a human as his wife?"

"No. Avery may not have given birth to me, but she is my mother. I love her."

"Where is your real mother?"

"She was taken by the leeches when I was a child," Sophia said.

He didn't offer his condolences, and she craned her neck to look at him again. "How did Draken keep half-breeds as his slaves? Were they unable to shift?"

She was finding it hard to believe that a Lycan, even a half-breed, could be captured and kept as a slave so easily.

His hand rubbed at his neck. "Draken has special collars for the half-breeds. They're made of silver. It keeps them weak and if they're even able to shift, the collar has silver points on the inside."

"Gods be damned," Sophia breathed. She could almost picture what would happen to the Lycan who tried to shift while wearing that collar. As soon as their body began to swell during the shift, the silver points would pierce their flesh and kill them.

She shivered lightly. Lycans were strong and had healing powers, but they were not immortal. A Lycan could not survive a beheading or being stabbed through the heart. The bite of another Lycan, if left untreated, had the power to kill them. And all Lycans, half-breeds and full-bloods, were particularly vulnerable to silver. A wound from silver would fester and become quickly infected in even the strongest of Lycans.

Shortly after her father had married Avery, Jeffrey had told her a story of a Lycan who'd been scratched with a silver dagger. It was a small scratch and barely bled, but within two weeks the Lycan was dead.

"It spread, Sophia. The silver causes an infection that cannot be treated, and our healing powers are useless against," Jeffrey had told her earnestly. "You must always be careful when you're near silver. Do you hear me, girl?"

She was both fascinated and terrified by the idea of a Lycan dying from a single scratch. She was plagued with nightmares for weeks and had woken her father and Avery nearly every night with her screams. She had begged and pleaded to sleep in their bed with them, a request that Avery indulged.

A small smile crossed her face. At the time, she thought her father's exasperation at having her share their bed for nearly ten nights was caused by her childish fear. It was many years before she realized the truth, and it had only made her love Avery more. She may not be Avery's child, but the Red had always put her own needs aside when it came to Sophia and Nicky, as well as her birth children.

When she had finally confessed her reason for the nightmares, Tristan had been furious with Jeffrey. It had taken many conversations and reassurances from Avery and her father before she had been comfortable sleeping in her own bed again.

She suddenly stiffened against Kaden and he pressed tightly against her. "What is it?"

"They're close," she murmured.

"That's impossible." He scanned the trees around them. "We've only been riding for a few hours. They would not have made camp already."

"I'm telling you they're close. The dagger – quickly!" She said.

He pulled the dagger from his belt and held it one hand as he used the other hand to unbutton the first few buttons of her shirt. He pulled her shirt open and rested the point of the dagger over her heart.

She couldn't stop the shiver running through her body as a snippet of Jeffrey's story came back to her. She stared down at the point of the dagger resting against her skin as Kaden murmured in her ear. "Don't move, Lycan."

CHAPTER 22

They came out of the trees, four black wolves that stood nearly as tall as the horse she and Kaden were riding on. Sophia's pulse was pounding, and she unconsciously leaned back against Kaden. She could feel his heart beating solidly against her back. Oddly, it comforted her a little.

He held the dagger against her chest as the Lycans bared their teeth at them. The horse they were riding on whinnied nervously.

"I am here to speak with Draken. I wish to propose a trade," Kaden said.

The Lycans snarled at him and Kaden waited patiently. She was trembling and Kaden tightened his grip around her waist, his fingers pressing against her ribs.

Finally, the four wolves turned and took a few steps into the woods before pausing and looking behind them. Kaden used the dagger to slice through the rope tying her to the saddle horn, and then surprised her by pushing her roughly off the horse.

She hit the ground with a loud thud, the wind knocked out of her, and he jumped from the horse and wrapped one hand in her long dark hair. He yanked her to her feet, and she bit back her snarl of pain as her hair pulled against her scalp. He held the dagger over her heart again and kept his other hand wrapped in her hair. Holding it tightly, he pushed her in front of him.

"Start walking, Lycan bitch," he snapped.

She growled at him but followed the wolves through the trees. It took them only a few minutes to reach the Lycan's camp. She felt more than heard Kaden's sigh of relief when he saw Bree sitting on the ground, her hands and feet tied together with rope. Two Lycans in their human forms were standing close to her, and they gave Kaden a surprised look.

"Kaden!" Bree cried.

"How did you survive the blade, human?" Draken drawled.

Kaden turned toward the Lycan emerging from one of the tents. "It'll take more than a sword to kill me, Lycan."

"Apparently." Draken stared at Sophia. "Hello, pretty one. Have you missed me?" He inhaled deeply before frowning. "I smell horse."

The four wolves shifted into their human forms and one of them said, "They were riding on a horse, Draken."

Draken inhaled again. "Did you see the others?"

Before they could answer, Kaden said, "There are no others. This one was treating my wound. I overpowered her and took her hostage. The other Lycans were out searching for my sister. It was easy enough to steal a horse and take this one with me."

"And then scampered off back to me?" Draken grinned at him. "Do you wish to go back to your old life as my slave then?"

"I am here to propose a trade," Kaden replied. "This Lycan bitch for my sister."

Bree gasped in horror. "Kaden – no!"

"Interesting." Draken looked Sophia up and down. "She is very pretty. I imagine she would look spectacular lying naked in my bed."

Kaden's hand tightened in her hair. "Do we have a deal then, Draken? I will give her to you in exchange for my sister's freedom. Let us go free, and you can do whatever you want with this one."

He shook Sophia roughly, the dagger pressing against her skin, and she growled as her eyes flashed green.

"No, Kaden!" Bree shouted. "I won't let you do this!"

"Be quiet, Bree!" Kaden snapped. He looked at Draken again. "Do we have a deal?"

Draken regarded them silently for a moment. Despite her efforts to remain calm, Sophia was shaking, and her body was swelling as her wolf tried to break free. Kaden yanked her head back and stared into her pale face.

"Shift and I'll shove this dagger into your heart. I swear to you." He spoke loud enough for the others to hear.

She took several deep breaths, and Kaden looked back to Draken. "Do we have a deal?"

Draken grinned at him. "Aye, human. We do. You may take your sister and slink away like frightened deer."

"Do I have your word that neither I nor my sister will be harmed?"

"But of course," Draken said. "You have my word that no harm will come to either of you. Of course, I cannot say the same for your pretty little bargaining chip."

His grin widened and his eyes glowed red. Sophia swallowed thickly as Kaden's hand tightened again in her hair for a brief moment.

Draken turned to one of his men. "Bring me a collar."

The Lycan disappeared into one of the tents. He returned

carrying a leather bag that he handed to Draken. Draken pulled both a collar and a small silver key from it. He unlocked the collar and started toward them.

Sophia shrank back against Kaden. Adrenaline was coursing through her veins, and her wolf was growling at her to shift. She ignored it grimly as Draken spoke.

"Hold her still, human."

Kaden's hand slipped from her hair and his arm wrapped around her body. He pinned her arms to her sides and held her tight. The dagger was still pressed against the skin over her heart and she shook and snarled at Draken as the large Lycan stopped in front of her.

Panting and growling low in her throat, Sophia pressed her head against Kaden's chest. She could see the sharp, silver points on the inside of the collar and it sent a fresh wave of fear through her. She was close to shifting and she tried desperately to control it. The thought of the silver being around her neck was making her panic, and the Lycan within her was demanding to be released.

"Be still," Kaden said into her ear. Although his arm was a hard band of steel around her, his hand had slipped under her shirt and was stroking the bare flesh of her lower back almost soothingly. She concentrated on his touch, the warmth and gentle motion against her skin helped to calm her, and she closed her eyes in defeat as Draken put the collar around her neck and locked it.

He dropped the key into the small leather bag and handed it to one of the Lycans before smiling widely at Kaden. "You may let her go now."

"My sister first. Untie her and bring her to me," Kaden demanded.

Draken nodded and one of the Lycans quickly sliced through the ropes that bound Bree. She staggered to her feet, rubbing at her wrists, and the Lycan dragged her to where Kaden was standing.

She wrenched her arm free and glared at the Lycan before looking at Kaden and Sophia. Anguish crossed her face and tears slipped down her cheeks. "Kaden, this isn't right. Please, I know you hate them, but Sophia is – "

"Be quiet, Bree!" Kaden said. He shoved Sophia into Draken and yanked his sister to his side.

"Remember your promise, Lycan." He glared at Draken, who laughed and stroked Sophia's long dark hair.

"Of course, human. You are free to go." He made a shooing gesture with his hand as he leaned down and nuzzled Sophia's face affectionately. She snarled at him, her bound hands tightening into fists, and he laughed and kissed her cheek where a bruise was visible.

"Oh, you're going to be a handful, I can tell." He kissed her bruise again before glancing at Kaden who was slowly backing through the trees, dragging Bree with him. "Don't worry, my pretty one. I won't bruise your lovely face like this oafish brute."

With a thin shriek, Bree turned on Kaden and struck him hard on the chest with her small fists. Surprised by her outburst, he stumbled back and released her. She started toward Sophia and Kaden reached out, just managing to grab the back of her shirt. He yanked her back into his arms, and she screamed again as she kicked and punched at him.

"No, Kaden! No!" She shrieked. "I won't let you do this!"

With a loud grunt, he picked up her squirming body and heaved her over his shoulder. He winced as she kicked him hard in the ribs and pounded on his back. Without speaking he turned and strode through the trees.

"No!" Bree screamed again. "Sophia! Sophia!"

Draken watched with amusement as Kaden disappeared

into the trees with the struggling Bree. He captured a strand of Sophia's dark hair between his fingers. He rubbed it gently before raising it to his face and sniffing at it. "You are so lovely. I can't wait to have you in my bed."

"Lord Draken?" One of the Lycans said hesitantly.

"What is it?"

"Are you really going to allow the slaves to go free?"

Draken traced the collar around Sophia's neck before turning to the other Lycans clustered together in a loose group. "I did give them my word. Did I not, Terrence?"

"Aye."

Draken studied his hands for a moment before returning his gaze to the Lycans in front of him. He pointed at two of the bigger ones. "Go and kill the slaves."

Sophia tensed against him before screaming, "Bree! Run! It's -"

Draken clapped a hard hand over her mouth and tightened his arm around her painfully. "Be quiet or I'll cut out your tongue."

The two Lycans shed their clothing and shifted into their Lycan form. As they started through the trees, Draken said, "Bring me their heads."

CHAPTER 23

"Put me down, Kaden! Put me down right now!" Bree was struggling against him, and he winced when her foot kicked him in the meat of his thigh.

He cursed and dropped her to her feet. She immediately punched him in the chest and made a break for the trees. He snagged her arm and yanked her to a stop, spinning her around and grabbing her shoulders.

"Enough, Bree. I will explain everything later, but for now we need to keep moving."

"No!" she shouted. "I will never forgive you for this, Kaden! Never! Sophia is my friend and I won't leave her behind with Draken. I don't care if -"

"We're not leaving her behind," he muttered. "Be quiet and trust me."

She gave him a cautious look. "What do you mean?"

There was a low growling behind her and her face paled. "Kaden?"

"Get behind me." He pushed her behind his large body and handed her the silver dagger.

She gripped it tightly as the two Lycans emerged from the trees.

"He gave me his word," Kaden said.

The Lycans growled in unison and stalked forward on stiff legs. One circled behind him and stared at Bree.

"Back to back – now, Bree," Kaden said.

He felt Bree's bony shoulders pressing into his back as she whipped around to face the Lycan creeping closer towards her.

The Lycans crouched as one as their growling grew louder.

"C'mon then, you cowardly dogs!" Kaden shouted. "What are you waiting for?"

The Lycans leaped and Bree screamed shrilly. There was loud snarling, and Kaden watched with amazement as a large grey wolf bulldozed into the Lycan leaping for him. It knocked it to the ground, and the wolf buried its snout into the Lycan's neck and tore it open before it could even whimper.

Bree screamed again and her small body was yanked away from his. He turned, shouting her name, and staggered back in surprise. The second Lycan lay dead on the ground, its head torn from its body, and James was pulling Bree into his arms. He lifted her small body against his naked one and rained kisses on her face and throat. She sobbed his name and clung to him.

"Are you all right, little one? Are you hurt? Have you been bitten?" James' voice was hoarse as he lowered her to the ground and scanned her anxiously. His fingers traced the bruise on her cheek.

"No, my lord. I am fine." She gave him a trembling smile, and he pulled her close.

"I love you, Bree," he whispered. "I love you."

"I love you too, James."

He wiped the tears from her cheeks. "Are you sure you're not hurt? Did he…"?

He hesitated and she shook her head immediately. "No, he did not. Kaden and Sophia -"

She stopped and Kaden watched as her eyes widened with panic. "Sophia! She is still with him! Please, we must go back before -"

She was interrupted by a piercingly loud howl of pain from Draken's camp. The large grey wolf barked impatiently as James cupped her face. "Stay here, Bree."

"I'm going with you," Bree gasped.

"No." He glanced at Kaden. "Keep her here."

Kaden nodded as James shifted and followed his father toward Draken's camp.

Bree paced back and forth for a few minutes before looking at Kaden. "We should go and help them. They don't know how dangerous Draken is."

"They can take care of themselves, Bree," Kaden replied.

She shook her head. "I don't feel right about standing here while they -"

There was an enormous howl of pain that seemed to go on forever before it abruptly cut out. Bree, her eyes huge and her face pale, twitched violently.

"James?" she whispered. She gave Kaden a brief guilty look. He had just enough time to realize what she was planning before she darted into the trees. Cursing, he raced after her.

DRAKEN SMILED AT SOPHIA AND TOOK HER BY HER BOUND hands. "Come, pretty one. Join me in my tent."

On legs that felt like wooden stilts, Sophia followed him into his tent.

"Sit, please. You are my guest after all." He motioned for her to sit down. She sat down on the floor of the tent and crossed her legs beneath her.

Draken gave her a pleased look and sat down beside her. He caressed her cheek before producing a knife from a sheath around his belt. She inhaled sharply but he simply cut the rope from around her wrists.

She rubbed her wrists and stared silently at him.

"Would you care for a drink, pretty one?"

She shook her head and scooted back when he leaned closer. A fleeting frown crossed his face and he placed his hand on her leg. She growled and he grinned as her eyes glowed at him.

"Do not forget the collar around your neck, my dear. I can't tell you how many of my half-breed slaves have forgotten and shifted." He made a noise of disgust in the back of his throat. "It's unpleasant to see what happens. Do you know that occasionally they just burst apart? Blood and guts rain everywhere. It's a terrible mess to clean up."

She swallowed, feeling the weight of the collar brushing against her throat, and took some deep, calming breaths.

"There, that's better." Draken stroked her hair again. "If you're a very good girl and do everything I ask you to do, I'll consider taking off the collar from time to time. Would you like that, my pretty?"

She didn't reply and he frowned. "You will answer me when I ask you a question. It's rude not to, don't you think?"

"Aye," she replied in a tight voice.

"I will treat you well, if you obey me without question." He eyed her hips appreciatively. "Your body was made to bear my young. You will give me many healthy pups – I know it."

"I won't mate with you."

"You will change your mind. The women I take to my bed always do." He winked at her, and she shuddered with disgust.

"Don't look like that, Sophia," he said. "You should not -"

There was a loud piercing howl just outside their tent, and the look of good humour dropped from Draken's face like a stone. He growled low in his throat and shoved her flat to her back with a hard push.

"Stay there," he snapped and ran from the tent.

BREE SPRINTED THROUGH THE TREES. SHE BURST INTO THE clearing where the Lycans had set up camp and stared around horrified. The air was filled with growling and howls of pain as the Lycans fought each other viciously.

She watched in terror as Nicholas leaped onto one of Draken's Lycans and knocked him to the ground. With a screaming growl of rage, he tore a wide hole into the Lycan's stomach. Blood and long loops of intestines fell from the Lycan's stomach, and it made a whining whimper of pain and grew still.

Blood dripping from his mouth, Nicky turned and ran for a Lycan that was pinning Marshall to the ground. James, his red fur glinting in the cold sun, reached him first and fell on the Lycan. He sank his fangs deep into the back of its neck. It yipped and twisted, trying to bite at James, as Nicky wrapped his mouth around the Lycan's back leg and ripped it from his body with a wet squelching noise. The Lycan squealed and dropped to the ground, as James raised his snout and howled loudly.

Draken burst out from his tent and howled with rage and disbelief. His body rippled and swelled, and he shifted. His clothes fell in tattered rags to the ground as a dark brown wolf, cowering at the edge of the campsite, barked frantically at him.

There was a low growling to her left and Bree turned to see a black wolf, it's very large and very white teeth glittering in the sun, running toward her.

KADEN RAN INTO THE CAMP AND STARED IN HORROR AT THE Lycan that was running toward his sister. He was too far away, and he screamed her name as the Lycan closed in on her. He watched as Bree stumbled backward and tripped over an exposed root. She fell onto her back and raised the silver dagger she still clutched in her right hand.

The Lycan snapped its teeth, saliva dripping from its mouth, and jumped. Before it could land on Bree and tear her throat out, Sophia appeared out of nowhere and dove at the Lycan. Still in her human form, she hit the Lycan in the side and drove it to the ground. The woman and the Lycan rolled on the hard-packed earth, both of them fighting for control as Kaden ran toward them.

THE LYCAN WAS BIG AND STRONG. SOPHIA FOUGHT TO GAIN the upper hand but the silver around her throat made her feel weak and sluggish. The Lycan scrambled on top of her, braced its heavy paws on her chest, and lunged for her throat.

Shrieking in fear and anger, Sophia buried her hands in the thick fur of its throat and pushed violently. The Lycan's mouth, only inches from her face, snapped viciously and its hot and rotting breath washed over her.

Arms shaking, her eyes glowing and her body trembling violently, Sophia strained to keep the Lycan from her throat. With a sudden burst of power, it lunged forward again, and she twisted violently to the right. Its mouth, aiming for the soft flesh of her throat, missed and sunk deep into the meaty flesh of her shoulder.

The pain was immediate and enormous. Sophia shrieked with agony as blood flowed down her arm. The Lycan snarled and dug his teeth into her shoulder, ripping and tearing at her flesh as she shoved futilely at its broad body.

It raised its head and grinned at her. Its teeth were dripping with her blood, and she snarled at it as it dipped its head towards her throat. She felt its teeth pressing against her throat above the collar, her body pinned by its weight, and then suddenly she was free.

She watched dazedly as Kaden, his large hands wrapped around the struggling, snarling Lycan's neck, pinned the wolf to the ground.

"Bree - the knife!" he shouted as the Lycan began to slip free of his grip.

Bree staggered forward, tossing the knife at him. He caught it neatly and drove it deep into the eye of the Lycan. The Lycan squealed sharply with pain and collapsed. Kaden pulled the knife free, wiping it clean on his pants, as blood poured from the gaping wound in the Lycan's face.

Sophia sucked in a gasping, whining breath as Bree dropped to her knees beside her. She made a loud cry of distress at the sight of Sophia's shoulder, and brushed Sophia's hair away from her face with trembling hands.

"Calm down, Sophia. You're all right, honey. Calm down – just relax," she pleaded.

Sophia hitched in another breath. The pain from her shoulder was radiating through her entire body, and she could feel the shift happening in reaction to the pain. Her body was swelling, and dimly she was aware of the silver points on the collar pressing against her thickening neck. A growl of pain and fear erupted from her throat as her fingernails lengthened, and hair began to sprout on her face.

"Kaden!" Bree shouted. "She's shifting! I can't stop her!"

Kaden crouched over her. His face was grim and pale, and he cupped her face roughly.

"Sophia!" he roared. "Look at me!"

His rough voice demanded obedience and broke through the haze of pain and the need to shift. She stared up at him as he squeezed her face. "Don't shift! Do you hear me? Breathe like I am."

He bent his head until his face was only inches from hers and took a deep breath through his nose. He blew it out through his mouth, his breath warm and sweet on her face. "Breathe with me, Sophia. Do it now."

The need to shift was fading. It was being replaced by a throbbing pain that made her want to cry and vomit at the same time, but she stared into Kaden's eyes and forced herself to mimic his breathing.

"In through the nose, and out through the mouth," he murmured. She took a deep breath through her nose and blew it out harshly, and he smiled at her. "Good girl. Do it again."

Kaden stared at Sophia's pale face. She pulled in a long breath through her nose and out her mouth and he rubbed his thumb over her cheekbone. "Another one. Do it, Sophia."

She sucked in another long breath as Bree looked around frantically. From the corner f his eye, Kaden could see Draken and Terrence bounding through the trees with a red wolf and a white wolf following them.

"James!" Bree screamed. The red wolf stopped and looked back at her. "Sophia needs you!"

He barked twice and the white wolf whined in reply. He barked again before turning back and, with one last look into the trees, the wolf followed James to the clearing.

Tristan appeared and dropped to his knees beside Sophia.

"Sophia, my sweet baby – you're going to be just fine," he said. His face was pale, and his hands were trembling as he reached out and took her hand.

Kaden, still straddling Sophia's body and cupping her face, said, "Bree, the key to the collar is in a brown leather bag. Find it."

Bree nodded and staggered away. Kaden smiled at Sophia. "Keep breathing, Sophia. In and out. Nice and slow."

She stared up at him, her eyes dark with pain, as her father squeezed her hand. "James is coming, my Sophia."

There was an angry shout and he was dragged off of Sophia. Nicholas pinned him to the ground, his hands around his throat, and stared grimly at him. "Get off my sister!"

"I'm trying to help her, you stupid dog!" Kaden said.

"Nicky! Stop!" Bree was back and she pushed at Nicky's shoulder. "He was helping her. Get off of him!"

Nicky squeezed his throat and then pushed away from him, kicking him harshly in the ribs as he strode back to his sister. Tristan and Marshall were pulling her into a sitting position, and she cried out as James sat down behind her and crowded up against her back.

Kaden sucked in his breath at the sight of the wound on her shoulder. It was worse than he thought. He could see torn muscle and nerves in the gaping wound, and blood was soaking into her shirt and pants.

The Lycan was dying. The others might be pretending she would be fine, but they were hours from their home. The wound was too large to bandage, and not even her Lycan healing powers could stop her from bleeding to death. She would not survive the trip back. Sophia had risked her life to save his sister, and there was a strange twisting in his gut at the thought of her death.

Nicholas ran to the nearest tent and brought back a blanket as Bree kneeled next to them and, her hands trembling, carefully unlocked the collar around Sophia's throat. She eased it from her neck and dropped it into the leather bag.

Kaden watched as James ripped the back of her shirt open, eliciting another cry of pain from her, and urged Sophia to relax against his naked torso. He put his arms around her and pressed both of his hands on the wound on her shoulder. She shrieked as blood poured out in thin streams between his fingers.

Tristan echoed her cry as he knelt next to his children. Nicholas wrapped the blanket around them both, and James kissed Sophia's forehead and cheeks repeatedly as Tristan stood and paced back and forth.

"She'll be all right, Papa." Nicky squeezed his father's shoulder, and Tristan gave him a naked look of fear.

"We need to get her home to Avery. She needs her mama as well."

"We will," Nicky said. "Just give him some time to heal her enough to survive the ride back home."

Bree stroked James' head and kissed his forehead before

rising and walking to Kaden. She hugged him hard. "Are you all right, Kaden?"

"I'm fine. Are you?"

"Aye."

He put his arms around her and held her gently as he watched Nicholas and Marshall patrol back and forth at the edge of the camp. They were keeping an eye out for Draken and Terrence, and Marshall whispered something to Nicholas as he passed him. Nicholas nodded grimly and continued to stare into the trees as he marched back and forth.

"Bree, the Lycan is dying," Kaden said in a low voice.

She shook her head. "No, James will save her. You'll see."

"What do you mean?" He frowned at her.

"James is a healer."

"A what?"

"He's a healer, just like his mother. He can touch people and heal their wounds or their sickness," Bree replied.

Kaden gave her a cautious look. "That isn't possible."

"It is," she insisted. "I was dying when James and Nicky found me in the woods. James held me until I healed. If it had not been for him, I would have died."

He continued to stare at her, and she smiled at him. "I know it sounds crazy, but it's true. She patted his abdomen through his shirt. "You were stabbed. Do you remember that?"

"Aye."

"James or Avery saved your life. One of them held you until your wound healed."

"Bree, it is impossible."

She squeezed him lightly. "Just trust me about this, Kaden. Sophia will live – you'll see."

Kaden stared at her doubtfully but didn't argue. She

believed what she was saying, he could see it in her eyes, and he sighed and stared at Sophia. The Lycan's eyes were closed, and her face was pale as James murmured in her ear and Tristan stroked her leg.

They waited almost an hour, the sun slowly dipping lower in the sky and Kaden growing more certain by the minute that Sophia would be dead soon. Her face was the colour of milk and she hadn't opened her eyes once since James sat down behind her.

Nicholas crouched next to James and Sophia. "We have to leave soon, James. It would be best to be home before dark."

James whispered something in Sophia's ear. To Kaden's surprise, her eyes fluttered open and she nodded weakly. Tristan unwrapped the blanket as Bree and Kaden drew close. As James removed his blood-streaked hands from Sophia's shoulder, Kaden's mouth dropped open.

"The gods be damned."

CHAPTER 24

B ree sighed with relief. "It's better."

"Aye," Tristan replied. "But not completely healed."

Kaden crouched down and stared in disbelief at Sophia's shoulder. The gaping wound had closed over, but her shoulder was swollen and bruised. James brushed it lightly with his fingertips, and Sophia gave a short cry of pain.

"We should wait a bit longer," Tristan said.

"No," Sophia whispered. "It's much better than it was. We need to go."

Marshall had disappeared into the woods and, as Bree knelt beside Sophia and kissed her pale forehead, he reappeared leading the horse that Kaden and Sophia had been riding.

Nicky eyed Sophia's shoulder. "We'll move faster if we shift."

Sophia shook her head. "I'm sorry, Nicky. I can't run on it."

"Sophia and Kaden can ride the horse and I'll ride on James' back," Bree said.

"No," Nicky said. "He's not touching her."

"It's the only way, Nicky," Sophia said.

Nicky gave Kaden a sullen look before turning to his father. "Dad, what do you think?"

"Sophia's right. She can ride with the human." Tristan stalked to Kaden and stared steadily at him. "If you hurt my child, if you lead that horse anywhere other than back to my home, I will tear you apart."

"Papa, stop it," Sophia muttered. "He won't do anything."

"He won't hurt her." Bree rested her hand on Tristan's arm. "I promise you, Tristan."

Tristan continued to gaze at Kaden and when he neither stepped back nor dropped his gaze, the Lycan nodded and went back to Sophia.

"Can you stand, sweet Sophia?"

"Aye."

James and Tristan helped her to her feet, and she clutched the ruined remains of her shirt to her chest. "I need a new shirt."

The naked Lycans looked at each other, and Kaden nearly laughed at the looks on their faces. He quickly stripped off his shirt. "Here."

Bree took it from him with a nod of thanks, and the others turned away as she helped Sophia shed her tattered shirt and slip into Kaden's.

"I'm ready," Sophia said in a strained voice.

Kaden swung into the saddle and leaned backward as Marshall, James and Tristan lifted Sophia into the saddle. She sat rigidly before him and he eased his arm around her waist.

"Lean against me. It will help with the jostling," he murmured into her ear. She leaned back against him. She was sweating and pale, and she moaned quietly when he repositioned her in the saddle.

"Tristan, are you sure this is a good idea?" Marshall asked. "We could camp here for the night. Keep watch for Draken and the other. James can heal Sophia completely, and we'll travel back in the morning."

"No. Draken may have more men," Sophia said.

"I doubt it." Marshall patted her leg gently. "Sophia, the pain will be very bad. Let James heal you further and -"

"No, I cannot stay the night in this place. Not with the stench of dead Lycans and," Sophia paused, and Kaden could feel her trembling increase, "and the memory of Draken telling me I would make a good mother to his pups. I want to be at home. I – I want to be with Mama."

"All right." Marshall patted her leg again. "We'll get you home to your mama."

Kaden watched, his hand tightening on Sophia's hip, as Bree went to James. The Lycan kissed her softly on the mouth, his hand lingering around her waist, and she smiled at him.

"Hang on tight, little one. I will be moving quickly." He stroked her long blonde hair.

"Aye, my lord." She kissed him a final time and stepped back as he shifted. He was one of the biggest Lycans Kaden had ever seen and even with James lying on his stomach, Nicholas still had to lift Bree onto his back. She leaned over him, her hands sinking into his fur, and he turned his head and licked her face. She giggled and patted him gently.

Tristan gave Sophia an anxious look. "If the pain gets too bad and you need us to stop, just say so."

"Aye, Papa." She smiled weakly.

"I love you, Sophia."

"I love you too."

The rest of the Lycans shifted and Kaden nudged the

253

horse forward. Sophia made a soft groan of pain, and Kaden moved cautiously behind her.

"Put your head on my shoulder and lean into me," he said. She did what he asked, burrowing her face into his thick neck, and he moved his hand from her hip and toward her shoulder.

"This is going to hurt, but it's better if I try and steady you while we ride. Are you ready?"

She nodded and he crossed his arm across her chest and quickly pressed his hand hard against her injured shoulder, holding her against his upper body. She gasped but made no effort to pull away, and he felt a grudging amount of respect for her. Her skin was hot and throbbing through his shirt, and he could only imagine how much pain she was in.

"Hang on," he said as the Lycans loped through the woods. He dug his heels into the horse's sides and did his best to keep Sophia from jostling around as the horse broke into a run.

———

SOPHIA MOANED AND KADEN PLACED HIS MOUTH TO HER EAR. "Do we need to stop?"

"No," she muttered. "But I need to straighten a little."

"Hold on." He slowed the horse until it was walking. The Lycans matched their pace, and Tristan trotted up to the horse and stared at them.

"It's fine. She just needs to adjust her position," Kaden said. The Lycan watched anxiously as Kaden cautiously released his hold on her shoulder.

He wrapped his arm around her waist. "Are you ready?"

"Aye," she gritted out between clenched teeth. Already, sweat was dotting her forehead and her tanned face was pale.

He lifted her in a smooth motion, pushing her more firmly against him, and she gave a hoarse cry of pain. Her entire body stiffened and then she slumped against him. Tristan barked sharply as Kaden felt Sophia's throat. Her pulse beat steadily, and he stared down at the Lycan.

"She's fainted. That's probably better for her."

The Lycan whined as Kaden urged the horse to move faster. Sophia moaned but didn't wake. He glanced down at her and, holding the reins in one hand, used his other to carefully brush Sophia's hair away from her face. He pushed her head into his throat again. She muttered something, her lips brushing against his skin, and he inhaled sharply as his arm tightened around her.

His cock hardened in his pants to push against her backside, and he thanked the gods that she was unconscious. He was attracted to the Lycan, had been since the moment he had woken to feel her hand on his stomach, and he cursed himself bitterly.

He hated the Lycans. It didn't matter that this particular Lycan had gorgeous dark eyes and soft hair. Nor did it matter that she had full breasts that were practically begging for his touch, and a curvy ass that was cushioning his hardening cock quite nicely. There was nothing good about Lycans. He would be wise to remember that, no matter how attractive they were.

He snorted angrily to himself. It had been over four years since he'd had sex, and this Lycan happened to have the body type he liked best. That was the reason for his attraction to her and nothing else. In fact, once he convinced Bree to leave these Lycans and she was safe, he would find a hundred human women who had full breasts and dark hair, to ease his need.

Your sister won't leave him. You're a fool if you think she will.

He sighed and took a quick look at the Lycans around him. None of them were looking at him, and he buried his face in Sophia's hair and inhaled deeply. Bree thought she was in love with the Lycan, but he would remind her of their cruelty. She was a smart girl and would understand that he was only doing what was best for her.

Kaden stared into the fire. They had arrived home nearly half an hour ago and Tristan had quickly carried Sophia into the house to her mother. It had been chaotic and loud, with those who were left behind anxious for answers.

Kaden expected that Bree would spend some time with him. He couldn't ignore the hurt he felt when, without a second look at him, Bree allowed James to pick her up and carry her out of the common room. The others seemed to have forgotten about him completely as they left the room in small groups. He'd been left alone to pace back and forth as a growing sense of unease built within him.

There was a sharp, excited bark and he smiled as Tia entered the room. She went to him eagerly and he scooped her up, petting her as she licked his hand and arm with her small pink tongue.

"You're a good girl then, aren't you?" He shifted her in his arms. "You're starting to get chunky. What have they been feeding you?"

"I let her eat whatever she wants."

He looked up to see the young girl that Draken had caught in the woods, standing motionless in the room.

"Hello there." He gave her a friendly smile. "You're Leta right?"

She didn't reply and he looked down at the little dog in his arms. "Her favourite food is rabbit."

"I know that!" The little girl snapped at him. She took a few steps closer and glared at him. "Tia loves me more than she loves you."

"Does she?" he replied mildly.

"Aye. She sleeps with me and she plays with me every day."

She traced her hand across the back of the couch. "I don't like you."

"You don't even know me." He smiled at her.

"I know you're going to try and take Bree and Tia away from us," she replied.

"And how do you know that?"

"I heard Mama and Aunt Maya talking. They said you would try and convince Bree to leave because you're afraid of Lycans."

"I'm not afraid of Lycans."

"You should be!" She snarled and he watched, amusement etching into his face, as she growled, and her eyes glowed at him.

"My brother loves Bree. He won't let you take her away from us." Her voice had become lower, and her fingers were digging into the couch. "I won't let you take her away from us."

"Leta!" Dani entered the room and she frowned at the young Lycan. "Stop it! Right now!"

Leta turned and snarled at her, and Dani took her arm and squeezed lightly. "Stop it, I said. You're ten years old and you're shifting like you're a little pup. What would your mother say?"

The young girl seemed to deflate in front of his eyes, and she looked back at him. He was surprised to see tears in her eyes as she sniffed and leaned against her cousin. "Don't let him take her away from us, Dani."

"Hush now." Dani stroked her long dark hair. "No one's going anywhere. Why don't you take Tia to your room for a while?"

"I want Mama." Leta sniffed.

"Your mother is with Sophia. You know that, honey," Dani said. "You can see her in the morning."

Leta sighed and Dani kissed her on the forehead. "I'll send your dad to your room, all right?"

"Aye." The little girl wiped the tears from her cheeks and moved cautiously toward Kaden. She held her hands out and he deposited the dog into her arms. She petted Tia's head as she stared at him with a tear-streaked face.

"Please don't take Bree away from us," she whispered.

He didn't reply, and she kissed the top of the dog's head before leaving the room. Dani smiled hesitantly at him.

"Hello, Kaden."

"Hello, Dani."

She eyed his bare torso with more than a passing interest. "You seem to have misplaced your shirt."

"I gave it to Sophia to wear."

"Oh. Well, why don't you come with me? I'll find you another shirt, and you must be hungry."

"I'm fine."

She rolled her eyes a little. "If you're anything like Aunt Avery said Bree was – I know you're starving. We have plenty of food and I was about to fix myself a snack. Come join me."

He sighed. "I would like to see my sister."

"She's with James. I imagine she'll be with him until at least the morning. They've been separated and they -"

"Aye." He held his hand up. "I get the picture."

She blushed and held her hand out to him. "Come with me to get a bite to eat, and then I'll show you to your room. You can speak with your sister in the morning."

He took her hand and allowed her to lead him out of the room.

CHAPTER 25

"James, I'm fine – really." Bree smiled at the Lycan as he wrapped the blanket tighter around her small body. He had carried her to the bathroom and drawn her a bath. They had actually bathed together, his large body squeezed in behind her small one, but he had stopped her when she had tried to touch and stroke his large body.

"No, little one. You need rest," he'd said.

She'd sighed and rolled her eyes, and he gave her a solemn look. "Bree, you could have died. If you had, I -"

"I didn't," she said as he rinsed first her body clean, and then his own. "I'm not hurt, and I'm back with you where I belong."

"Aye, where you belong," he'd whispered as he carried her from the bathroom and to his bedroom.

While they were in the tub, someone had left a tray of food in their room and although she hinted that she wanted him to take her to his bed, he insisted she eat first. He'd hardly eaten anything, and she had to urge him to eat some of the meat and bread.

Now, she tried to hide her frustration as he tucked the

blanket between her body and the chair she was sitting on, and then added more wood to the fire. He was hovering over her like an old woman when what she really wanted was to be riding him in his bed. She stood and let the blanket fall to the floor, leaving her standing naked in his bedroom.

"Bree, what are you doing?"

"I'm going to bed. You said I needed rest remember?" she said innocently.

"Aye, you do." She felt a ripple of satisfaction when his gaze lingered on the blonde curls between her thighs.

"You should probably carry me to the bed. I'm feeling a little weak."

His brow knitted with worry, and he was standing beside her and lifting her into his arms before she could say anything else. He carried her to the bed and slipped her under the covers before sitting beside her. He brushed her hair back from her face.

"Maybe you are hurt internally again," he spoke distractedly as his fingers traced her head and shoulders.

"Perhaps," she replied. "It is sore."

"Where is it sore?" He asked.

"Here." She pointed to her shoulder and he leaned over and placed a gentle kiss on it.

"And right here." She stroked her collarbone and he placed a path of warm kisses along it.

She moaned softly and he eyed her suspiciously. "Bree -"

"It hurts here too," she said. He gave her another suspicious look before kissing her upper chest.

"Here." She traced her bare breast with the tip of her finger.

"I know what you're doing, Bree."

She smiled sweetly at him. "You don't want to help me heal, my love? That seems unkind."

He gave her a dry look before placing a light kiss on her breast. "There."

She shook her head. "No, m'lord. It still pains me greatly."

He couldn't stop the small smile from crossing his face. "Does it now?"

"Aye, it does." She cupped the back of his head and tugged it toward her breast. "Again, my love."

He sucked her nipple into his mouth and circled it with his tongue before sucking firmly on it. She arched her back, pushing more of her firm flesh into his mouth, and he cupped her other breast in his hand, pulling lightly on the hardened nipple.

"Oh, James," she sighed as her hands threaded restlessly through his hair.

"Where else does it hurt, little one?"

"Here." She rested her hand on her lower abdomen, and he blazed a trail of kisses down her ribs to her belly button. He circled it with his tongue before dipping the tip of it into her navel. She jerked and giggled a little as he gripped her hips firmly.

"Where else?"

"Lower," she whispered.

"Where?"

"You know where."

He smiled at the blush that was rising in her cheeks.

"Show me."

Her fingers trembling, she spread her thighs and touched the soft curls between her legs. "Right here."

He leaned down and nuzzled his mouth into the soft blonde curls. He kissed her and she moaned and arched her hips up.

"Is that better?" He asked, staring up at her.

She gave him a look of frustration. "No. Lower, m'lord."

He took her hand and placed it over her warm core. "Show me."

"James…" Embarrassment was flooding through her.

He kissed her inner thigh. "Show me want you need."

Moaning softly, she parted the lips of her pussy and ran her fingertips over her wet and swollen clit. "Kiss me right here."

He bent his head and licked a warm path over her clit and fingers. She cried out, and he captured one finger in his mouth and sucked hard on it. She trembled and moaned as he released her finger and licked across her clit again.

"Gods be damned," she muttered in a soft, hoarse voice.

"Do you like this, little one?" He asked before stroking her with his tongue a few more times.

"Aye, very much," she panted. Her hands tangled in his hair and she pushed on his head.

He made a low laugh and pushed her thighs wide. Holding her steady with his large, warm hands, he began an intense assault with his tongue and lips. He tasted and licked every part of her warm core as she wiggled and sighed and cried out beneath him. He probed one finger deep inside of her as he rasped his tongue across her clit and with a harsh cry, she arched her back and climaxed. He licked and sucked at her eagerly until she was pushing him away.

"Please!" she gasped.

He slid up her body as her thighs wrapped around his hips. He entered her with one gentle thrust, and she closed her eyes and bit at her bottom lip as he stretched her fully.

"You're so warm and tight, Bree," he murmured in her ear. "I love being inside of you."

He cupped her face before beginning a slow rhythm inside of her. "Open your eyes."

Her eyes fluttered open, and she stared up at him as he kissed her lightly on the mouth. She wrapped her slender limbs around him and met each of his strokes as he buried his face in her throat.

"I love you, Bree," he whispered into her skin.

"I love you too, James."

KADEN STARED AT THE TWO WOMEN IN THE KITCHEN. IT WAS the next morning and he had woken before dawn. He left his room, not willing to admit that he was a little surprised the Lycans had not locked him in, and made his way to the kitchen.

He was surprised to see people already up and milling about the kitchen. The lady of the house, he couldn't remember her name, but she had long red hair and a kind face, was standing at the sink and washing dishes beside a plump, older woman.

"Good morning, Kaden." She smiled at him before turning to the woman beside her. "Marian, would you go to the pantry and grab some potatoes? Sophia loves fried potatoes, and I'd like to make something special for her."

"Of course, m'lady." The lady dried her hands and glanced curiously at Kaden before exiting the room.

"How are you feeling?" The redhead asked as she finished washing the last of the dishes.

"Fine," he grunted. "I've forgotten your name."

"I'm Avery."

"You're Sophia's mother."

"Aye, I am," she confirmed.

"She doesn't look much like you." He waited to see if she would tell him Sophia was not her child.

She smiled again. "She does seem to favour her father in looks. Why don't you have a seat? Are you hungry? Marian and Nadine will be starting to cook breakfast soon but if you'd like to eat now, we can find you something."

He sat down at the table, wincing a little at the pain in his side, as Avery sat gracefully in the wooden chair opposite of his.

"No, I can wait to eat with the others," he replied. "How is she?"

"She's much better. Tired, but nothing a day or two of rest won't fix." Avery stared at him solemnly. "Sophia told me how you saved her life. How you killed the Lycan about to kill her, and then stopped her from shifting. I can't tell you how grateful I am to you for saving the life of my child. If there's anything I can do to repay you…"

She trailed off and then reached out and patted his hand quickly. He moved his hands to his lap and cleared his throat. "You can convince your son to let Bree leave with me."

Avery smiled at him. "But who will convince Bree?"

"I will," he replied.

"Will you?" she said. "I'm not so sure about that. Where will you and Bree go? You have no money and no place to live."

"We did just fine before. I will find us work."

"My husband tells me that this Draken escaped. What if he hunts you down again?"

His brow darkened. "I will kill him."

"He has a large pack, does he not? Would it not be better to have others who are willing to help you?"

"Why would your family be willing to help?" he replied.

She frowned at him. "This Draken took Bree from us and nearly killed our daughter. He is now as much of an enemy to us, as he is to you."

He didn't reply and she traced her fingers across the top of the table. "Did you know that we have no slaves here? That the humans work for us of their own free will and we pay them wages?"

"Aye."

She stared thoughtfully at him. "We could use help in the barn. We've acquired more horses in recent months and it's a lot for Ian to take on."

"What are you asking?"

"I'm offering you the chance to work for us. You would earn wages and have a roof over your head and three meals a day."

"Have you spoken with your husband about offering me employment?" he asked.

She grinned a little. "My husband trusts my judgement. And I do not need his permission to hire someone to work in our home."

He rubbed at his jaw. "Thank you, but I think it's better if Bree and I just move on."

She held up her hand. "Don't answer right away. Take the day to think about it."

"I won't need the day."

Marian returned from the pantry with a bowl full of potatoes. Avery smiled at him. "Spend the day with us please. Bree will not be able to travel today anyway. She needs rest after what happened. You both do."

He nodded. He stood up, his hand pressing briefly against his side, and left the kitchen.

Avery stared thoughtfully at Kaden's retreating back as Marian gave her a worried look.

"Avery, is he taking Bree from us?"

Avery shook her head. "No, Marian. I am certain that Bree will not agree to leave with him and will do whatever she can to convince her brother to stay. Even if Kaden does somehow convince her to leave, you know as well as I do that James will never allow him to take Bree away. He thinks of her as his mate, and you know how the Lycans are when it comes to their mates."

She gave Marian a wry look and Marian smiled. "Aye, Avery. I know."

———

"MAY I SPEAK WITH YOU?"

Kaden looked up. He had gone straight from the kitchen to the common room, and it was only a few minutes before he was joined by James.

"Where is my sister? I wish to see her." He stared steadily at the large redhead.

"She's sleeping. She is tired and needs her rest. You can see her later."

Kaden's temper flared at the dismissiveness in the Red's tone. He scowled at James. "She is my sister, and you cannot keep her from me."

James gave him a cool look. "I know she is your sister, but she is my mate."

"Your mate? She is human, not Lycan – we don't refer to each other as mates," Kaden said. "Besides, I don't remember seeing a ring on my sister's hand."

James flushed. "I love her, and soon enough she will belong to me."

Kaden glared at him. "Belong to you? She is not some

dog that you can tame and bend to your will. She can make her own decisions."

"Stop twisting my words, human," James growled. "Your sister and I will be married. She loves me and you know it. You will not be able to convince her to leave."

"Don't be so sure of that, Lycan," Kaden snapped. "It has been just my sister and me for many years. If you believe that my sister will choose you over me after only a few short months, you're in for a surprise."

James growled, his eyes flashing green and his hands rolling into fists. "I will not allow you to take her away from me. Do you understand? I want what's best for Bree and I don't -"

"What's best for Bree?" Kaden scoffed. "You barely know her. You have no idea what's best for her. I have been taking care of her for her entire life."

"Aye, and a fine job you've done of it too. She spent what – two years as a slave for the Lycans? What did you do to protect her when they were hunting her? If it had not been for me, she would be dead right now."

"I did everything I could to keep her safe, and I won't allow you to just take her from me," Kaden shouted

"You have no say in it!" James' voice was rising. "She belongs to me now, not you, and -"

"She is not your property!" Kaden said angrily. "And if you think that I will sit idly by and watch as you destroy her life, you're wrong!"

"You'll have to kill me before I let you take her from me. Do you understand, human?" James' body was swelling, and his large frame was shaking with anger.

"I'm not afraid of you, Lycan," Kaden snarled. "I don't -"

"Stop it, both of you!" Bree's voice broke through his cloud of rage, and James whipped around to stare at her. He sighed harshly at her white face, and the way her body was shaking with fear.

"Bree, honey, I'm sorry. Don't be afraid."

"I'm not afraid!" She snapped at him. "I'm angry. I don't belong to you, James."

He blinked in surprise and behind him, Kaden snickered loudly. Bree turned on her brother. "Nor do I belong to you, Kaden. I'm an adult, and I can make my own decisions about what or who I want."

"Bree -"

"Be quiet, Kaden!" she shouted. He took a step back, staring at her in astonishment.

"I've had enough of both of your ridiculous behaviour." She glared at them. "I understand that you both are looking out for me, but that doesn't give you the right to argue like spoiled children over how I will live my life."

She turned to James. "I would like to speak to my brother in private."

He frowned. "Bree, that isn't a good idea."

"James, he's my brother. He's not going to hurt me for the gods sake. Please, give us some privacy."

James hesitated and her face softened at the look of hurt on his face. She cupped his face. "Do not look at me like that, my love. I will join you shortly."

He took her hand and squeezed it. "Do you promise?"

She smiled at him. "Of course, I do."

She stood on her tiptoes and placed a gentle kiss on his mouth. He returned her kiss and gave her a brief, hard hug. "I love you, Bree."

"I love you too."

He continued to stare at her, holding her against his body, and Kaden snorted disdainfully. "Go on, Lycan. You're dismissed."

James tensed against her and she scowled at her brother. "Stop it, Kaden."

With a final glare at her brother, James turned and left the room. Kaden smiled at him impudently as Bree approached him. She shoved him hard, and he winced as he stumbled back.

"I said stop it, Kaden."

He gave her his own look of hurt. "Bree, what's happened to you?"

"Nothing has happened to me. I won't be treated like some object for the two of you to fight over."

He glared at her. "The Lycan treats you like you're his property. He told me himself that you belong to him, that you're his – his mate. Are you honestly okay with that?"

She sighed. "Kaden, the Lycans are different from the humans. They can be overly protective and possessive of their loved ones. James knows that I do not actually belong to him. It is just his way of letting others know that we are together. When James calls me his mate it means only that he loves me, that he -"

"Loves you? Bree, the Lycans are incapable of love. You should know that better than anyone!" Kaden ran his hand through his hair in frustration. "You spent two years being tortured by Lycans, and yet now you're professing your love for one? Have you gone mad?"

She squeezed his arm. "You cannot paint all Lycans with the same brush, Kaden. These Lycans are not like Draken. They are good and kind and they love their family the same way we love ours."

"I do not believe that."

Now it was her turn to look frustrated. "Now who has gone mad? These Lycans risked their lives to save me from

Draken. Sophia offered herself as a bargaining chip. James and Avery saved your life for the gods sake!"

She shook him lightly. "When I first came here, I was like you. Even though James had saved my life, I didn't trust any of them. I tried to run away. I was attacked by faeries in the woods and they risked their lives to save me. They have been nothing but kind to me since the moment I met them."

"Bree, he was only being kind to you because he wanted to sleep with you!" Kaden said.

She shook her head. "You're wrong, Kaden."

"I am not. You are young and naïve to the ways of men. The Red wanted what you had to offer and like a fool, you gave it to him. Gods, Bree! He is a Lycan! Every time he takes you to his bed, he could kill you. Did you even think of that?"

She paled and stepped away from him like he had slapped her. He knew immediately that he had gone too far, and he gave her a pleading look. "I'm sorry, Bree. I did not mean that. I'm just – I'm tired and I'm confused, and I don't understand how you can trust the Lycans after everything they have done to you."

She crossed her arms over her torso and stared silently at him for a moment. "Listen carefully to me, Kaden. James would never hurt me. Not in his bed or anywhere else. And before Draken showed up, James and the others were devising a plan to rescue you. They were going to go to Draken's home and save you – a man they had never met – because you were my brother and because they think of me as part of their family. I did not ask them to rescue you, they volunteered."

He gave her another look of confusion. "It doesn't mean they have your best interest in mind. I'm your brother – I love you and I want to keep you safe."

She smiled at him. "James loves me too."

"Please, Bree. We cannot stay here. It isn't safe."

"Aye, it is. Draken is still alive. He will come after us again. You know he will."

"Which is why we should leave. Draken knows where we are."

"And where would we go? I only have a little money, and you have none. How long will we survive on our own?"

"We did just fine on our own before. I kept you safe, did I not?" He said.

"Aye, you did. And I will always be grateful to you for that. I know how difficult it was for you to care for me after our parents died. I know that I would be dead if it wasn't for you."

"Then trust me and leave this place with me, Bree," he pleaded. "I will take care of you."

"I won't leave him, Kaden," she said. "I love him and cannot live without him."

"So that's it then? You're choosing him over me?"

"I'm not choosing anyone. I love you both equally."

He tried one final time, the desperation evident in his voice. "Please, Bree. If you love me the way you say that you do, then you will leave this Lycan and come with me."

She smiled sadly at him. "If you love me, you will not ask me to make such a choice."

He felt a rush of shame and stared down at the floor. "I'm so tired. I'm tired of being afraid. I'm tired of being hungry and cold and worried that the only person I care about is going to be hurt."

She put her arms around him, and he bent and buried his face in her neck. "I'm so sorry, Bree."

"I know, honey."

He raised his head and stared gravely at her. "I can't stay with the Lycans. You know I cannot."

She sighed. "I know. But will you do me a favour?"

"What?"

"Stay for a few weeks. You're tired and you need to rest. Take some time to regain your strength before you leave. Please."

"You want me to see that the Lycans are good and can be trusted. You believe if I stay here, I will become friends with them like you have."

An image of Sophia, her dark eyes full of pain and fear staring up at him as he urged her to breathe, flickered through his head. He shook his head to clear it and stared at his sister. "It will not work, Bree."

She smiled at him and rubbed his arm. "I'm asking you to stay because you need rest and because I have missed you."

He bent and kissed her on the forehead. "I will stay for two weeks and then I'm leaving."

"All right," she said with a hint of resignation. "I love you, Kaden."

"I love you too, Bree."

CHAPTER 26

James sighed with relief when Bree entered their room. He had told her brother that Bree would never leave him, but there was a small part of him that was filled with doubt. He gave her a nervous smile as she closed the door and leaned against it.

"Are you all right, little one?"

"Aye."

He gave her another nervous look and she smiled at him. "I'm not leaving you, James."

He couldn't hide the relief on his face as she crossed the room and wrapped her arms around his waist. "I love you and I want to be with you."

He kissed the top of her head before resting his chin on it. "Did you convince your brother to stay?"

She didn't reply and he stared down at her, his chest tightening at the look of sorrow on her face. Tears glinting in her eyes, she shook her head. "He said he would stay for a couple of weeks but then he was leaving."

"I'm sorry." He rubbed her back as the tears slipped down her cheeks.

"Me too."

Feeling guilty, he tightened his grip on her. "Maybe once he sees how happy you are with us, he'll want to stay."

"I doubt it. My brother hates the Lycans. I knew he did but I was hoping that he would…" She shook her head. "It does not matter. He's made his choice and I've made mine."

"Bree, I don't want you to regret -"

She put her hand over his mouth. "Stop, m'lord. I will never regret my decision to stay with you."

He suddenly lifted her until she was eye level with him. She smiled and stroked his face softly before kissing his nose. "I love you."

"I love you too." He gave her an earnest look. "Will you marry me, Bree?"

She blinked at him, her mouth dropping open a little, and he hurried on. "I don't have a ring and I guess I should be down on one knee but I -"

He set her on her feet and smacked himself on the forehead. "Gods, I'm making a mess of this, aren't I?"

He startled her by suddenly dropping to one knee and gripping her hand. "I love you, Bree. Will you marry me? I'll buy you the prettiest ring I can find, and we'll have a big wedding and I'll take you into the city to buy a wedding dress. Or you can wear pants – I don't care. I just want you to be my mate, I mean, wife. I promise I'll take care of you for the rest of my life and -"

"James, stop." Her cheeks were still wet with tears, but her eyes were shining with happiness. "Aye, I'll marry you. And I don't need a ring or a fancy wedding. I just want you."

She bent and kissed him hard on the mouth, and he scrambled to his feet and picked her up. She squeaked in surprise as he spun her in a circle. "I'll do whatever it takes to make you happy, Bree. I promise you."

"You already make me happy, James." She kissed him. "Let's tell your family."

"They're your family now too, Bree." He whirled her around once more before setting her gently on her feet. "Come, we will tell them over breakfast."

"YOU MUST BE THE YOUNG BREE'S BROTHER THEN?"

Kaden looked up at the older man who was coming down the center aisle of the barn. After his conversation with Bree, he had escaped the house and went to the barn. He had lost his appetite and he knew the Lycans would soon be gathering for breakfast. He had been petting the large black stallion the Lycans had given him to ride, when the man came clomping out from the other end of the barn.

"Aye, I am."

"You don't look like her." The man eyed him up and down before wiping his hand on his pants and holding it out. "I'm Ian. I work for the lord Tristan."

Kaden sighed with relief. The old man was a human then. The Lycans would never have one of their own kind working for them. He shook the man's hand. "I'm Kaden."

"Good to meet you."

Kaden was pushed forward by the nose of the stallion and he grinned a little and turned back toward it. He petted its head and the stallion butted him lightly in the chest.

"The others will be eating breakfast soon," Ian said.

"I'm not hungry."

"Well then, make yourself useful and brush Samson. Tristan has so many horses now that I'm having trouble keeping up with the work."

Kaden took the brush Ian was holding out and brushed

Samson's shiny coat. "Aye, the lady of the house mentioned that to me."

"Did she now?" Ian had moved into an empty stall across from him and was shovelling out the old hay and manure. "Tristan has been promising me an extra man for weeks now, but he's been a bit preoccupied as of late."

Kaden grunted in reply and continued to brush down the stallion. Ian kept up a steady stream of chatter as he worked, and Kaden was surprised to realize that he found the old man's chattering to be soothing.

"How did you come to work for the Lycans?" he asked when Ian paused to draw breath.

Before Ian could answer, the door to the barn opened and Sophia stepped in and smiled at Ian. "Breakfast is ready, Ian."

Ian leaned his shovel against the side of the stall and wiped his hands again. "Is it?"

"Aye and Marian said she wasn't bringing it out to you. She said it was time for your weekly visit to the house."

Ian laughed. "I guess I'd better go then."

He nodded to Kaden and stopped to give Sophia a brief hug. "I'm glad you are all right, sweet Sophia."

She smiled and kissed the old man's cheek. "Thank you, Ian. Please tell the others to start without me. I'll be there in a minute."

He nodded and gave Kaden a wave before leaving the barn. Kaden stepped out of the stall and latched the door carefully before joining Sophia in the middle of the aisle.

"Hello, Kaden."

"Hello, Sophia. How's your shoulder?"

"Much better." She frowned when he reached up to put the brush on a shelf on the wall and flinched. His hand rubbed at his side.

"Are you hurt?" She took a step forward and reached out

278

to touch his side before stopping.

"It's nothing."

"It's obviously not nothing," she replied. "I saw you flinch. Is it from the stabbing?"

"No."

"Show me."

"It's fine, I said." He glared at her and she glared back at him, her dark eyes flashing fire.

"Let me see your side, human."

"For the love of the gods…" He rolled his eyes and lifted his shirt briefly to show her the dark bruise on his side.

"A little gift from your oafish brother." He rubbed the bruise, his gaze darkening as he remembered how the one named Nicholas had kicked him in the ribs.

"I'm sorry." To his surprise she actually did look sorry. "My brothers can be… protective."

"Aye, I've seen the way your brother *protect*s my sister."

She frowned. "What do you mean?"

He gave her a dry look. "He treats her like she's his property. Like he owns her."

"It isn't like that. James loves Bree and would do anything for her."

"As long as she does what he tells her, is that it?"

She blew her breath out in a frustrated snort. "No. Perhaps you should not make snap judgements about people until you actually get to know them."

"You're not people – you're Lycans. And apparently, you've all fooled my sister into believing that your brother is good for her."

"He is good for her," she said. Her cheeks were flushed, and her nostrils were flaring as her anger with him grew. "And perhaps you don't like my brother's possessiveness for Bree because it reminds you of yourself."

"What's that supposed to mean?" He glared at her as she stepped closer to him.

"You know exactly what it means," she said. "You're more similar to my brothers than you care to admit."

"Now who's making snap judgements," he grunted.

"I know men like you, Kaden. Hell, I live with three of them. You would be just as protective of your woman as my brother is."

"There's a difference between protective and controlling," he said.

"And my brother knows the difference."

"No, he doesn't."

She stepped closer and glared daggers at him. "Aye he does. He loves Bree and only wants what is best for her. Sleeping in fields, starving, and hiding from Lycans like Draken, is no way for her to live. But that seems to be the best you can offer her."

His temper snapped and he pushed her back against the barn wall. He cupped her head tightly in one hand and lowered his face until it was only inches from hers. "You should be careful what you say to me, Lycan. I've killed your kind before."

"Aye." She spoke breathlessly, but he saw no fear in her eyes. "You keep reminding me of that."

His hand tightened in her hair and his gaze dropped to her mouth. Her lips were pink and full, and he watched fascinated as her tongue slicked across the bottom one. He could feel her breasts pressing against his chest and her warm breath on his face. Lust was growing in his belly and his hand tightened in her hair as his gaze flickered back to her eyes. The dark lust in them matched his own and his cock hardened in response.

He pressed his pelvis against her, trapping her between the wall of the barn and his hard body. She inhaled sharply when she felt his cock against her, and her hands came up to rest against his chest. Perhaps she meant to push him away but at the first touch of her hands, his pelvis thrust against her again and her fingers curled into the material of his shirt.

He bent his head until his mouth was nearly touching hers. "Why are you here, Lycan?"

She licked her lips again, and it was sheer willpower alone that stopped him from kissing her.

"I wanted to say thank you for saving my life," she whispered.

When he didn't reply she took a shuddering breath. "Thank you for killing that Lycan and for helping me control the shift. I would have shifted if it had not been for you."

———

SOPHIA STUDIED KADEN AS HE PRESSED HER AGAINST THE barn wall. If Kaden hadn't pulled her back from the brink of shifting, she would be dead right now. She owned him an apology and she had done so. Why was she not pushing him away and returning to the house?

She frowned a little. She wasn't sure the human had even heard her. He was still staring at her mouth and she squirmed against him. Her movement made his erection brush against her abdomen and she was helpless to stop her soft moan. He smiled at the sound and her heart thudded fiercely in her chest.

She should be pulling away. He was a human who hated Lycans and he had threatened to kill her.

He also saved your life, remember?

Instead of moving away, she tilted her head and parted her lips in silent invitation. His nostrils flared and his mouth dropped down onto hers so suddenly she gasped. His tongue plunged between her lips, seeking out hers, and she moaned into his mouth and sucked hungrily at his tongue.

He groaned and pressed his body against hers. His hand moved to her ass and he squeezed it hard before sliding down to her thigh. He lifted her leg around his hips, pressing his cock against her as she dug her hands into his broad chest. He kissed her hard, his mouth demanding a surrender that she willingly gave him. He explored her mouth with hot licks and swipes of his tongue before nipping at her full bottom lip.

His hand left her thigh and wormed its way under her shirt. At the first feel of his callused hand against her bare breast, she cried out and arched her back. His fingers traced her nipple, and he moaned hoarsely when it hardened under his fingertips. He pulled her head back and kissed the column of her throat.

"Kaden," she gasped out.

At the sound of her voice, he stiffened and then abruptly pushed away from her. He turned away, his hands clenched into tight fists and his shoulders hunched.

"Kaden, I -"

"Leave me," he muttered.

"I'm sorry I should not have done that."

"Leave me!" he shouted.

She hurried to the door of the barn and opened it. She hesitated as the cold air washed over her. She risked a glance behind her, and her breath caught in her throat. Kaden was staring at her, a combination of lust and anger boiling over on his face, and he was squeezing the top of Samson's stall so tightly his knuckles were white.

"I'm sorry, Kaden," she said.

He continued to stare at her, and she swallowed nervously. "You should have my mother look at your bruise. She can heal it for you."

She left the barn, closing the door behind her, but even then, she could feel his hot gaze burning into her back.

"A TOAST!" NICHOLAS STOOD AND RAISED HIS GLASS. "To James and Bree. May they live a long and happy life together, and may their marriage be full of love, laughter, and many pups."

"To James and Bree!" The others in the room echoed before clinking their glasses together.

Bree stared at the people gathered in the kitchen. In only a few short weeks they had become like family to her, and she could feel her heart swelling with love and gratitude for them.

"Mama, I'm going to need a new dress for the wedding!" Dani crowed excitedly to Maya as Leta, with Tia in her arms, skipped up to her father.

"I'll need a new dress too, Papa!"

"Will you now, Leta?" Tristan lifted her into his arms and gave her a mock frown. "And how will you get this new dress?"

"You'll buy it for me," she replied sweetly, and Tristan laughed and kissed her on the forehead.

Avery stood next to Bree and stroked her long blonde hair. "I'm so happy for the both of you, sweet Bree."

Bree stood and hugged the Red. Avery returned her hug and then kissed her on the cheek as Bree smiled at her. "Thank you, Avery."

"I'd like it if you called me mama." Avery brushed her hair back from her face. "Unless you would rather not?"

Bree blinked back the tears threatening and shook her head. "No, I – I would like that very much."

"Good." Avery hugged her again before James tugged Bree towards him.

He pulled her on to his lap, and she put her arms around his shoulders and grinned happily at him. "I believe your family is more excited about this wedding than we are."

"Aye. They do love a good party." James laughed but Bree's face had paled. She was staring at the doorway to the kitchen.

He followed her gaze, his grip tightening about her waist when he saw Kaden standing in the doorway.

"You're marrying him?" he said hoarsely as the others quieted.

Bree stood up and took a few steps toward him, stopping when he backed away. "Aye, I am."

"When were you going to tell me?" He gave her a look of hurt, and she made a soft soothing sound.

"I'm sorry, Kaden. I should have told you first."

"How could you?" he whispered. "How could you marry a Lycan?"

"I love him. You know that." She took another few cautious steps forward and he held up his hand.

"Don't come near me, Bree. I – I don't even know who you are anymore."

"I'm still your sister and I love you," she replied before holding out her hand. "Come for a walk with me, Kaden. We'll talk and -"

"No. I need to be alone."

She gave him a pleading look. "Promise me you won't leave, Kaden. You promised you would stay two weeks."

His gaze flickered briefly to Sophia. "Aye, a promise I now regret."

He turned and stormed from the kitchen. Bree made a low cry of distress and chased after him. He banged out the front door and ran across the yard to the barn, disappearing inside of it. Before Bree could follow him, James had caught up to her. He tugged gently on her arm, pulling her to a stop. She stared up at him, shivering in the cold air, and he pulled her into his embrace.

"Give him some time, Bree. It's a shock to him that's all. He'll come around."

"Will he?" she said. "I'm not so sure, James."

"He will." He rubbed her arms and kissed her forehead. "You learned to trust us and so will he."

"If he leaves and Draken finds him…" she gave him a look of misery.

"We'll convince him to stay. We Lycans can be very loveable when we put our minds to it." He paused. "Well, most of us. Maybe Nicky and I should stay away from him for the first little while."

She laughed in spite of herself, and he grinned and kissed her again. "Come, little one. It's cold out and you have a wedding to plan."

"Aye, I do."

He took her hand and led her back to the house. "Do not worry. It will all work out in the end. Your brother will accept us, and we'll be married soon. Trust me, all right?"

"I trust you. But what about Draken? He's still out there and he knows where we are. What if he comes back?"

He squeezed her hand. "If he's wise, he'll never set foot on our lands again. But if he does, we'll be waiting for him."

As he led her toward the house, he smiled down at her. "Come, little one. This is a day to celebrate with my family – our family now."

She smiled at him. "Aye, our family."

DARK MOON EXCERPT

(BOOK THREE, RED MOON SERIES)

Copyright ©2014 Elizabeth Kelly

"He is a handsome man, is he not?"

"I hadn't really noticed."

Avery smiled at Sophia and stroked her dark hair. "Dani seems quite taken with him."

"Aye, she does." Sophia stared out her bedroom window. Kaden and Dani were standing next to the barn, and she watched as Dani threw her head back and laughed before resting her hand on Kaden's arm.

"It's driving your Uncle Marshall crazy."

"Why? He is married to a human. Why should he be bothered that his child is infatuated with a human?" Sophia asked.

Avery shrugged. "I think it's the fact that Kaden hates Lycans."

"Dani is as human as he is."

"True. But her father and her brother are not."

Sophia didn't reply. Kaden's sister Bree was engaged to her half-brother James and like it or not, Kaden would soon have a very close relationship with the Lycans. She sighed.

She understood why Kaden hated the Lycans. He and Bree had been kept as slaves by a Lycan named Draken. James and Nicky had stumbled onto Bree in the forest after she had been attacked and hunted for sport by Draken and his pack, and James had used his healing powers to save her life.

It had not taken long for Bree and James to fall in love and when Draken had come after her, bringing Kaden with them, Bree had offered herself in exchange for Sophia's sister Leta. The young girl had been captured by the powerful Lycan, and Draken had quickly agreed to the exchange. Kaden was stabbed and left for dead by Draken, but James and Avery healed him. Once he was healed, they set out after the pack of Lycans to save Bree.

Sophia shivered. It had only been two weeks since she nearly died at the hands of Draken and she couldn't seem to shake her fear.

Everything went according to their plan. Kaden offered Sophia in exchange for his sister and Draken, instantly taken with Sophia and eager to make her the mother of his pups, agreed. Once Bree and Kaden were safe, James and the others attacked the Lycan's camp and saved her.

That's not exactly true. Kaden saved your life. He killed the Lycan about to tear your throat out, and he stopped you from shifting with that silver collar around your neck. If it hadn't been for him, you'd be dead right now.

"Sophia? Are you all right, my love?" Avery's warm hand stroked her back through her shirt and Sophia took comfort from her touch.

"Aye, I am fine."

"Are you sure? Leta said she heard you crying out last night."

Leta's bedroom was next to hers, and Sophia forced

288

herself to smile at her mother. "I'm fine, Mama. I just had a bad dream."

Avery squeezed her waist. "Tell me about it."

Sophia hesitated. The dream had been awful. She was back with Draken, the hideous silver collar around her neck, and his hot breath blowing on her face as he leaned over her.

"You're mine, Sophia." He'd smiled down at her as his teeth lengthened and sharpened. "You're mine."

She'd woken from the dream, sweating and afraid, and couldn't fall back asleep. She laid in her bed, staring out the window as the darkness faded and the sun rose in the sky. She supposed it didn't help that Draken had escaped before they could kill him. The Lycan was out there somewhere and it would be foolish to think that he would not attempt to take his revenge.

She shook her head. "No, Mama. It was nothing."

She watched, her stomach tightening with what she refused to admit was jealousy, as Dani took Kaden's arm. He glanced briefly at the house - she could have sworn he was staring directly at her - and then followed Dani into the barn. Sophia had kissed Kaden in that very barn, had felt his erection against her abdomen and his hand on her breast, and try as she might she couldn't forget the way it had felt.

It was ridiculous. The man hated Lycans and she had never once mated with a human. Not that she was opposed to the idea of mating with a human, she had just never met one that interested her.

Kaden interests you.

She snorted angrily. That might be true, but Kaden had made it perfectly clear he wanted nothing to do with her. He'd kissed her in the barn because she had practically thrown herself at him. It hadn't taken him long to come to his senses, and since the moment he pushed her away he hadn't spoken a single word to her.

She realized Avery was still watching her and she cleared her throat. "Dani will be upset when Kaden leaves tomorrow."

"If he leaves," Avery said.

Sophia stared at her. "He will, Mama."

Avery shrugged. "He may not. He loves his sister very much. He may find it more difficult to leave her than he realizes. He has been here two weeks and even he has to admit that Bree is very happy with us. He has seen for himself that not all Lycans treat humans the way that Draken did."

"He hasn't spent any time with us. The last two weeks he's been with Bree or Dani, or in the barn helping Ian with the horses. He's been actively avoiding anything to do with our family."

"That's true," Avery said. "But the last few days, Bree has gotten him to agree to eat dinner with us. It's a step in the right direction."

Sophia snorted. "He stares at his plate, eats his dinner, and leaves. He won't speak a word to any of us unless he has to."

"He just needs more time. You remember how Bree was the first moon she was here. She was terrified of anyone she thought to be a Lycan."

"Aye, but she was only frightened of us. Kaden hates all of us."

"Does he? I'm not so sure about that," Avery replied.

Sophia frowned at her. "What do you mean?"

———

Avery stared thoughtfully at Sophia. She had seen the way Kaden looked at her child when he believed no one else was watching. And Sophia might avoid Kaden more than any of them, but Avery wasn't blind. The others had attempted to gain Kaden's trust over the last two weeks, even Nicky had been friendly and polite, but Sophia hadn't bothered. In fact, to anyone watching, she projected a clear dislike for the large human.

Avery smiled a little. Sophia might have fooled her father and her brothers, but she couldn't fool her mother. The slight reddening of her cheeks, the frequent subtle glances at Kaden whenever he was near her, and the way her eyes darkened when she watched Dani and Kaden together were unmistakably clear. Something had happened between Sophia and Kaden, and both were doing their best to keep it from the others.

"What do you mean, Mama?" Sophia said again.

"Nothing, my sweet. Only that perhaps Bree will still be able to change his mind." Avery stretched up to kiss Sophia's forehead. "Come, it's almost dinner. Let us join the others."

Kaden smiled at the young girl standing next to him. He liked Dani, she had a happy, bubbling personality that was infectious, but he was growing distinctly uncomfortable with the way their relationship seemed to be turning.

She touched him at every opportunity, just small presses of her hand against his arm or his back, but he recognized it for what it was. Last night at dinner she had wormed her way into a seat beside him and spent the entire meal brushing her thigh against his. He had subtly shifted further and further to his left until he was practically sitting on his sister's lap.

Bree had given him an odd look but rather than try and explain with Dani's father staring suspiciously at him across the table, he had just hurriedly finished his meal and excused himself to the barn.

He grinned a little to himself. It was painfully obvious that Dani's father Marshall did not approve of his daughter's crush. Kaden was almost tempted to sleep with the girl just to anger the Lycan.

He stared down at Dani's pretty face. Who was he trying to fool? The girl was an innocent, and he wasn't the type of man who would use a woman in that manner. Besides, pretty as she was, she wasn't his type. Her slender body and blonde hair did nothing to stir his lust. He liked his women dark haired, with full and lush curves a man could get lost in. Wide hips to hang on to when the sex turned frantic and rough, and full breasts that overflowed in his hands.

Sophia's face flashed in his head and he automatically looked at the wall of the barn. He had pushed her back against that wall, had kissed her full mouth and ground his cock against her. He could still remember the feel of her breast in his hand, the way her nipple had tightened against his palm, and her low voice moaning his name.

He looked away quickly as his cock started to harden in his pants. Gods, he was going crazy. Thinking about having sex with a Lycan was pure madness. Besides, he was leaving tomorrow. He would never see the Lycan again.

Dani was chattering to him and he smiled and nodded, only half-listening as his thoughts turned to Bree. He couldn't convince her to leave with him. He had, in fact, known it was useless after the first few days and stopped pressuring her.

Bree loved the redheaded Lycan and, as much as Kaden hated to admit it, it was obvious that James loved her. Bree spent much of her time the last two weeks with Kaden and he was surprised by James' lack of objection. He'd given Bree her space and her freedom to visit with her brother, and Kaden had no sense that the Red was doing it as a way to win his favour.

He told Sophia that James was trying to control his sister, but he realized his mistake after only a few days. It was clear, even to him, that the Lycan would do anything his sister asked. It would have amused Kaden to no end that his tiny baby sister had such a powerful Lycan wrapped around her finger, had it not been for his deep-seated hatred for Lycans in general.

And fear, a voice deep inside his head whispered. *You can deny it all you want, but you fear them as well.*

He nodded at something Dani said and stared down at her blankly. He did fear the Lycans. He hated that he did, knew that it made him weak, but he had spent two years as their slave and his entire body was proof of their cruelty. His chest, back and thighs were covered with the reminders of their whips and their claws. Even now, away from Draken's home, he could feel a shudder run through him at the memory of being chained to the pole like a dog.

His hand rubbed at the skin on his throat. The band of pale skin, the only reminder of the collar he had worn around his neck for over two years, was still there. He wondered if it would ever go away or if it would brand him forever as a Lycan slave.

"Kaden?"

He realized Dani was staring at him oddly and he made himself smile at her. "Aye?"

"Were you listening to me?"

"I'm sorry, I was, uh…"

He was saved from replying by the appearance of Leta at the barn door.

"Uncle Marshall is looking for you," she said to Dani. She was holding Tia in her arms and she frowned when the small dog barked excitedly and wiggled from her grip. Tia ran to Kaden and he scooped her up, petting her head as she wagged her tail and licked at his hands.

Dani sighed. "What does he want?"

Leta shrugged. "I don't know. He just asked me to come find you."

Dani frowned and then turned to Kaden. "I'll see you at dinner?"

"Aye."

She hesitated and before Kaden could step back, she stood on her tiptoes and kissed him lightly on the cheek. Blushing a little, she hurried past Leta who stepped out of the way but didn't follow her out of the barn. She kept a careful distance from Kaden and stared at him warily.

"I still don't like you," she said.

He grinned. "No? Why not? I'm not taking Bree away from you."

"I know! Bree would never leave me – she loves me. And my brother." She added as an afterthought.

His grin widened. Despite the fact that she was half-Lycan, he liked the girl. Other than Sophia, she was the only Lycan who had made no effort with him at all in the last two weeks. Although she refused to leave Bree's side the first few days, she'd spent most of the time glowering at him as he visited with his sister. After a few days she mysteriously disappeared, and he had questioned Bree about it.

His sister smiled a little. "She's in trouble for being rude to you. Avery and Tristan aren't allowing her to spend time with us until she learns better manners."

He laughed. "How long before she cracks and starts being nice to me?"

Bree giggled. "You have no idea how stubborn Leta is. When her parents told her what they expected of her, I guess she vowed she would never be kind to you and that she couldn't wait until you left, and she never had to see your ugly human face again."

He had snorted laughter as Bree poked his side in a friendly way. "She lost horse-riding privileges for a week and was sent to her room without supper for that little outburst."

"So that's why I haven't seen her glaring at me in the barn lately." He had grinned.

Now, he crossed his arms across his chest and arched one eyebrow at her. "Why such a dislike for me, young Leta?"

She pursed her lips together and stared silently at the ground. He'd decided she wasn't going to answer when she suddenly blurted, "Because you're making Bree sad."

He frowned. Bree hadn't said a word to him about leaving. She had seemed to make her peace with the fact that he wouldn't stay, and she had not appeared upset to him. Her acceptance had hurt his feelings and, in a way, made it easier for him to leave.

"It's true." Leta mistook his silence for disagreement. She forgot herself and moved deeper into the barn to stand in front of him. "She cries when you're not around."

"What do you mean?"

"She cries! She cries to Mama and to James almost every day. She's sad because you won't even stay for the wedding."

She gave him a cautious look. "I wasn't spying. Don't you tell Papa that I was spying because I wasn't. I just – just happened to hear them when I was playing in the closet in Papa and Mama's room."

"I won't," he promised.

She stared gravely at him. "You're not a very nice person. I thought you would be nice like Bree but you're not."

Surprisingly, her words stung him a little. "I am a nice person, Leta."

"No, you're not," she insisted. "You won't even stay for your own sister's wedding. That's mean. You're mean!"

"Leta!"

The young girl whirled around. Sophia had entered the barn and she frowned at her younger sister. "What did Mom and Dad say about being respectful to Bree's brother?"

"He's mean!" Leta was starting to cry. "He's making Bree sad and he doesn't even care!"

Sophia started toward her and Leta backed away until she bumped into Kaden. He steadied her with a hand on her back, and she turned and growled at him.

"Leta!" Sophia said and the young girl slumped to the ground and began to cry. Sophia sat beside her and gathered her into her arms. "Hush, Leta. Don't cry."

She glanced up at Kaden. "I'm sorry, she isn't usually like this. The thing with Draken frightened her very much, and things have been different around here lately. She's excited about the wedding and I think she's overtired and over-stimulated."

Leta crawled into her lap and continued to sob. "Please don't tell Papa I was bad, Sophia."

Sophia stroked her dark hair. "Honey, you know that Dad told you specifically to be respectful to Kaden. You weren't. There are consequences for your actions."

"They won't let me ride again for another whole week!" Leta wailed. "I'll die, Sophia. Die!"

Kaden sighed. The girl's dramatics would have been funny if it wasn't so obvious that she was truly upset. He crouched beside them and touched Leta's shoulder lightly. "It's all right, Leta. I know you didn't mean to be rude. You were just being honest, right?"

She sniffed and nodded. "Aye."

"I'll make you a deal. I'll ask Sophia not to tell your father if you promise to help Ian brush the horses after I'm gone. There are too many for him to brush by himself."

She eyed him carefully for a moment and then nodded again. "I promise."

"Good." He straightened as Sophia kissed Leta's cheek gently and then stood, pulling the young girl to her feet.

"Dinner is ready, my love. Go and wash up."

Leta left the barn and Sophia turned to Kaden. "Um, dinner is ready," she said awkwardly. "Will you be joining us tonight?"

"Aye."

It was the first time they had been alone together in days, and his gaze flickered to the wall where they kissed. He cleared his throat and glanced back at Sophia. She'd followed his gaze and was staring at the barn wall. Her cheeks were pink, and her tongue darted out to flick nervously at her upper lip.

She looked at him and her blush deepened. He stared silently at her and after a moment, took a step towards her. She backed up a step and smiled uncertainly at him.

"Is it true what Leta said? Is Bree upset?" he asked.

She gave him an odd look. "Of course, she is. You're her brother and she wants you to stay."

"For what? She has your brother now. She has no need for me." Even he could hear the jealousy in his voice.

She stared impatiently at him. "Loving my brother does not mean she doesn't need you, Kaden. You don't strike me as a stupid human but you're certainly acting like one."

He glared at her. "I'm not being stupid. I'm being realistic. Bree no longer needs my protection. Why would I stay?"

"You stay because she loves you. You stay because it's

foolish of you to leave when you have no money and no place to go. My parents are willing to hire you to work with Ian in the barn. You could earn a wage, be a free man, and have protection from Draken."

He scoffed. "Another reason Bree should be leaving with me. I know you believe that your family can protect us from Draken, but you don't know him the way that we do. His pack is large and he's crazy. And now," he stepped closer and took her arm in a firm grip, "it's not just my sister and me he wants, but you as well."

He rubbed her arm with his thumb. "You think you're safe. You believe that Draken cannot harm you but you're wrong. Your family has no idea what he's capable of."

"All the more reason for you to stay," she replied. "You can help us. You know what he's capable of."

"Aye, I do," he whispered. He was standing so close to her now that his chest brushed against her magnificent breasts.

"Do you want me to stay?" he said.

She nodded.

"Why?"

"I – what?" she said.

He lowered his face to hers and she parted her mouth for his kiss. Instead of kissing her, he rubbed the ball of his thumb across her lower lip. She moaned, her breath warm against his face, and he stared mesmerized at the hint of her straight, white teeth. "Why do you want me to stay?"

"Because Bree wants you to stay," she whispered.

"Is that the only reason?" He slipped his thumb between her lips and she closed her mouth around it and sucked.

He made a quiet groaning noise and slipped his other hand around her to cup the back of her head. He slid his thumb back and forth in her mouth, feeling the wet heat of her tongue and lips holding him firmly inside of her.

His cock was rock hard, his breath coming in harsh pants, and he couldn't look away from her dark eyes. They were changing, flecks of green appearing, and he watched fascinated as the dark brown changed to a light, clear green.

"Is there another reason you want me to stay, Sophia?" he said.

He started to pull his thumb from her mouth, and she tightened her lips around it, stroking it roughly with her tongue until he groaned again.

"Tell me," he whispered as he pulled his thumb out of her mouth.

"Kaden, I -"

"Gods be damned, it's cold out there tonight. You sure you want to leave when it's this cold?" Ian came ambling through the doors at the far end of the barn and stopped short when he saw Kaden and Sophia locked together.

Sophia pulled away from Kaden and ran to the door. "Dinner is ready," she called hoarsely before disappearing into the darkness.

Ian stared shrewdly at Kaden. "Sophia's a pretty girl."

"Aye." Kaden started for the barn door, ignoring the grin on Ian's face. "Are you coming for dinner or not?"

"Aye, I am." Whistling softly, Ian followed him out of the barn.

ABOUT THE AUTHOR

Elizabeth Kelly was born and raised in Ontario, Canada. She moved west as a teenager and now lives in Alberta with her husband and a menagerie of pets. She firmly believes that a person can survive solely on sushi and coffee, and only her husband's mad cooking skills prevents her from proving that theory.

For more information about Elizabeth, check out her website at

www.elizabethkelly.ca

facebook.com/EKellyBooks

twitter.com/ElizabethKBooks

instagram.com/elizabethkelly_author

amazon.com/Elizabeth-Kelly/e/B00EOHZ0MS

bookbub.com/authors/elizabeth-kelly

ALSO BY ELIZABETH KELLY

Tempted Series

Tempted

Twice Tempted

Forever Tempted

Breathless

Tempted Trilogy (Books 1-3)

Red Moon Series

Red Moon

Red Moon Rising

Dark Moon

Alpha Moon

Pale Moon

Red Moon Bundle Books 1 – 3

Red Moon Bundle Books 4 – 5

The Recruit Series

The Recruit (Book One)

The Recruit (Book Two)

The Recruit (Book Three)

The Recruit (Book Four)

The Recruit (Book Five)

The Recruit Series Bundle Books 1-3

The Recruit Series Bundle Books 4-6

Saving Charlotte

Shameless

The Fairy Tales Collection

Broken

An Unlikely Seduction

Holiday Romance

The Christmas Wife

The Christmas Rescue

The Christmas Nanny

Sordid Games

www.ingramcontent.com/pod-product-compliance
Lightning Source LLC
Chambersburg PA
CBHW071110250626
47159CB00002B/675